Hauzer's Brat Haus

A tale of crime, dog romance, German sausages, beer, and high adventure.

by Rick Poore

Chapter One

Allow me the honor of a brief introduction: I am known by many who fear my presence and a few who consider me their friend as Bertrand Chauncey. I have an exceedingly lovely partner in my personal and professional ventures who goes by the name of Ms. Chessie Beretta. Whether or not those names stem from any root in reality is of little consequence, but I must admit the use of a bit of poetic license in their construction. As is customary, our original monikers were affixed at birth by our parents, who failed to envision the fearless lifestyle we were born to lead. But all this self-promotion will get us nowhere. There is little I enjoy more than to share a good tale, especially one in which I survive. But I must confess a tendency, on occasion, to embellish the saga just a bit, for theatrical effect. So, in the interest of accuracy and efficiency, perhaps I should turn over the storytelling duties to another close associate. Unusually close, some would say…

Bert Clauster here. Glad you could join us. I will explain about Bertrand in a few minutes. For now, pull up a chair, pop a cold one, and let's go for an adventure. Let me give you a quick background to keep the confusion level under the legal limit. I consider myself a full-blooded American dude. One of millions of aspiring American youth flailing along, trying to live up to their full potential. My long aimless run after college used to bother me, despite my suspicion that I was an upstanding member of the vast majority. I also had a strong suspicion that there was more to life than a career shuffling electrical components in the back of a Kansas City warehouse. I least I hoped there was. Two years down… forty-three to go. Scary thought for a twenty-four year old single guy. I guess that was before I teamed up with Bertrand Chauncey. I do not worry too much about that long aimless run any more.

You see, back in 2003, when George W. Bush was busy telling the Iraqi people to brace themselves for a shitstorm of capitalistic freedom that would transform their deeply oppressed masses into a hoard of wealthy fast-food entrepreneurs, I took up with State Electric Supply, Inc. performing the highly skilled task of stocking the warehouse shelves with electrical gadgets that arrived by freight truck five times a week. After college I was in pretty good shape; a decent looking dude, although my self-appraisal could be seen as somewhat subjective. I was twenty-two at the time and fresh out of a brilliant four-year college career spent traversing the University of Kansas campus from keg party to keg party. I would elaborate on the glory of this pursuit, but there is precious little of it I can remember, except for one week spent in Watkins Mill State Park campground with a Swedish exchange student who spoke almost no English. Ya, shore. But let's save that for another venue.

The State Electric job was mindless and excruciatingly boring after the first week or two. But after graduating two-hundred twenty-third out a class of two-hundred seventy, I realized my talents acquired from the English Department of University of Kansas did not gain me access to the ranks of well-compensated corporate executives. For some obscure reason, my folks still suffered under the delusion that I might someday make a meaningful contribution to society. They had a friend who ran State Electric who was willing to take a chance on 'Herbert's boy'. Yep, dad was a Herbert. Some weird family obsession with the Bert thing. Something about old dead great grandpa Bertros, and they wanted to keep the Bert thing going. That was the excuse my folks laid on me when I was old enough to get ribbed at school for being 'Bert the Squirt'. Always comforting to have a chunk of old dead Pappaw inside somewhere. So now Herbert's boy Bertrand, commonly referred to as Bert, great grandson of Old Dead Bertros, unloaded boxes of electrical supplies and fixtures in the back of a cold warehouse on the south side of the tracks in Kansas City, Kansas. How had society ever functioned prior to my meaningful contribution?

State Electric was the model of efficiency, a profitable stalwart of the community, providing a valuable addition to the local economy and source of employment for generations. The warehouse aisles were clearly organized and labeled. The stocking codes even followed a logical pattern that could be easily learned in an hour or so, even by an underachieving English major. The retail section of the business, up in the front where it was warm and bright with the glow of hundreds of display fixtures illuminated over the sales counter, was even more organized and spotless. Intelligent, efficient staff quickly navigated through the inventory files to locate, price, and deliver whatever ceiling fan or box of wire nuts might be needed. I think that is how State Electric managed to compete with the sprawling home improvement monstrosities; by offering a significant reduction in the legwork and hassle factor.

My job was far too mindless and left far too much time for an active imagination to slip through the radiating cracks in the wall of shear boredom, so I began to fall into a parallel fantasy life at times. Slipping for short periods during the day into another lifestyle, one of clandestine operations designed to give me, Bertrand Chauncey Clauster, the kind of adventure and challenge he so richly deserved. Eventually, I dropped the Clauster part during the fantasy sessions, and went with Bertrand Chauncey. The name 'Clauster' could be too easily associated with *'clauster-fuck'*, making it an inappropriate name for high adventures. Chauncey might be associated with *'chancey'* which seemed much more in keeping with my daring diversions.

But this was all just harmless fantasy, the type of distraction any of us might use to keep the claws of monotony from gouging out our soul. Bertrand Chauncey the Great Adventurer would always slip back to being Bert Clauster the Stock Boy the minute I heard the backup beep-beep-beep of the delivery truck, cautiously inching backwards into the loading bay to dock with the warehouse doors. Time to be a good boy and play my part in making State Electric the model of efficiency that our beloved community has come to expect. God forbid we put the ten-gauge Romex in the twelve-gauge rack, or stock the 150-watt heat lamps with the fluorescent bulbs, or accidentally stick the forklift tongs through the back of the goddamn truck. That would be a very un-State Electric type of thing. That would be more like U.S. Army Division of Supply Requisitions and Quartermaster Supply Centralized Shipping and Receiving Central Division type of thing. And I thought we really didn't need much more of that.

But after the truck drivers slammed down the roll-ups, latched the doors, and headed back to Dallas or Detroit or Denver or wherever all that stuff comes from, Bertrand Chauncey slipped out through the cranial cracks and ran amuck in his private fantasy world of high adventure. I recall one Tuesday afternoon when the dashing Bertrand Chauncey envisioned the crates all nicely filled with lovely lamps and lights, except for one, specially marked by shadowy Russian operatives, with tins of fine Russian caviar cleverly concealed within the housing of wall heaters. This was not your ordinary, run of the mill rot-gut caviar slurped up by common congressmen at private yacht club parties. Nosireebob. This was the good stuff. Destined for small silver plates handcrafted by Thomas Jefferson and served by small beautiful Asian women to those handful of people who truly held the reigns of world power in their crusty claws. Bertrand Chauncey wondered who those handful were. And why were their claws crusty? Could they be shadowy elements of the underworld? The dashing Bertrand Chauncey worked to fill this particular gap in the fantasy. Maybe lobbyists? Wall Street executives? Insurance company leaders? The Chinese elite? Perhaps. Somebody had to be yanking the puppet strings attached to the duly elected pinheads. Got it! Maybe the big oil executives! Very good possibility.

But then I formulated the image of large white men from Texas wearing immaculate, starched cowboy hats and boots made from the skin of some endangered lizard standing around a cleverly concealed private board room filled with cigar smoke, gawking at small beautiful Asian women. Could these crackers actually be swilling caviar from plates made by Thomas Jefferson? That image was disturbing, spoiling the fantasy session for the day, and then I was back. Good old Bert. Efficiently carrying a box of 120-volt receptacles up to the sales counter so the lovely Claudia Auckland could efficiently issue a sales invoice to Grambler Construction. Just playing my part as a small spoke of the great wheel of American Free Enterprise. What a proud tradition. Those oil execs will just have to wait for their expensive illegal caviar, Bert's got shit to do.

And so it went, for a long while. The work was mindless, but the daily slips through the cracks got me through it OK. It was fun running rum with Bertrand through the crowded streets of Antigua, being chased by dark-skinned cops in white shorts with automatic weapons. Swinging pendulum style across the face of a high rise in Rio to access a 'secure' room full of priceless diamonds. Sipping exotic drinks on the veranda of a plush resort in the Bahamas with the stunning heiress of a banking magnate. Oddly, I began to notice the stunning heiress bore a striking resemblance to Claudia

Auckland from the sales counter. I passed this off as a mere coincidence and continued my daily forays into the exciting world of Bertrand Chauncey, International.... what? International Playboy? No, too 1960s. International Adventurer? Not broad enough. Traveler? Sounded homeless. International Stock Boy. Yeah, I guess that's about it. And back to being Bert I would morph.

One summer afternoon, sometime about the middle of my second year working in the back of State Electric warehouse, an odd incident occurred that caused a tectonic shift in the monotonous cycle of boxes coming and going all day. After unloading a large truck full of dull colored pallets of various electrical gadgets, I peered around the loading bay corner to investigate the destination of a medium-sized brownish dog that ambled past. He was a friendly looking guy, of questionable lineage. I like dogs, and often confide life's secrets and desires to perfect dog strangers, as I find this infinitely more rewarding than having these deep inner feelings ignored by some self-absorbed platinum-haired exotic dancer. Plus, talking to strange dogs is much cheaper, and considerably less sleazy.

Turned out the pooch was headed for the tracks behind the warehouse, so I followed him back there to confide some secrets and desires, in the event he was in the mood to listen. As it happened, the mutt was preoccupied with a non-descript patch of dirt between the tracks and the building. "Yo, Poochie, wassup with you?" Poochie took a gander at me and went back to sniffing the dirt. So I tried, "Tu hables Espanol, que?" No response from the dog. "Du bist un schnauzer, ya vol?" I tried a few more grammatically flawed foreign phrases I had picked up in my school years, but still failed to make the link with whatever language was coursing through his mutt brain. I took a closer look at the dirt patch and noticed something a bit off. Nothing much at first, but when you stood back a few feet and looked at the broad view of the scene, the eye could pick up a faint square outline, nearly brushed away. In fact, it wasn't even an outline as such, more of a square area about four feet across that showed light brush marks. The clean, fresh gravel seemed a little out of place, given the location next to the tracks with the typical railroad detritus scattered about. Here and there outside the square were pieces of broken bottles, a few old spikes from a track repair job, some candy wrappers from a train worker's lunch, and an old moldy wet garment of indistinguishable origin. But nothing at all inside the square brushed area. It had been recently disturbed, but some effort had been made to brush away any sign.

"What's down there, boy?" The dog side-stepped around the little square and started to scratch at the dirt. Before my four-legged buddy could comment, a Transit Motor Freight truck banked into view at the entrance to the loading area and gave a quick air-horn blast to announce its arrival. I bid farewell to my new canine acquaintance, "Hasta luego, cochorrito!" A blank stare from the dog, perhaps insulted by the use of the diminutive form of the phrase, or else confused by my lack of an authentic Latino accent.

Back at the salt mine, the truck had successfully mated with the loading orifice, albeit ass-first, and was awaiting my help to impart his electrical load. The driver of such trucks are often affectionately referred to as 'cab-lizards' and driver Jimmy did not stray far from this image. With a stained John Deere cap strategically locked in an awkward angle across his balding melon, and baggy jeans flying at half-mast down his wide-load backsides, Jimmy crawled up the ramp to the dock and passed his usual greeting. "Don't nobody work 'round here but me? Whose ass do I hafta whoop to get this bitch unloaded?"

"Nobody back here today but me, Jimmy, and I'm on break for another four hours. Might wanta drag those pallets out of there on your own." I had to give him a little something back after the warm manner in which he always greeted me. "And for the sake of God, wait till I get out from behind you, 'cause that butt crack of yours is giving me vertigo. Somebody's gonna slip and fall in there one of these days and need search and rescue to recover the body."

"Oh hell, Bert, you can kiss my butt crack. Get off'en your ass and fire up that fork. I gotta blow some dust off the road, goddamit." It was always nice to see Jimmy. Of course, this affectionate banter was repeated nearly verbatim with each successive driver. If one of them had said, "Bert, lovely to see you... new hairstyle?" I would have called 911, and then passed out. So, the cycle repeated, the fork lift was fetched, and the pallets drug backwards out of the shiny metal box trailer, and Jimmy stood by and watched, while hocking snuff spit out between the dock and the truck. These were my 'colleagues' during my years at State Electric. My peers. Jimmy the Cab Lizard and Bert the Stock Boy, working side by side to crank forward the gears of commerce. No wonder I talked to dogs.

Poochie came back around later, after the crates were disgorged into their numerically coded shelves. I saw him gnawing on something vile out by the loading dock and went to say bonjour. "What have you got there, stinky?" This time the dog acted protective and took off for the back of the building with the gross-looking chunk in teeth. Sharing his lunch was not in the program, evidently. I followed along and found him back at the weird square spot, and saw he had unearthed the disgusting chunk of meat from the center of the square. He dropped the mess and gave me a look, like he knew he had been caught pocketing money from the collection plate. The gnarled meat chunk was hanging off a brownish red bone, and was lying by the dig. I thought he had unearthed somebody's deceased pet, or maybe some poached deer carcass that had been quickly buried behind the warehouse to keep the game warden off the trail. "You are definitely not coming home with me, Poochie. That's disgusting." I pronounced 'that's disgusting' like Paul Lynn sitting in the center square of Hollywood Squares every time he got a question that could be vaguely interpreted as having anything to do with sex among senior citizens or bodily functions of chimpanzees. Then Paul would make a face and laugh like it really was sort of disgusting, but he might like to give it try after the show. For unimaginable reasons, this made Paul Lynn my favorite square.

I gave the chunk a nudge with my toe, checking for clumps of hair that might give a clue as to the origin. Strange looking bone for a deer. I flipped it over. That one absent minded action might have been the pivotal point in my otherwise sedate life. I could have left this stinking dog chew-toy for the pooch and gone back to shuffling recessed overhead floodlights. None of my damn business what rotting carcasses are buried out back. No, I did not grasp the magnitude of my morbid curiosity until it was too late, and the meaty mess was flipped upside down, revealing a mangled finger attached by a tendon to the end of a finger bone. Uh oh. Either this dead animal had some very warped DNA strands, or some unfortunate fool had gotten the deep-six treatment. Poochie whined at my feet and looked on with interest. "We've got some serious issues here, pup."

Just about then, I heard a low growl from the pooch and saw him focus on something across the track, next to an empty boxcar covered with unintelligible graffiti created by young urban artists. It was a thickly built man, only slightly smaller than the boxcar, staring our way without making a movement. He was not a railroad worker or boxcar hobo, but dressed in tight dark clothes, and wearing shades. The hair on my neck stood up. The hair on Poochie's neck stood up. The hair on that mangled knuckle stood up. Slowly, the man shook his head... side to side, several times. *'NO.'* OK, I get it, mister. That simple gesture conveyed a whole lot of message. And it was unmistakable. *NO* phone calls... *NO* police... *NO* press... or *NO* life. OK. I nodded back to acknowledge that I received the silent message, and the dark man turned on his heels and disappeared behind the boxcar. I waited for him to appear from the opposite side, to see if he got into a car, or met someone else, but he did not reappear.

I was thinking fast, *'What now? Call the cops? Disregard the warning and spill the beans? Shut up and pretend it never happened? It's just an old bone. I did nothing wrong... yet.'* I had a serious decision to make. I had to weigh the options carefully. There might be some painful consequences if I fuck this up. Poochie helped with the next move. He sidled over, picked up the bone, and dropped it into the excavated hole he had created earlier. Then, with impressive persistence, he proceeded to rake all the dirt back between his legs and over the bone. "Smart boy." OK, so that's the way we roll. One of the most terrifying and important decisions of my young life had just been made by a medium sized brown mutt with questionable culinary discrimination. So, with the conclusion of that unique event, I returned to the warehouse and began filling an electrical supply order for Hasbrook Brothers Construction, who were evidently starting another trophy house for some lucky schmuck who ferreted out the magic pathway to government housing subsidies.

That order took a little longer than expected to fill. I kept having to pull out wiring boxes that were the wrong gauge, get the right ones, replace cases of beige receptacle covers with white ones, and so forth. Could have been a little distracted, maybe. I knew it was bad when I checked the order one last time and found my lunch bucket in the crate. This is not good. Those guys at Hasbrook would have eaten my lunch. Got to forget this mess and focus on work. Good luck, Bert.

With the recurring mental image of the mangled finger, I decided to skip lunch altogether, and spent the rest of the afternoon considering my options. It essentially boiled down to two. Choice One: Call out the gendarmes. Choice Two: Shut the fuck up. Preferring not to join Finger-Boy in the hole behind the warehouse, I decided Poochie made the right call, and cover it up for now. Go with Choice Two. If they got wise, I could always plead ignorance. *'Sure, I saw a dog with a bone. Any crime there? Sorry, not a forensics expert, that's your call. Guy by the tracks? Maybe. Should I call the cops when I see a guy by the tracks? Come on guys, let me outta here! I'm just Bert the Stock Boy. I've got shit to do.'*

Or I could have gone with Choice One, call out the troops. *'Hi officers, glad you could come over. Good to see you. Actually, you need to dig up this spot out back. I think there's a body, or at least parts of one, in a hole. No, I didn't put it in there. How did I find it? Oh, well, the dog told me. Or showed me, I mean. Sorry. A little nervous. Why am I nervous? Oh, no reason, just found finger bone this morning and had some weird guy in dark tights giving me the fish-eye. And I figure this little conversation with you guys is going to get me stuck in the heart with a railroad spike. So, there's really no reason to be nervous. No, I do not drink heavily, although I am considering starting. No, I do not have any disagreements with State Electric Management. Well, except for their infuriating habit of consistently failing to stock Snicker Bars in the vending machine. No, I would not consider murdering the assistant manager for this. Look, am I a suspect now? Come on guys, let me outta here! I'm just Bert the Stock Boy. No, wait... don't let me outta here. Bucky the Bagman is out there waiting for me. Oh shit! I'm screwed.'*

What I needed was some professional consultation. Some sage advice to guide my actions and keep me clear of Bucky the Bagman. Some wise and experienced mentor to throw an arm around my shoulder and say, *'Bertrand, old boy, the answer is right there in front of you.'* Hmm... who is calm, cool and collected in times of high-anxiety? That's it! Bertrand Chauncey! The answer was right there. What would Bertrand Chauncey do? Bert is a Domestic Clauster-Fuck. No wonder he's nervous. Bertrand Chauncey, on the other hand, is an International... what? Still could not pin that one down. The 'International' part was set. The next part was just not coming through. But I had some hope. Slip through the cracks and take a look at things from my alter-ego point of view. What could it hurt?

'So, what say we take another gander at the situation?' (Bertrand had begun to think in a vaguely English accent, as it seemed appropriate when dealing with clandestine operations, beautiful Asian women, high caliber automatic weapons, and partially exposed body parts.) *'Good call, old boy. Keep a wrap on this thing till we gather a smidge more data. Illogical to putt one's self in harm's way, unless of course, you stand to profit in some manner. No sense getting your bloomers in a bunch over a dog bone, now is there? Let me think this situation out with you for a bit. Might be a bit of fun in this one for us, you suppose? The key here is to recognize an opportunity when so presented.'*

And so it went for the rest of the day. Bertrand Chauncey conjuring solutions to transform an apparently serious situation into a jaunt in the park. When I finally punched out at five, I checked in with the front desk, just so someone could later say, *'My God, I saw him just a few minutes ago! And he looked so lifelike!'* in case I never made it to my pickup. So I stopped at the sales counter and waved, "Bye, Claudia. See you in the morning."

Claudia was subtly gorgeous, not 'supermodel-train-stopping' looks, but more of a 'rest your head in your hands and take a nice long look' sort of looks. She wore a long plaid skirt as she swirled past behind the sales desk. She was getting ready to head out too, and was shuffling the day's invoices into their respective filing bins. Her image would occasionally drift into Bertrand Chauncey's fantasy world, but she had never seemed personally inclined to drift into Bert Clauster's Stock Boy world. "You won't see me tomorrow, Bert. Not unless you are working Saturdays." She smiled up at me like I was a dunce. The way Archie Bunker would look up at his son-in-law Michael and say *'Meathead, they ain't no peer group, we goin' fishin' in a boat!'*

"Right, Claudia. Forgot. Been a little distracted this afternoon." I started to move toward the front door, but turned around on a whim when I realized we were the last ones to leave. "Want me to wait and walk you out to your car?" I hoped this came from some chivalrous cavity within my soul, and not from some cringing instinct to keep someone nearby in case Bucky the Bagman decided to start pounding railroad spikes in tender places.

"Sure, Bert. Give me a minute to file this away." Oh, wow. At least one thing had gone right. I was taking beautiful Claudia out to her car. Nice little bonus to accompany my last minutes on earth. While she finished the filing, I flipped the switches on the wall panel that controlled the hundred or so overhead display fixtures, and the front office went dim. Yep, the lights might be going out in more ways than one. Silliness. Come on Bert, this is pathetic. What about the opportunity thing?

"Right-o. Off we go," I let that slip out loud in a badly exaggerated English accent as we pushed through the front glass doors and Claudia turned back to click the lock for the weekend.

"Jolly good!" she replied when she picked up the English theme, and then hooked her arm through mine and we started across the parking lot to her red Honda Accord. Wow. That was interesting. She had picked up the fantasy theme without hesitation and gone with it. That was kind of cool.

I decided to stick with it and see where it went. "Dangerous place out here by the rail yard, you know. Can't have a beautiful young lady such as yourself attacked by venomous dogs, now can we?" Claudia giggled, and gave my arm a squeeze. I caught sight of something coming from behind the car, "Good heavens, there's one now!" Poochie had ambled up, fortunately without his preferred snack food, and introduced himself by sniffing Claudia's backside.

Without the slightest hesitation, she bent down and scratched his ears and looked around for an ID tag. "Hello, little guy. Who belongs to you?" Poochie had no collar, but seemed content to be fawned over by Claudia. I would have liked to project myself into that dog about then. "He's adorable," she crooned.

"Don't be fooled, Miss, these beasts are trained to lull their victims into a sympathetic stupor and then launch their fangs into your jugular like the French invading Poland." I was not at all sure if the French ever invaded Poland, but it seemed like something an English swashbuckler might say. International Swashbuckler? Better... but not quite right.

She continued to pet the pup, but smiled up at me, shifting back into her best aristocratic English accent, "I have my doubts as to the ferocity of this particular beast, Bert."

Bert? Who was Bert? That sounded so wrong. "Bertrand, if you please. Bertrand Chauncey, at your service." I made a deep bow and lightly kissed her hand as she stood near her car door.

She feigned a swoon, and I steadied her as she spoke, "My gracious, Mr. Chauncey, where have you been all my life?" Even with the fake swoon, this was extraordinarily encouraging, and I do not think I would have broken out of Bertrand Chauncey mode even if Bucky the Bagman had been charging towards me riding a rhino.

"Why Miss, I've been at your beck and call all this while." I delivered this with a smile as I kept her hand, opened her door with the other hand, and drew my arm in a theatrical sweep towards the seat.

She slid into the seat but left her door open for a parting word, "Sir, you have been most gallant. I do hope I might see you and your noble beast again."

My noble beast? Poochie? "It would be an honor. I shall not sleep until then. Or perhaps I shall sleep, but I shall not eat, I swear it is so. Or perhaps I will eat, but only some fish-and-chips and a pint or two."

She busted into giggles at this, closed her door and rolled down the window to wave goodbye. "Until then, Bertrand Chauncey." And she was off, gliding out of the parking lot like a red wave of heat, leaving me standing alone and wondering what just happened. Yesterday I was shoving circuit breakers into a shipping crate, and now I was cloned into a cross between Sam Spade and Sir Lancelot. And from the looks of things, I owned a dog.

Chapter Two

As I stood in the parking lot, feeling rather warm and proud of myself, I decided to take another chance. I walked around to the passenger side of my truck and opened the door. The dog followed behind and paused. "Load up!" In he went like it was standard protocol, perched himself on the seat and waited for me to climb aboard. "Settles that, I guess. Looks like we partner up, Poochie." The mutt gave a low growl and shot me the once-over. "What, you don't like Poochie?" I got a glare. "OK, fine. We need a new name, before I get bit." This required some thought. I had no idea the mutt was so sensitive. Hell, I was shocked he even spoke English. "Let's see, you like beautiful girls, and you like to eat human parts." Nice image, I thought, like something out of a horror movie. Sure... Silence of the Lambs. "Got it. Henceforth and hereafter, thou shalt be known as 'Hannibal the Hound', faithful defender of maidens, and occasional consumer of spare body parts." I reached across the seat and dubbed Hannibal lightly on each shoulder with an ice scraper. "Go forth, Hannibal, and do good deeds." Hannibal looked pleased with the new title. He smiled and looked out the window for maidens, ready for the next adventure. So be it.

As I started the engine and got set to wheel towards my low-rent apartment across town, I noticed a small note stuck under the windshield wiper. It was written on an old State Electric receipt that looked like it had flown out of some contractor's truck into the parking lot, because it appeared to have the impression of a tire tread across the face of it. Written in large letters it read simply: *'Pecker Head. Do Not Fuck Up.'*

Cute. Eloquent and to the point. So far, Bucky the Bagman had given me one shake of the head and six words. I felt like we were becoming fast friends. All the words were even capitalized! That had to count extra in our relationship, I thought. And such elegant stationary. Who does this shitweasel think he is? *Pecker Head*? That was a little strong. *Dipshit* would have been reasonable. Even *Dirtbag*. But, *Pecker Head*? Definitely over the line. No sense getting this friendship off on the wrong foot. Something had to be done. Bertrand Chauncey would never sit idly by and accept such an insult.

Under the seat was an old notepad from an electrical supplier, and I scrounged around and found a ball-point pen in the glove box. "How do we convey the proper sentiment to our new acquaintance, Hannibal?" He laid down to await my decision. "Ah, yes. Casual and patient. Good call, my aromatic friend." It was getting a little ripe inside the truck.

I turned the ignition back off, cranked the windows down and sat back to author Bertrand Chauncey's reply:

Dearest Bucky.

What a pleasure to see you today. Good to know the city's felons still have the superior taste to bury their victims in discreet locations. One bit of advice, if I may be so bold, next time dig a hole more than six inches deep. What were you using, a spoon? I deeply appreciate your advice regarding my occasional propensity to 'Fuck Up', but must take umbrage with the endearment 'Pecker Head'. Really. After all we've been through. It saddens me.

In the future, please see fit to address me by my full name, to avoid any unfortunate misunderstandings that might lead to your physical discomfort.

Most sincerely,

Bertrand Chauncey...

I reread the note and checked the signature line. It seemed to need something, so I embellished it a bit;

... and Hannibal

I liked the new touch. The note had flair. It was perfect. It was nuts. I was giving some murderous psycho my name? Well, it was not really my name, so to speak. He could have figured it out anyway by walking into State Electric and looking at the old 'Employee of the Month' posters. I had a couple pinned up there.

Hadn't done anything in particular, just managed to keep the fork-lift tongs out of the truck doors for a couple of months. So, no big secret there. I guess being an arrogant jerk would at least throw Bucky off temporarily. Maybe he had a sense of humor. Maybe not. At least I had not called the troops to investigate the scene. And the Hannibal part might really shake him up. He would have to stop and ponder that a bit. *Who the heck is Hannibal? This Bertrand dude looks like a putz, but Hannibal sounds dangerous.* I smiled. Hannibal smiled.

One small problem. How to deliver the note. I doubted if I could find Bucky sipping a latte at Starbucks, reading the Wall Street Journal while texting his boss that Freddie the Frog was sleeping with the fishes. I started the truck and pulled backward out of the space. Hannibal sat up and turned to look out the side window toward the corner of the warehouse. "Another good call, partner." I swung around to the corner and stopped by the edge of the lot, folded the note into a triangle and got out. Bucky was not at his previous outpost, so I slipped the note under a rusted railroad spike and set it on top of the dig, knowing he might return to enhance his handiwork before someone got wise. I got back in with Hannibal the Hound and took a long look around for any movement. Nothing.

No shots rang out. No car chases ensued. No sirens wailed in the distance. We just drove off, wondering if that last move was entirely sane. The note was fun, no doubt. But just maybe not incredibly bright. For one thing, it tied me to the crime. I could no longer plead ignorance, as I just signed a note admitting knowledge of the shallow burial. Very certainly not incredibly bright. About a half-mile from State Electric, I decided to turn around and go back for the note. I was still traveling parallel to the railroad switching yard, along Seventh Avenue, when I pulled into the Shop-n-Stuff parking lot to spin around and reverse my previous lack of judgment. One of those pesky coincidences popped up again, another in what now seems like a rather remarkable series of inter-connceted events. Right there in plain view next to the '*Return Carts Here*' rack was Claudia's red Honda Accord.

"By Jove, Hannibal, we seem to be running an unusual streak of good fortune today!" I figured Bucky the Bagman would not take a chance picking up the note back at the railroad tracks till darkness fell, so I wheeled into the next space and piled out of the truck. "Sit tight, Noble Beast, and I shall return in triumph." Hannibal showed no sign of being disturbed at being left alone in a strange truck. I kept the windows down, trusting my new partner would deter any potential truck thieves that may covet my dilapidated Ford F-100 with a mere 270,000 miles on the odometer. But I suspected I could have kept the keys in the ignition, put the signed pink slip on the dash, and taped a large "FREE!" sign on the door and still been perfectly safe. Besides, the aroma exuding from Hannibal would have been deterrent enough.

It occurred to me on the way into the Shop-n-Stuff that I was in actual need of some Shop-n-Stuff. Like dog food. And a dish. Maybe a collar. And some industrial dog shampoo. Did they allow dogs in my apartment? Jeez, how could they not allow dogs? Fleas and chiggers were the primary occupants. The place was once declared unfit for low-income housing by the city planning commission. It was a yellow brick block of apartments that had been shoddily constructed in close proximity to the rail yards, on the opposite end of town from State Electric. They discovered that the foundation concrete had been mixed with surplus oatmeal to save money, which probably worked reasonably well in the short-term. But Vista View Apartments were strategically located atop the oozing quagmire of a former wetland, prior to being bulldozed into reluctant submission by my forefathers whose legendary vision of progress did not include any flat area of land left unplowed or unpaved. The unfortunate combination of a bog for an understory, oatmeal for a foundation, and 1350 fully loaded freight cars per day vibrating the earth in all directions gradually encouraged my humble domicile to list about six degrees to the west. From the front view, it looked like all the fat people were having a party over on the starboard side of the ship, and we were preparing to take on water. This slight inconvenience caused the city planners to refuse the use permit for low-income housing, a formality that would have allowed the apartment owner, one Francisco Rodriguez Hernandez Shapiro, owner of 29 other marginal complexes, to secure city tax subsidies for each unit. This subsidy far exceeded the market rental value of the dumps in question. Francisco Rodriguez Hernandez Shapiro failed to understand that the city planners must ultimately answer to the mayor, who was running a tight mayoral race at the time and needed the Hispanic and Jewish vote to ensure his victory in November. Francisco Rodriguez Hernandez Shapiro was asked to erect large placards in front of each of his 29 pestilent accommodations to help swing the Hispanic and Jewish vote. The city planners assumed, with limited accuracy, that my landlord must have considerable sway with both groups, given his ethnically diverse name and the fact that the majority of his tenants belonged to one group or the other. The campaign sign request was ignored, as Francisco Rodriguez Hernandez Shapiro did not think election placards would enhance the ambiance of his dwellings, and failed to make a direct link from the billboards to his application for subsidies. He apparently had the political insight of a fruit-bat.

As I pondered these issues on my way into the Shop-n-Stuff, I remembered seeing Francisco Rodriguez Hernandez Shapiro at my complex one time, trying to prop up the south wall of the apartment complex with four-by-fours. But he had not shown his face near there since, so I doubted if keeping Hannibal would make any waves. Besides, once Hannibal had his shampoo, who could have resisted such a face? Had to keep him from eating any more people, though. That particular culinary faux-pas would definitely endear him to very few people.

I looked up and down the grocery aisles for Claudia, but did not see her near the front of the store. The place was enormous, and people sometimes lost touch with relatives for years inside there, before a chance tearful reunion in the produce department. Instead of developing a grid search to track her whereabouts, I decided to let fate take her course, and develop a grid search for dog food instead. After only one wrong turn into the Horrific Stench of Soap Products aisle, I located the giant bags of kibble and considered my choices. May as well go for volume, a forty-pounder would be a good start. Something told me this partnership was not a temporary setup. But which brand, and what flavor? I looked for '*Human Arm Flavor, With Real Bits and Pieces of People's Personal Parts that Dogs Love!*'... but they were out. Thinking back to Anthony Hopkins, I settled on '*Lamb and Liver*', the perfect combination for Hannibal.

The dog paraphernalia was stashed on the opposite side of the aisle, so I loaded up on the basics; two big sturdy plastic bowls, a blue collar made out of webbing, and two large bottles of '*Good-Boy*' doggy shampoo with flea resistance. '*Good-Boy*' was purported to make my doggy '*Glow!*' and I wondered if it had any nuclear waste material mixed in. I formed a mental image of confronting Bucky the Bagman in a dark alley, with Hannibal beside me, fur sticking straight out in all directions, glowing a faint orange color in the night. *'Don't fuck with me, Bucky, or Hannibal here will light up your world.'* I was growing increasingly pleased with my choice of partners. Or was it Hannibal's choice? Hard to say.

I passed up the leash rack after some consideration. It did not seem quite appropriate to keep one's partner on a leash. But I wondered about whether Hannibal might get bored and wander off to wherever he came from. I thought, if he did, then he did. He is his own master anyway, not me. His decision. A voice called from behind me, "Why, Mr. Chauncey, what a surprise to see you!" Claudia had come up the aisle and was smiling broadly. I was glad she was addressing Bertrand Chauncey, as she had barely noticed Bert Clauster for nearly two years.

"Miss Auckland, what a pleasure." I bowed deeply, trying to look as English as possible.

She sized up one of my shopping items, "I see you are stocking up for the venomous beast. Aren't you afraid of being bitten?"

"Terrified, my dear. Hence the purchases. Bribery can be an effective tool, when dealing with these nefarious types. Got to negotiate on their level, you see. Lull them into a sense of complacency and then ply them with kibble. Remarkable what secrets can be learned after a stout bowl of chow." She looked like a French painting, standing there in her plaid skirt, hair shining in the Shop-n-Stuff fluorescent lighting, leaning on her cart with that melting smile. I could hear myself talking with her, but it was all coming from somewhere else... maybe *someone* else. I felt incredibly detached to whoever was joking and laughing with this beautiful lady, so unlike the nervous sputtering dunce that should have been in his place. I remember that it seemed so effortless. That is how it must have been for the handsome self-confident types I had envied all my life. Effortless.

She switched to my side of the aisle, reaching across to the shelf for a can of Friskies chicken flavor cat food, "And you, Mr.

Chauncey? What devious interrogation methods are required to ply secrets out of you?" She smiled as she plunked the cat food can into her cart that contained what appeared to be disturbingly healthy food items.

"My heavens. I'm afraid I must admit, much the same method has often been embarrassingly effective on me." I hung my head pitifully.

"Really? All I need to do is offer you a bowl of kibble and I can learn all about this mysterious Bertrand Chauncey?" Was this an offer? Whoa! This Chauncey dude was on a definite roll today. This was so unexpected that Bert almost blurted out, *'Oh hell, yes, you can ply me with kibble... or water... or cheap beer, or just about anything!'* But fortunately Bertrand caught up with the thought before it could be said.

"Perhaps. But I require a fine kibble. To loosen my tongue, I require a delicate mixture of chow simmered with brochette of beef, with flavors of chateaubriand, and perhaps a crystal bowl teeming with sparkling mineral water." That got another encouraging reaction, with a delicious laugh from her.

"I may have to dig deep in the recipe book for that dish, but let me see what I can do. Come by tomorrow night and I'll bet I can have you talking like Chatty Cathy by the time we have dessert." Claudia Auckland was asking me out. Or more specifically, asking me in. *In* was even better than *out*. Either way, this was a major coup on my part. Bert Clauster was pin-balling around off the ceiling, but Bertrand Chauncey casually retrieved the new plastic bowl from his cart and held it out for Claudia's consideration, "Shall I bring my own china?"

Another glorious giggle escaped as she replied, "No, Mr. Chauncey, I think I may have a spare. Here's the address... a little after seven?" She was writing out a note along the blank portion of her shopping list. She tore it off and slipped it to me with a lovely smile. I took the note and mustered a supreme effort not to melt into a puddle of goo in the middle of the pet food aisle. After a thought she added, "... and bring along the ferocious beast... what was his name? I don't think you ever mentioned it."

"Indeed. He is known as Hannibal the Hound. But I must warn you, I cannot be responsible for his actions, for his preference in cuisine lacks certain refinements that might otherwise make him a more pleasant dinner guest." I thought back to Hannibal's lunch choice earlier in the day and worried about his table manners. But what else would I do with the mutt while I was being wined and dined (or kibbled and watered)?

Claudia did not seem concerned with Hannibal's lack of social graces, "Hannibal will be fine. He and Cecelia can become fast friends and find other interests to amuse themselves during dinner."

Cecelia? "Might I assume that Cecelia is of the feline persuasion, judging by your recent selection?" I pointed into the cart at the Friskies can. I felt proud of my deductive powers at that point, picking up on the subtleties of minute details, and swiftly processing the data to arrive at a stunningly incorrect conclusion.

"Actually, no. Cecelia is my Irish setter."

"I see, well, she has a beautiful name." I was confused.

"He."

Now I was very confused. "Excuse me?"

"Cecelia is a *he*." Claudia appeared to be serious. "He is very sweet, but seems to have a serious... um, gender issue."

"That explains the cat food?" That did not explain the cat food.

Claudia paused to consider a response, "No, that would be Cecelia's... um, species issue. Cecelia thinks he is a female cat. Refuses to eat anything from the dog food department. On the bright side, he is meticulously clean and seldom barks."

As strange as this conversation had become, it seemed, oddly, to conform to the general theme of the day, so it did not surprise me much when Bertrand Chauncey immediately replied, "Good show. Had a neighbor once with a white cockatiel that was convinced he was an iguana. Sat about all day on a sunny window ledge trying to snap flies out of the air. Most amusing bird."

Claudia seemed amused as well. "Mr. Chauncey, I am very much looking forward to continuing these stories over kibble tomorrow evening."

I took this as my cue to do something dashing, so I took her hand for the second time in the hour and gave it a kiss. "Until then!" I took my leave by reversing the direction of my Shop-n-Stuff cart nimbly, pushing off hard toward the registers, and jumping onto the cart rail with one foot while extending the other back horizontally, one hand raised forward like superman, and sailing down along the pet food displays looking like the prow ornament of a schooner. I could hear that delicious laugh all the way to the registers.

Back outside in the parking lot, a freight train was chugging past at a moderate clip, heading west toward my apartment end of town. Once, in the previous spring, I had ridden one of these freight cars back to the apartment after work when my truck refused to start. I had waited for a nice slow-moving string of boxcars to pass and then hopped on one of the passing ladders. It was so easy. Hobo Bert riding the rails, wild and free! All very romantic till we got to the apartment area and I began searching for a good landing spot to bail off the boxcar. To complicate disembarking, the train's pace had picked up to around 30 mph, and the railroad-ties were whizzing by at a blurring rate. Amazing how few soft-looking spots are provided along railroad tracks. I chose the crossing of a side-street, with flashing guard-rails in horizontal position and bells ringing to warn approaching motorists that an extremely large object might sputz their Subaru into a grease spot if they try to cross. But at least the side road provided something paved and smooth, rather than the creosote soaked ties and herbicide infused gravel. I remember that my exit lacked the type of grace and balance I had hoped for, as I tried to keep my legs moving as quickly as my body. Once my feet made initial contact with the pavement, I had several seconds of suspended forward momentum to contemplate the inevitable consequences. I might have made it intact, but the crossing bar blocked my trajectory and it hit me in the groin, spinning me over like a foul ball flying off the top of a baseball bat. I impacted the front of Chevy Suburban full of soccer kids who all went into a wild uproar of laughter and hooted mercilessly until the train passed and Soccer Mom drove them quickly across the tracks toward their pizza party, leaving me to scab over at the curb.

In the Shop-n-Stuff parking lot, I got back to the truck while thinking, *'That was Bert Clauster bouncing off the bumper, not*

Bertrand Chauncey. Bert is the subject of ridicule and amusement for soccer brats... Bertrand Chauncey is the subject of intrigue and mystery'. Even Claudia had wondered about the mysterious Bertrand Chauncey. He would not have bounced... he would have jumped lightly astride a passing convertible, slipped casually into the passenger seat beside a stunning swimsuit model, produced a rose from his vest and said, *'Fabulous of you to pick me up. Could I possibly make it up to you this evening?'* There were a few logistical difficulties with making this particular fantasy flow seamlessly. The convertible would need to be traveling dangerously close to the train, in the same direction. And the driver would need to be on the right side of the car, leaving the passenger seat next to the train. Maybe she was driving an English Austin Healy. Or the whole scene could take place going the other direction. What if she had the top up, if it was raining? But no doubt Bertrand Chauncey would have worked out such minor details in mid-air.

Hannibal was sitting patiently in the seat, watching the world go by, as I loaded the goodies into the back and swung into the driver seat. "Great news, my friend! I have a date with the beautiful Claudia Auckland tomorrow night!" He looked at me with skepticism. "And you, my smelly canine associate, have a date with a very disturbed dog." His skepticism deepened. "Do not fear, Noble Beast. I want you to exhibit tolerance and open-mindedness. This sort of thing happens within the best of families." This was met with an icy glare from Hannibal. *'Speak for yourself,'* seemed to be the best translation I could make.

"Did I mention that your date tomorrow, Cecelia, also considers himself to be a female cat? Eats smelly tins of tuna-flavored gruel and coughs up hairballs with some regularity." I added that last part for shock effect. It worked. Hannibal collapsed into a curled heap on the seat and tucked his head into his tail, utterly disgusted with the image. "Do try to be cordial, won't you? I'm sure she will find you attractive... or he will... whatever." This was bordering on animal cruelty so I relented, "Come on, mate, it will be worth some laughs, at least. The owner is a peach... you remember, Claudia, the one who scratched your ears back at the shop?" Hannibal shot me a quick glance with one eye, but kept his head tucked away. Maybe I should have softened that delivery a bit. I could have left out a few details to keep the suspense up a bit. Keeping Hannibal in the dark might have made for a more interesting scene on our arrival Saturday night. I envisioned Hannibal's introduction to Cecelia, *'Good God, Hannibal! I had no idea Cecelia would turn out to possess that kind of appendage. Shocking! And the way she licks herself! Himself? Whatever! My boy, I am as flabbergasted as you.'* But I could not have done that to Hannibal. Maybe to one of my old college roommates, sure. They deserve getting cornered into a blind date with a gay cat-dog. In fact many of them have. But Hannibal seemed above that sort of juvenile prank, so his sudden disposition of disgust with me and my arrangements was justified. I endeavored to brighten his mood, "Let's go home and bust out the feed bag. You in?" That elicited a lukewarm grunt as Hannibal raised up to look around when the truck roared to life.

I was thinking about the complexities of having a dog versus the potential benefits as I backed out of the grocery parking slot. Negative aspects included the forty-three bucks I just laid out for dog goodies, versus the potential benefit of having girls like Claudia coming over to say, "He's *soooo* cute!" As I swung back forward I noticed a familiar small piece of paper under the wiper. Uh oh. Looked a lot like the last piece of paper I found there after work. This one turned out to be an old grocery receipt, rather than from State Electric. Oddly, it too had a tire imprint across the face. I was going to have to buy Bucky some Post-It-Notes. What class of hit man has to scrounge around in the gutter for scraps of paper to print his implied threats? Has prevailing wage for thugs dropped to this level? Has no one convinced them to try collective bargaining?

> *Nice Babe Pecker Head*
> *Maybe She Gets It Two*
> *After Im Done With Her*
> *Its Your Tern*

There he went with the capitalization again. No comma after Babe. Misuse or misspelling of the adverb *too*. No apostrophe in the contraction *I'm* or *It's*. Misspelling of *turn*. Bucky was not only underpaid, he was illiterate. Bagman school was simply not producing the quality of goons they used to in the old days. Still, the note sent a bit of a chill through me. I made a mental list of some implied messages:

1. Bucky the Bagman was probably watching me right then.

2. Bucky must have seen Claudia with me in front of State Electric, seen me write the note, then gone back for it.

3. Bucky then followed me to the grocery with apparent ease.

4. Hannibal was a wuss for not biting him when he got close to the open window.

5. That stupid dipshit act with Bertrand Chauncey had just gotten Claudia involved in some very dark stuff.

6. I was also in deep pigeon poop.

I looked around quickly, expecting to see the dark clothes and dark shades peering out from behind a mini-van. *'Come on out, Bucky. Drag your Mastodon carcass out where I can see you.'* My hands were shaking on the wheel. I had made some fairly serious mistakes in the past couple of hours. Somebody out there had a very limited sense of humor, along with the scholastic achievements of a water buffalo. My humorous problem solving turned out to be humongous problem causing. All the elation of being invited to dinner with Claudia was turning into rising bile in my throat. I was about to get her killed... or worse. Bucky seemed a little too interested in her great looks to assume he would have the common decency to just shoot her. If I had only walked away from Hannibal and that disgusting bone he dug up. Even after that, I could have pretended it was just another scrap from the butcher. But that dickweed Bertrand Chauncey had to strut up and take charge. Rescue the Noble Beast, sweep the girl off her feet, and then leave a signed note for some felon telling him to stick it all in his ear. Brilliant.

No sign of the Mastadon, so I pulled to the far corner of the parking lot to weigh the situation. Maybe I should just lead him over to my ramshackle apartment and show him around. *'Hey Buckster, glad you could make it. Lemme show you around. Key is right here on this nail in the corner. Wanna beer?'* No doubt he would follow me there. I wondered if I could spot him behind me, if he followed along. I'm sure I never saw him behind me on the way to the grocery... but then, I wasn't looking very hard.

I started to pull out to the avenue and give Bucky a good shake around town, but I stopped before reaching the exit gap and pulled back around into a lane that more or less meandered around the entire Shop-n-Stuff complex. I spotted Claudia's red Accord still by the cart return rack. I kept moving past it till I was able to make a left turn behind the gigantic grocery outlet where the big rigs congregate near the cooler room doors. I made a bat-turn between a couple of Shop-n-Stuff delivery rigs, and snuck back out to the edge of the building where I could just barely get a peek of Claudia's car. I could not let this chimp-turd follow Claudia. I was also not sure what to do if he did. Call the cops? *'Hello, 911? Yeah, emergency. There's this guy, all in black, no idea who he is... let's just call him Bucky for now. Anyway, I'm at Shop-n-Stuff and Bucky just pulled right out onto the avenue behind this girl I know. Can you believe it? Yeah. Come quick.'*

That conversation seemed to lack the urgency required to force the typical 911 operator out of their lethargic stupor. *'Oh yes sir. I understand. I have the National Guard moving in with Blackhawks as we speak. And just for the record, what might your name be, Romeo?'* OK, no emergency calls. I was over-reacting. I hoped I was over-reacting.

I spotted Claudia heading to her car. She loaded up the trunk, and pulled out into the lot, and of course I was just overreacting to nothing. Except that black sedan that had been parked along the outside berm the whole time was moving out behind her! Yep, that was Bucky all right. Oh, crap! He's going for her, not me. Oh, crap, crap, crap!

"What do we do, Hannibal?" No response from my partner. He just shifted over in the seat and leaned against his door like he might take a snooze. "Big help, there, Watson. I could use a little input here." The problem with Hannibal, I learned later, was not that he failed to provide input at critical times, he was just subtle about his delivery. I pulled the truck around the building and shot down the space towards the exit where Claudia was just turning onto the avenue parallel to the passing freight train. Bucky's black sedan was closing the gap to the exit point, but a jacked-up Jeep Cherokee roared out of the other lane and cut him off before he could pull out behind the red Honda. I could hear the sub-woofers pounding out of the Jeep and watched Bucky edge impatiently up to the back of the Jeep.

Hannibal continued his nonchalance by leaning at an even greater angle against the door as I sped toward Bucky. I had no clue what to do to prevent him from following Claudia. Hannibal gave a quick woof and I glanced over. "You want me to bark at him?" All I got was an *'Oh, please,'* look. "You want me to... do what? Lean on him?"

"Woof."

As the black sedan prepared to pull out, I punched my old Ford up from behind, mashed in his right-rear quarter panel, and spun him around facing the curb. I was sure Claudia missed all this, as I saw her disappear into the evening traffic. My truck was sandwiched in between the sedan and shoppers piling up behind me, trying to get home with their sacks of groceries. On the advice of a stray dog, I had just smashed up the vehicle of the thug who wanted me dead. Even more brilliance. Nowhere to go at this point. Might as well get set to get the snot kicked out of me. Bucky was already out and heading back to me. I leaned out casually and greeted him, "Hey, look who's here. What an honor! It's Bucky the Bagman!"

The guy was thick as a refrigerator, so he sort of waddled when he walked up to the truck window. Hannibal sat calmly by me and took in the confrontation with detachment. "Whadda fug you think you're doing! You fuggin' crazy? You're the little pecker head that's been sniffin' around where he don't belong!" He was leaning into my face outside the door and raging mad, face red with fury. I had the strangest thought as he stood there, blowing flecks of spittle into my face, *'Maybe he will kill Bertrand and leave me alone!'*

"Oh, now, there you go again with the pecker head thing. Why don't we search for a grain of creativity here, shall we? Remember... didn't we discuss this very thing in our last correspondence?" I smiled broadly and awaited his reply. It was not forthcoming. He just stared at me with his great gaping mouth open.

After a few seconds, a few more invectives must have been processed through that dense cranial block of his and he restarted, "I oughtta jerk your worthless ass outta that truck and pound the crap outta your worthless ass!" A bit redundant, but his point was clear.

"Now, now, Bucky. That's twice you used the term 'worthless ass' in same sentence. If you can't speak fluidly and with a little more creativity, I suggest you hold your tongue till you have fully formulated your thoughts." I was now prepared to die, right in front of the Shop-n-Stuff. But somehow, I felt like it was Bertrand that was about to get hammered. Bert was hiding behind him somewhere, poking this huge moron with a sharp stick, just for laughs. As reckless as it seems now, I felt safe hiding behind Bertrand, like I was not going to feel the pain when my head was twisted off and rolled out into traffic like a grapefruit.

"The name ain't Bucky, pecker head! Who the fug is Bucky?"

"Good heavens! My mistake. Since you were so prompt in returning my first missive addressed to 'Bucky', I naturally assumed I had guessed correctly. Please forgive me, but we have not been formally introduced. I'm Bertrand Chauncey. And who might you be?" I stuck my hand out the window in greeting, wondering if I would see it ripped from the socket and used to beat me senseless. Bucky... or whoever he was... continued to gape mutely at me, struggling to get his mental footing in this unfamiliar territory.

About then, one of the frustrated shoppers behind the crunched sedan laid on the horn and hollered out his window, "Move it, Magilla, I got ice cream melting in here!" Bucky moved with alarming speed to the silver Prius waiting two cars back. The alert driver was able to get his driver side window up in case Bucky was thinking about jerking him out that portal, but failed to perform the same duty for the back window, into which Bucky shot a thick, hairy arm and extracted a half-gallon of Dreyer's Mocha Almond Fudge ice cream that he then smeared across the windshield and hood of the Prius.

"There you go, Asswipe. Now you don't got to worry about your fuggin' ice cream." He turned back towards me as I considered an appropriate comment.

"Ever been in an anger management seminar?" I offered calmly. His big paws were back resting in my window that I had not bothered to roll up. Mocha almond ice cream was dripping from his hairy knuckles onto my floorboard. I continued, "Look, we can either call the cops to come have look-see at this little fender bender, or we could both pull over to the Palm Frond Saloon over there, have a cold beer and figure out the next move. Cops might already be on the way after your little food fight with Asswipe back there." The Prius had squeezed out of the line and was bouncing over the curb at the edge of the parking lot to escape the crazed gorilla that attacked his grocery bag. "'Asswipe' was a nice touch, by the way. Very creative. I think you may have some potential after all."

To my utter astonishment, the big maniac grunted, "Thanks". He actually mistook blinding sarcasm for a compliment. He added, "OK, let's get over to the Palm Frond. Park out back... and don't try to take off on me, you hear?"

"My dear boy, it was me who came crashing in to you, remember? If I wanted to run, I had ample opportunity to do so prior to this unfortunate mishap." It seemed that both Claudia and I were destined to live a bit longer. My assailant had calmed himself a bit, and was actually prepared to have a discussion regarding our predicament at a local watering hole. Perhaps things were brighter than they seemed. At least, from the looks of things.

Chapter Three

The Palm Frond Saloon was within sight of the Shop-n-Stuff complex, almost attached to the back corner, except for a narrow delivery alley that separated the two architecturally mindless pieces of urban sprawl. Both structures, along with most of the rest of the strip-mall enterprises in the vicinity, had been expelled from the intestines of the 1970's building boom that transformed Kansas City from a major urban center to an exceptionally ugly major urban center. The Palm Frond Saloon had not been the original tenant. In 1974 an enterprising older Asian fellow named Chung had the insight to construct and finance The Happy Hanger Dry Cleaners near the grocery, for the convenience of middle-class suburban housewives to pick up the hubby's shirts on the way home from the grocery. This stunning bit of business foresight was abruptly derailed by the newfound popularity of permanent press shirts that diminished the profit margins to the point that most of the dry cleaning businesses were forced to supplement their income by selling powerful Asian remedies made from the powdered remains of nearly extinct animals. Adaptive business management.

After a 1989 police raid involving the Bureau of ATF, INS, FBI, and the KCPD, the Happy Hanger was shut down and eventually transformed into a second-hand clothing store given the original name 'The Second Saver'. Six months later the new renters, two elderly ladies from Minnesota, realized that it took a lot of fifty-cent shoes to pay the rent on commercial storefront. One night, they loaded up their 1966 Buick LeSabre and disappeared, leaving the front door of the Second Saver unlocked and a large 'FREE' sign taped to the front window. Despite the significant markdown, most of the stained garments donated by widows of recently deceased train-yard workers failed to attract any takers, and the landlord had to pay to haul three truckloads of soiled garments to the city dump.

Ironically, the next venture that opened in 1992 was a strip club called the Pole-n-Hole, where there was very little demand for clothing at all. This enterprise fared considerably better, as the demand for incoherent young naked girls was not likely to be upstaged by some modern advancement in technology and the cash flow could have covered rent on the White House. But even the most solid business plan cannot account for the self-righteous indignation of the right-wing conservative religious masses. Despite clear demonstration of demand for this entertainment venue, a large number of local Fundamental Baptists became so enraged at the success of the Pole-n-Hole, that they began to picket the parking lot with signs that read '*Protect Our Daughters*' and '*Shame on Sinners*'. This demonstration had a chilling effect on the stripping business, due in part to one particularly vehement Baptist who camped in his car every night taking home videos of all customers and then posting them on a local public access television channel, where ratings went through the roof. After that, you could safely allow your infant children to play unattended in the parking lot of the Pole-n-Hole. They folded within a year.

The Palm Frond Saloon opened for business in late 1993 and retained the same managers that ran the strip club, trying to salvage some of the clientele from the previous successful venture. This decision allowed the Palm Frond to retain a certain strip-club ambiance that was further enhanced by the brass pole still affixed to the stage behind the bar, ostensibly for historical value. There were, however, known to be impromptu performances that occurred late on weekend evenings, but these rumors were hardly the foundation for moral outrage. Most of the public display of shock and disgust was diluted by calming words from the new Fundamental Baptist preacher, Pastor Habbersham, telling his flock to focus on the needs of the hungry and the poor. This diversion was necessary so that Pastor Habbersham could continue to focus his Saturday night evangelical attention on the tragically under-dressed Tyffany. It is rumored that he has been spotted after midnight at the Palm Frond Saloon, staggering out of the club with his shirt unbuttoned. Just reaching out to the troubled youth of our community.

I dutifully aimed my pickup toward the designated area, pulled through the delivery alley between the club and the grocery and found an open spot near the back entrance. The dented sedan backed in next to me and Bucky extracted his mammoth girth from behind the wheel and waited at the rear entrance door for me to join him. I left Hannibal in the seat again and reluctantly slid out. The air had the smell of decaying dumpster detritus and stale beer; the kind of stench that can get a Kansas City drunk all teary eyed and sentimental.

"Pleased you could join me, er... once again, I seem to be at a loss for a name?" He stood holding the door open. On the back of the door was an impressive air-brushing of an enormous palm frond arching gracefully over a leggy blond with a martini glass in her hand. They had apparently not strayed far from the old Pole-n-Hole theme.

"Mack." He delivered this syllable as if he were using it to break a rib.

"Of course. I might have known. Please excuse the Bucky label, needed something catchy and I thought..."

"Shut the fug up and get inside, smartass." Well, at least he had a name now. Probably not a real name, but he could not take offense at being called 'Mack' since he brought it up.

"OK, Mack, after you." I motioned for him to enter, but he did not move so much as a knuckle from the door.

"Wrong. You first. Last thing I need is some fancy little puke sticking me in the back with a knife."

"Fancy little pecker head, you mean. Really, Mack, I thought we were beyond all that."

"Move it, before I die of thirst." We entered the gloom of the bar, me first, and took a couple of chairs at a little table away from the bar. We both seemed to understand that chatting it up with the bartender was ill-advised at this stage.

The bartender, an enormous round walrus of a guy with facial hair to match came around the end of the bar, tossed a couple of Top-Side Ale coasters across the table and said "What's your pleasure?"

"Ah, my pleasure would be to sip a frosty beverage while enjoying a deep tissue massage from Cindy Crawford while laying naked on a private beach in the Caymans." This bit of mirth was met with a blank, unsmiling stare from Wally, so I added quickly, "...or a Bud draft."

Mack looked up and ordered, "Same." Wally rolled his eyes and returned behind the bar to draw the beers. Safely out of earshot,

Mack began, "So, we got issues, here, Chauncey." He leaned across the table and gave me a hard stare to convey the gravity of this statement.

"Yes, I agree. Looks like we missed happy hour by fifteen minutes."

"You know what I mean, smartass. You seen somethin' today you shouldn't have oughtta seen. We gotta do somethin' about that, don't we?" This was beginning to sound like something out of a low-budget 1960s gangster movie.

"I quite agree, Mack, we need to discuss several of the mistakes you made during your recent foray into the undertaking business." This zinger was timed perfectly as Wally returned with the two drafts and plopped them down unceremoniously on the coasters. Mack could not blow up without raising some alarm from the bartender. I continued, "Thank you, sir. Nothing like a frosty pint of lager to take the edge off the travails of the day, what say?"

The confused bartender stood by the table staring blankly at me. "Where in hell you from, boy? You sound *fern*."

I realized the word Wally was striving for was '*foreign*', so I took his perceptive conclusion as a compliment to my affected accent. "Why yes, my good man, Great Britain, to be sure. Bertrand Chauncey, at your service. And who might you be?" I rose and extended my hand in greeting while wondering why I offered all this information to a complete stranger.

He shook my hand, probably out of reflex, and added, "Walter. Folks here call me Walt. Welcome to the Palm Frond. You boys travelin'?" He eyed Mack and probably hoped he was traveling. Mack looked like he could throw the beer cooler through the wall.

I almost fell out of my seat. "Walter? You must be having a spot of fun with us. I was just saying to my business associate here that you look like a 'Wally'. Ever go by that particular nickname, Walter?"

"Nope, not since kindergarten. Sounds homo. I'll stick with Walt, if you don't mind." He returned to the bar without digging any deeper. No sense prying into the private affairs of two paying customers, unless they volunteered it on their own. Business was business, and money from some English poof was as good as money from the next guy.

I turned my attention back to Mack. "Look, Mack, we need to get past this scene out of Scarface. You might be a tough guy, no offense intended, but you're no Tony Montana. You've made some serious errors in your recent work, and I have resisted the temptation to turn you over to the authorities, at great risk to my own reputation. Now please do me the courtesy of dropping the insults and threatening little notes and admit that my recent restraint has saved you considerable trouble.

Mack was taken aback by my turn on offense. The change in his expression told me I had the upper hand for the moment and he knew I had spoken the truth. Still, he felt like he needed to play the role of the thug, so he ventured, "What about the car? Boss is goin' to skin me for that. Whadda fug you have to go and mash in the car?"

I could tell his heart was not in the attack, so I let him off easy. "Mack, what was I supposed to do? You took off to trail a very sweet girl; who knows nothing about any of this, by the way. You give me a note that makes me think there may be some reason to suspect you capable of bodily harm and perhaps sexual deviance, so I give you a little nudge to spin your attentions in the opposite direction, so to speak. You can't blame me for trying to protect Claudia. None of this is her fault, and I could not let you frighten the knickers off her for something I had done."

Mack's reaction showed the argument was gaining some footing, so I continued, "Besides, I was not the one who got tired of digging and decided that an inch is as good as a mile. I suggest that you consider refining your tactics before the Bobbies come and incarcerate you."

"Yeah, my cousin got incarcerated in an apartment fire one time, and he came out looking like a piece of bacon. And who's Bobby?"

"Incinerated," I replied with as much patience as I could muster.

"Yeah. That too." My God, it was going to be tough sledding. "OK. So I might have buried the stiff a little shallow. How was I supposed to know your little dog was gonna dig him up? Jeez, I do everything just perfect, like Mr. Perez wants, and I still fug it up. And now I gotta take the car with the big dent in the back and explain all that. I'm gonna get shit-canned over this. I gotta explain this to Mr. Per... oops." He caught himself in mid-sentence and looked up to see if maybe I had missed the name. "You didn't hear nothin' about no Mr. Perez, you understand?"

"No, no, Mack, nothing at all. And I never saw that rotting finger bone the dog unearthed, and you and I are just old college pals from Cambridge, reminiscing about our adventures on the cricket field." The thought of seeing Mack with a cricket bat would certainly put the opposite team in hasty retreat.

"You talk American, you hear. I don't know nothin' about crickets or Bobbies or no pints of loggers," he was beginning to work up another rage, so I tried to tone down the rhetoric a shade.

"Sorry, Mack. Look, my point is, if I intended to turn you in, I would have already done it by now. I have had ample opportunity to call the police, and yet here we sit, having a pint of lager... er, *beer*, and trying to work out a solution so that we can both continue with our lives."

He sagged down into his seat, both massive hands wrapped around his mug, looking truly pitiful. "I s'pose," Mack replied, resigning himself to his fate, whatever it was. After a few moments, a different thought seeped slowly into his consciousness, "So how come you never went to the screws with all this? How come you're sittin' on this deal so cool and calm and all?" He looked over expectantly and pulled a long drink out of his beer that emptied half the glass.

"Mack, let's just say I have a vested interest in keeping a low profile for the time being. Inserting myself amid the bustle of a murder investigation, with all the associated newsprint photos and live-action coverage on the local television, well, that might become somewhat detrimental to my interests." I did not have the foggiest idea what Bertrand Chauncey was babbling about. He seemed to have taken on a life of his own and left Bert Clauster out of the loop. It was somewhat disturbing to listen to this rambling dialogue without any clue whatsoever as to either the source or the direction. I was sitting in a dark drinking establishment of negotiable integrity, careening off in some parallel universe, operating under the ruse of a fictional English rogue, befriending an educationally challenged behemoth thug named Mack. Interesting day.

What might pass for a smile came across his face. "You running some weed out of the old electric store, Chauncey? Maybe something stronger? Hey? I seen them trucks coming and going every day. You tryin' to tell me nothin's in them trucks but light bulbs? That's a lot of light bulbs!"

"Yes, yes, you've got me there, Mack. State Electric is a front for a massive marijuana distribution system run by a Lithuanian cartel. I, myself, am Lithuanian, but have undergone intensive facial surgery and linguistics training to complete the subterfuge."

Mack sat back in shock. "No, shit. You've got one of them things that enrich uranium in the warehouse? That's some serious shit, there, buddy."

My turn to sit back in shock. "Oh, no, Mack. I believe you are talking about a *centrifuge*, and we do not have one... yet. Anyway, we are not making bombs or selling weed. I was being sarcastic."

"You mean you was being a smartass again, right?"

"Well, yes. But don't take these things personally. It's just the English manner of discourse. We often banter about, saying outrageous things just to hear the sound of them." That seemed almost exactly what Bertrand Chauncey had been doing. Saying outrageous things at random, just to enjoy the reaction to them. It felt like a dangerous method of communication, but I was at an utter loss to reverse the process, especially sitting across from the Human Wrecking Ball. Better stick with Plan A for now and see what consequences arose.

Mack leaned across the table and whispered, "OK. You tell me what bullshit you got going in the warehouse, and I tell you what bullshit I got goin' with Mr. Perez. That way, can't neither one of us stick it to the other one without messin' his own deal." Mack looked over for my response. Actually, Mack made a very reasonable observation. Perhaps I underestimated his mental capacity. A little low on the vocabulary, perhaps, but not without some street intuition. He had survived to this point somehow.

"OK, Mack, but not here. Wally might have sharp ears. Let's take a peek about the front for the local constables and then clear out to a more appropriate setting."

"Jesus, you talk like a fag." Mack pounded back the remainder of his beer, I left a five for Wally, and we slipped out the back door of the Palm Frond Saloon. The stench of dumpster smacked into us like the backdraft of a forest fire. I told Mack to sit tight by the truck while I checked around the front to make sure the Mocha Almond Fudge incident had not precipitated a police response. No sign of the local boys in blue, so I returned to find Mack scratching Hannibal's head through my truck window. "Nice dog. He don't smell too good, though."

"Yes, Mack, I am keenly aware of his aroma. Could be related to his choice of cuisine for lunch, remember?"

"Oh, yeah. Forgot about that. Probably should have bagged that a-hole up and flung him in the river like the last two." The last two? Great. Mack was a mass murderer, not your garden variety common single murderer. I might have known.

Once again, I did a quick mental count on the transformations that had occurred during the day. I had: a) discovered portions of a dead body in a shallow grave, b) forfeited innocence in the matter by failing to report the discovery, c) acquired a medium-sized brown mutt and named him after a notorious cannibal, d) switched personalities into a loquacious English chap with a penchant for questionable business dealings, e) negotiated a social liaison with a remarkably attractive young lady, f) caused a collision in a crowded parking area, g) befriended a large psychopathic murderer and then prepared to take him into strictest confidence regarding the fictitious illegal enterprises of my alter ego. And it wasn't quite dark yet. Plenty of time left to liven up the day.

Chapter Four

Mack followed Hannibal and I across town to a small public park where vigilant moms and a few somewhat less vigilant dads supervised their children's mayhem across a few acres of grassy, tree-lined open space carved out of the center of a housing development. All the surrounding homes were built by the same developer, who had enormous respect for the individuality of the future buyers by altering the configuration of the attached garages slightly on every other home, and instructing the painting crew to reverse the color combination of the trim and siding on a house-by-house rotational pattern to give the units a truly unique quality. The repetitious color patterns resulted in the common practice of weary or intoxicated residents walking into the wrong house, usually two, four, or sometimes six doors away. On returning from those late night business meetings at the Fen Sui Massage Palace, they seldom noticed there was something out-of-place about the furniture. *'Honey, I'm home. Wow! Did you have your hair done?'*

In the little park, we found a bench overlooking a complex series of brightly colored plastic chutes where the neighborhood urchins were busy exchanging childhood diseases. Hannibal went merrily off to make friends and mark the playground equipment. One particularly rambunctious little boy saw us parked on the bench and came scampering over before being detected by whoever was on watch. He stopped in front of Mack and stared at him intently. "Are you a *predator*, mister?" the little tyke inquired of my massive companion.

Before Mack could react to this perfectly reasonable inquiry, an urgent call came from the window of one of the ubiquitous mini-vans lining the edge of the park. "Timmy, come here... NOW! Timmy, get over here this instant!" Timmy should have pointed out to his mother that even with exceptional foot-speed, the human body was incapable of traversing fifty meters of open grass in an instant, thus making her demand impossible, allowing him ample technical grounds for ignoring the request.

Perhaps he realized this conundrum, because Timmy did indeed ignore her request, cocked his head sideways, and patiently awaited Mack's response. "Naw, kid, not me. Not with kids anyway. Kids I like, it's the adults that tend to tick me off." Seeing that Timmy was practicing selective hearing loss, and in immediate danger of being consumed whole by some enormous pervert, Mommy had exited the mini-van and was stomping furiously toward the bench to retrieve her spawn.

The kid saw her coming and decided it might be time to hasten his departure. He smiled at Mack and said, "Yeah, I know what you mean," and with that he spun around and dodged his mother's grasp, running in a great arc towards the road.

There was not a car in sight, but the trajectory nevertheless had the desired effect on Mommy Dearest. "Timmy!!! NOOOOO!!!" She was howling in terror as she raced across the grass in hot pursuit of her beloved rascal, who had no intention of dashing out across the road. Near the curb, Timmy shot like a squirrel up one of the planted water maples near the mini-van and scrambled to safety in the upper branches. Mother Inferior caught up and stood beneath the tree, raving like he had narrowly escaped a brush with death, and demanding he "Come down here this instant!" Yet another physically dubious feat.

For the first time since our meeting I heard Mack laugh out load. He damn near fell off the bench laughing. That got me going and we both cackled like fools sitting there watching this boiling mad soccer mom hollering up a tree at the invisible little rogue. "I do believe that child is destined for greatness, don't you Mack?"

"No doubt about it. Already got the world by the tail, and couldn't be more'n about ten." Mack slouched back after a minute or so, his troubles gradually flowing back around him like a mudflow. "Chauncey, I never meant to get in this deep with Perez. It started out he just wanted me to tag along on some of his deliveries downtown."

"What kind of deliveries, Mack?"

"I don't ask too many questions, but mostly the usual stuff. Sometimes it was somethin' small and heavy, sometimes maybe a package of somethin' soft. Who knows? The stuff didn't have a fuggin' packing slip. And I don't give a shit what Perez is shipping out, all I know is he keeps me in the dough when I make the drop. I remember the first time he sends me out on my own. He gives me this fat envelope to hand deliver to a guy behind the ticket counter at the train station. No escort this time, like it's my show, you know? So I asks him what's in the envelope. He smiles and says, 'Mack, it's a fuggin' engine block from a Studebaker.' So I shrug and figure it ain't none of my business and I take the thing down there and pass it off to this little short fat guy looks like Danny DeVito. He looks around, and then passes me this other skinny little envelope to take back to Perez. For this I get two nice new hundreds from Perez. Shit, that's more cash than I ever seen in one place in my life, so I'm fuggin' hooked." Mack had his head down now and I could tell the words were pouring out painfully.

"Then it got worse. Perez sent me out on more jobs, but not such easy ones. I remember the first time he had me rough a guy up. Sent me over to this little Italian restaurant with some cash for dinner. I do as I'm told, have a plate of linguini, and then ask to speak to the owner about an issue with the meal. We go to 'talk' in his private office out back and I have to bust his arm. Then I have to say, '*The 20th, Tony. Every month*'. That's it. Bust his arm, deliver the line, and head for home. For this Perez slips me five hundred bucks. He tells me how good I'm doin', that I'm moving up the ladder. Shit, I never moved up nothin' in my life. Just moved from one fight to the next. Never even got outta high school cause of the fights. I'd get back in for a week or two, some cocky football star would make a joke about my momma being a gorilla, and I'd put him in traction for a while so he'd have time to think about my momma. With Perez for the first time I feel like maybe I'm good at somethin'. It ain't like I'm a doctor or nothin', but I felt pretty good about all that money for a while. All I gotta do is knock a few heads together once in a while, and I'm rollin' in the dough. Used to do that shit for free in school. Never lost a fist fight in my life."

"No, Mack, I expect not." This story was amazing. It seemed true enough, primarily because I did not think Mack had the imagination to lie about it, and he could have never memorized such a dialogue. I wondered, though, why he had chosen me to unload on. I was thinking about asking him when he decided to continue on.

"It was OK then... nothin' too bad. The guys I busted up, I figured they had done some evil shit to somebody, or I wouldn'ta got sent over on one of my visits, right? But I made a lot of visits to a lot of guys. Even a couple of girls. Them, I just held up in the air for a minute or two, till they got the message from Perez. Then I let 'em down and left. I was glad I didn't have to do no more to the girls. That ain't right." Mack looked down at his feet.

"The only time I ever seen Mr. Perez get pissed at me was when he sends me over to this nice little neighborhood address and tells me to slip in behind the house and plant a claw hammer in the head of this big yellow dog out back. I tried to get Perez to let me plant the hammer on the owner instead, but he gets all worked up and tells me to get the fug over there and deal with Fido before he plants the hammer on me. I get the message and take off for the suburbs, looking for the house. I get there and it's this big fuggin' place on a hill. I park a block away, pack up my hammer and head for the house. I'm feelin' like shit about this one already, and when I get around through the gate to the back I get knocked on my ass by this big goofy yellow dog must weigh as much as me. He's sittin' on top of me, lickin' my face and barkin' like crazy. I think he wants to play, so I grab a stick beside me an' toss it across the yard for the mutt. He's off after it, so I pull out the hammer and figure I'll clock him in the noggin when he brings it back." Mack looked like he might melt through the slats of the bench.

"You didn't clock the dog, did you, Mack?"

"Naw. I couldn't do it. I raised up with the hammer, but the big mutt just wanted to chase it. He couldn't figure why I wouldn't throw it. Plus I seen a bunch of little bikes and skates and stuff out there, and I start thinkin' about them kids comin' home to find Fido... and, well... I give up, Chauncey. I just give up and went back outta that yard and got back to my car and tossed the hammer in the back and drove back to where I meet Mr. Perez downtown. That's when he gets pissed and starts in on me being weak and actin' like a pussy. Maybe I should'a gotten hot and busted his nose, but I didn't do nothin'. Just stood there and listened to Perez call me a loser at the top of his lungs." Mack was staring at the dirt between his feet.

I realized Mack was not quite as mean as he looked. "That would explain why Hannibal never tried to bite you when you placed the note on my truck." Hannibal was making the rounds around the park again, rechecking for scents, and investigating scraps of paper for food crumbs. He must be getting hungry by now, it was late and almost dark. The kids had all filtered out of the park, most of them hauled off to their respective mini-vans by their parents after seeing Mack and me lumber up. Timmy had taken his sweet time coming down out of the tree, only after his exhausted mother threatened to leave him there with the 'two weirdos' over on the bench.

"Hannibal? That the pup's name?" Mack cheered up a bit as Hannibal recognized his new moniker and trotted over to say hello. Mack scratched his ears and smiled. "He don't smell too bad out in the open."

I was feeling bad for Mack, in spite of his dubious habit of rearranging people's appendages. He got caught up in a bad little corner of the world, and had no idea how to work his way out. Everything he did worked himself deeper into the trap, and it sounded like this Perez guy knew exactly how to use Mack to cover his own ass. "Mack, I could use help getting this hound in the bath. Dinner is on me if you can lend a hand. We can continue this chat at my flat."

"Your what?"

"Apartment, Mack, sorry."

"You talk like a fag."

"I know, Mack. Product of my upbringing."

"In Lithuania?"

"Never mind. Let's go." We headed for the vehicles. Hannibal loaded up again, looking happy with his romp around the park. Mack slid in to his recently dented black sedan and pulled out behind me to trail me to my 'flat'. I again marveled at the turn of events in the past few hours. Added to my growing list of events for the day was a large homicidal maniac following behind my truck, being intentionally led to my residence where I intended to employ his assistance in shampooing a dog. My head was spinning.

When we arrived in my parking area I noticed my 'flat' was not very flat, ironically. It was still listing to starboard. In fact, there was not a single surface inside or out that could have been accurately described as 'flat'. Mack extracted himself from his car and stood at the walkway looking up at the building with his head cocked to one side to gain a more sensible perspective on the scene.

"Yeah, I know," I commented to pre-empt the inquiry. Mack shrugged, lifted the forty pound sack of dog food from my truck bed with one hand, and followed me up the stairwell to number 234, my humble domicile. I worked the lock and swung the door open for Hannibal to race inside. He tore around the place, checking for dogs, cats, food, anything exciting and found the place thrilling, with wonderful smells of composting laundry, molding pizza crusts, and unwashed dishes. Hannibal found no dogs to wrestle, no cats to chase, and no body parts to consume, but he still seemed impressed with the dog-like ambiance of my residence. It does not bode well for my housekeeping habits that I felt embarrassed to show this mess to Mack, a man who breaks bones for a living.

Mack took a look around the living room and said, "Wow. What a place. You need a girlfriend. Or maybe a maid."

"Thanks, Mack. Glad you approve."

"You might wanta clear this crap outta here before you bring sweetie-pie over." I missed the reference, but Mack elaborated, "You know... the parking lot babe I seen you with this afternoon."

"Right. That would be Claudia. Look, Mack, we need to discuss her involvement in this little arrangement we seem to be developing. If we are going to cooperate with each other to resolve our problems to our mutual benefit, I must insist she be extricated from the situation."

Mack looked back with a dark expression, "Translate that from fag to English."

"She has to be kept out of this, Mack. No more threats... no more trailing her car. She cannot ever hear a single word about anything we discuss. Agreed?"

"Sure Chauncey, I never meant nothin' to begin with. It told you I don't like leanin' on the ladies. I wouldn'ta done it, but I figured you had the goods on me, and you might shut the fug up if I knows where she lives. So, I took off after her... till you crunch my car. Ain't even my car, Chauncey, it's belongs to Perez. He's gonna have another one of his fits when he sees that." Mack started to get fired up again about the car, but his previous rage had lost some steam over time and it sounded more like a plea for help, rather than a threat of violence.

"OK. We have an agreement. I'll trust your word on this." It sounded strange as soon as I said it. How exactly did I know that? "Mack, does this Perez jerkwad have a first name?"

"Near as I can figure, it's Antonio. He don't ever use it, but I heard a guy say it once downtown. I think it might'a been his cousin or somethin'. You gotta help me get clear of Perez, Chauncey. Guy like you could figure a way outta this mess. You're in this deal too, you know." He was right about this, of course. If I had been an innocent bystander before, any chance for such detachment had dissipated hours ago. "And another thing... you gotta come clean about your little warehouse operation. Deal's a deal."

"Yes, I remember. But first we better get this pooch washed up before I lose my lunch."

"Yeah, well if you're so worried about the stink in here, maybe you should do your damn laundry." He pointed over at a jumbled heap of dirty clothes piled high beside the bedroom door.

"Touché, Mack. Come on; grab that bottle of shampoo in the grocery bag. I'll get the tub filled up." I rounded up a stack of previously used bath towels while filling the tub with luke-warm water. Mack stood by with 'Good-Boy!' shampoo bottle in hand. I whistled for Hannibal, expecting the next process to require a maddening pursuit through the house to capture the dog and wrestle him into the tub. Hannibal, however, continued to surprise me by racing into the bathroom and leaping unassisted into the tub of warm water where he calmly immersed himself up to his nose. The intolerable smell I had previously noted elevated itself to a new dimension when mixed with the warm water, and I dove for the wall switch that operated the exhaust fan. The fan produced enough noise to drown out the lead singer at a punk-rock concert, but made no improvement to the air quality in the bathroom.

"Mack... quick, pour some shampoo over him while I rub it in. Holy Mother of Churchill, this dog reeks!" Mack did as requested, and dumped half the bottle over Hannibal who appeared to be enjoying the attention. All my previous encounters with dogs and baths involved bare-fanged resistance and snarling determination to fight till the bitter end. Hannibal actually appeared to be smiling again. I mistook this expression for one of joy at the luxury of a good warm bath, but I found out quickly that Hannibal had another motive for his amusement. Once the shampoo was worked thoroughly into his thick fur, frothing him into a giant sudsy ball, I turned to boast to Mack, "Piece of cake, Mack. Hannibal loves it!" That was apparently the cue for Hannibal to end his bath and he vaulted out of the tub and careened around the apartment spraying suds and water in all directions.

For the second time that day, I heard Mack bust out laughing. "Yeah, Chauncey, he's havin' a fuggin' blast!" Hannibal shot past me again and headed for the bedroom. I caught up with him standing in a puddle in the center of my bedspread, still smiling. I wrapped him in a couple of towels and returned him to the tub to rinse him off, keeping a closer eye on him to prevent escape. Mack finally quit laughing and helped dry him off. I let the water out of the tub and gathered up most of the towels, rugs, clothes, and bedspread that Hannibal had soaked during his rampage. I went back to the bathroom once the water was drained and took a look at the tub. It appeared to have been recently used to mix potting soil. A thick lining of dirt and hair stuck to all vertical surfaces and an inch of disgusting muck settled on the bottom. Mack looked in, "You should wash your dog more often, Chauncey."

"I'll deal with this debacle when we get back. Shall we go in search of fine cuisine?"

"No thanks, Chauncey. I'd rather eat first."

"Right. Guess I better feed the pooch first." I tore open the dog food bag and filled the new bowl with '*Liver and Lamb*' chow. Looking over the carnage across the apartment I realized that sooner or later, I would have to do some laundry. I changed into marginally cleaner clothes and we headed back out, leaving Hannibal behind, munching contentedly. We took Mack's car, despite the altered fender. "What's your fancy this evening, my dimensionally excessive friend?"

"What?"

"What preference might you have for dinner?" I realized that I might have to find some linguistic compromise that would prevent continual translations.

"Got to steer clear of them queer fancy restaurants. You might like 'em, what with all your fag talkin' and whatnot, but I tried one once, with Mr. Perez. He drags me into this fancy little pink joint, some fairy French name like Chateau Peppi Le Pew or somethin'. He thinks it's some kinda treat cause I done a good job smackin' this a-hole car salesman around. I guess the guy came runnin' in to pay off his mark draggin' one leg and with one arm in a sling. Perez said I deserved a little reward. I'll tell you somethin', Chauncey, I could go for years without no more rewards like that dinner. Bunch of little slimy slugs floatin' around in this little cup of goop. Tasted like boiled cat turds in a cuppa snot. Ain't no wonder them French fuggers are little bitty bastards. I'd starve to death over there if that's all you get." Mack was driving along making a face like he just swallowed a stinkbug.

"Mack, I couldn't agree more. The French seldom prepare anything edible. On the rare occasion they do, they fail to supply sufficient quantities. I've got just the place for you. I often take my meals there, and I think you will find the food extraordinary and the quantities sufficient, even for you. Take a left up here by the corner." Mack obliged and we passed a few blocks of small older houses mixed in between homes converted to business use, most of which would only last a few months before changing hands to the next entrepreneur trying their luck at the cut-flower or bicycle repair business. At the end of the third block was a similar sized older house with a small sign hung from the porch that read 'Hauzer's Brat Haus'. The whole block smelled fantastic, as Hauzer cooked his bratwurst and sauerkraut in the back and the exhaust fan distributed the smells to the entire neighborhood. I doubted anyone ever complained because the brats smelled like heaven, and Hauzer looked like a German Panzer tank. I made a mental connection from Mack to Hauzer due to their similarity in size. When Mack mentioned his preference for large quantities, the Brat Haus seemed like the logical venue.

We passed through the front door into a converted living room with a few small tables scattered around, mostly occupied by boisterous patrons with half-full beer mugs and baskets of brats. We found a corner booth in the next room and I watched Mack fold his frame into the seat. Hauzer spotted us and came over to greet us. "Vat da heck you do here, Bert? I haven't zeen you all dis veek! You go on ze Veight Vatchers, ya?"

"Hey, Hauzer, meet my friend Mack. Mack this is Hauzer." Hauzer smiled and thrust out a huge hand to shake with Mack who returned the greeting as some of the nearby furniture rattled with the gesture. Introducing these two characters was like witnessing a truck wreck.

"Ya, zure glad to meet a big fella like you! Two or three more like you and maybe I get rich!" Mack smiled up and took a menu from the huge owner. "You two give a vistle ven you ready vor a good homemade bratvurst." And Hauzer motored off to accost other guests and refill a few beer mugs.

I settled on the Brat Haus Special knackwurst and a draft pilsner while Mack ordered two beer brats with kraut and a pitcher of Hefeweizen. I pictured my week's paycheck being signed over to Hauzer for the tab, but I had made the deal. Mack had fulfilled his end of the bargain by helping with Hannibal, and I was stuck the dinner tab.

After a few minutes, the first bratwursts and beers were delivered by Delores, an ironically thin, sandy-blond waitress who asked Mack how many glasses he would need for the pitcher. "None. Pitcher's fine." She shrugged, set the pitcher in front of Mack, and sauntered back to retrieve someone's order from the kitchen. Mack took a long swallow out of the side of the pitcher and pronounced the brew fit for consumption by expelling a foam-filled belch. "Good beer."

"Glad you approve. Wait till you taste those brats." Food and beer raised Mack's mood considerably, and he continued to relate tales of illegal business deals and the consequential brutality that seemed to inevitably follow most of Mr. Perez's transactions. There were no worries about being overheard by one of the other patrons, because Hauzer's sausage grinder was busy in the attached room grinding away on some animal carcass, gradually transforming raw meat, bone and guts into perfectly delectable bratwurst. He made all his own sausages and brats, according to 'rezipee from ze old country', but I never asked what went into that grinder back there. Some things are best left unthought about.

I continued to mull over the predicament that Mack, and now me, were in. It almost seemed like Antonio Perez set up deals that were destined to fail, just so he could use his muscle to make a point.

I was confused as to the financial foundation of this business plan. Even if bouncing bowling balls off the brainpan of some backwater drug dealer gives a guy a rise, how can you maintain long-term viability in the gangster market if your clients are all critically injured?

"Mack, when you adjust the facial features of these fellows, how many ever get back to Perez with the payoff?"

"Oh, I dunno... half, I guess. Some of 'em take off. Don't never see 'em again, 'cause they figure next time there won't be no Mr. Nice Guy. Some come back to Perez with the cash, but them ones Perez hits for more and more, till they get tight and can't pay no more. I pay 'em another visit, and they go too... sooner or later. Mr. Perez, he ends up runnin' all of 'em off. If they stick around and still don't come up with the payoff, then... well..." Here Mack paused before finally continuing quietly, "...then Perez has me fix 'em up like your friend behind the warehouse." I realized I shouldn't have pressed the issue with Mack, because his lighter mood was now slipping into a much darker corner.

"Look, Mack, you have to get out of this gig. I'll help you find a way to end this ordeal without getting put in jail or killed by Perez. Just try not to kill anybody else till we come up with a plan."

He raised up and gave me a doubtful look. "How you gonna do that, Chauncey? Mr. Perez, he's got eyes all over the country. I think he's related to half the guys in Florida and most of California. He sits here in the middle, shipping stuff both directions to his brothers and cousins and uncles and who the fug knows who. Guy like me kinda stands out in a crowd, you know. I can't just give the guy the finger and walk off. I got a lot of dirt on Perez that might be of interest to the local coppers. If I was to bolt on Perez, he'd have me at the bottom of a lake by sunset." If Mack was upset by his predicament, it had no effect on his appetite. He was well into his second brat and showed no sign of slowing down. The pitcher was dry when Delores came back around to check on us.

"One more pitcher for you, Stud?" Mack looked up and smiled at the tiny waitress who seemed impressed by the size of the massive thug. I guess when you live off of tips in Hauzer's Brat Haus you get good at sizing up your benefactors. His huge intimidating frame seemed to have the opposite effect on Delores.

"I s'pose, yes ma'am. And maybe one of those knocker wieners like he had."

Delores, who was wearing a ubiquitous white waitress smock with a nametag that read '*Delores*,' shouted over her shoulder toward the kitchen, "One knocker wiener and another pitcher for Sasquatch!" She turned back around to me and added, "Anything else for you, hun?"

"Thanks, Delores, I'm good here." I could not imagine consuming three enormous brats in one setting, but maybe washing them down with a couple gallons of beer helped. Delores trundled off to fill the pitcher while Mack watched her go with a smile across his massive mug.

"Mack, where do you usually meet with Mr. Perez? You said somewhere downtown. Does he have an office there?"

"Dunno. Well, maybe, but I never seen it. Perez calls me up and says '*Meet me at Tara's*' and I go there, or wherever, order a coffee or somethin', and Perez shows up a little later. He gives me the job to do, and I go off and do it. Once I'm done, I got this number for Perez and we meet up at some other spot to hand over the cash. If there ain't no cash, I tell Perez and he tells me to go back and fix it so the guy remembers the deal better."

"Got any idea where he operates from? Got to be nearby if he meets at the same area every time. Does he get out of a car, or just walk up to Tara's?"

"Just walks right up, usually. I seen him once across the street, standing behind the newspaper stand, peekin' around like he was hidin' from somebody. He was lookin' over the cafe to see if I was alone, I figure. After a bit, he comes on across the street, stops again outside the window and looks over everybody in the joint before opening the door. Then, he just comes on in, plops down, and says, '*Mack, good to see you. Give me some good news.*' I give him the news, he lays a few bills on me, slaps me on the back, and off he goes, happy as a clam. Except those times when I fug up, and then he's not so much fun. Like with the yellow dog."

Mack thought quietly a moment and then continued on, "One other time I was looking around downtown for some new shirts. I got problems findin' shirts big enough for me, so I'm about a block from Tara's I guess, outside this little clothes joint, and I notice some guy looking down at me from a balcony across the street. It looked like Perez, but when I wave up at him, he disappears into the building without so much as a nod. Like he don't know me. Kinda pissed me off a little. Then I think maybe it was some guy looks like Perez... but I dunno. Looked a lot like Perez."

"Do you remember which particular balcony he was on?"

"Sure, no problem. I remember the clothes joint, cause I bought this shirt I got on from the old lady in there. Nice old white-haired broad, kinda reminded me of my ma." Mack was smiling again, lost in some distant memory of his mom, I supposed.

"Jeez, Mack you never told me you had a mom."

He glared back at me, "Whadda fug you think, I hatched outta egg?"

"Sorry, Mack, just never pictured somebody scrubbing behind your ears and sending you off to kindergarten in your new knickers."

"Yeah, well, I didn't get born this big. Took till sixth or seventh grade. Once I started growin', I thought I would bust before I stopped. Ma used to try to feed me salads and crap like that, but it didn't do no good. I would'a gotten big eatin' cardboard. By the time I was twelve I was around two-hundred pounds. Now I'm close to three. Kids used to call me names like that waitress done. Sasquatch. Magilla Gorilla. You know. I'd get mad and bust their head open, and off I'd go to some hole-in-the-wall school for bad kids. Never could keep outta trouble back then. Shit, still can't keep outta trouble, looks like." He was back in a hang-dog mood for a few minutes, till Delores came back around with edible reinforcements, and Mack perked up as she approached.

"Here you go, Grizzly. Lemme know when you're ready for more. I'll send Hauzer out with a truck to stock up." Delores had sidled up to Mack and was leaning up against his giant frame after laying out the brat and beer. If Mack had any reaction to Delores calling him Sasquatch and Grizzly, he never gave a hint of it. In fact he looked like a kid with a stack of birthday presents in front of him as he ripped into his third brat. "You oughtta feed this feller more often, he's half-starved."

"Naw, he just likes your cooking, Delores. This is my friend Mack. Mack, Delores."

Mack got up out of his seat and took Delores' tiny hand and said, "Very pleased to meet you ma'am."

"Don't be callin' me ma'am, Grizz, hell I'm younger'n you. And it ain't my cookin'; that would be Hauzer's department, but I'll dang sure take credit for pourin' the beer." Mack continued to hold onto Delores' hand until she finally pulled away and retrieved something from her apron pocket. "Listen, Stud, here's our special card. After nine brats, you get number ten free. Just get the card punched when you check out. Course, we didn't mean for you to use one up every time you sit down." Before she passed the card over to Mack, she scribbled something on the back, and punched out three notches in the little square boxes printed along one edge. "You're my kinda customer, big boy," she said as she gave him a pat on the chest after slipping the card into Mack's shirt pocket. With that, Delores spun around and left Mack standing by the booth with his mouth hung open like the back of a cargo plane.

"Mack, sit down, you're blocking the aisle." He looked down at me as the words sank in, and then gradually refolded himself into the booth. I think his three hundred pound estimate was a few biscuits short. He retrieved the punch card from his shirt pocket and checked the note on the back.

"Damn."

"What?" I asked.

"Delores Kingston... 633-6639."

"Well... congratulations, I think." Mack was staring at the card, trying to comprehend the ramifications of this latest turn of events.

"Damn," he repeated out of a fog.

"You sure you're not enraged by her cute little pet names? You seem to be the subject of her amorous advances."

"Don't start that shit again, Chauncey."

"Sorry, Mack. I mean, you see fit to open most people's cranial cavity for the Sasquatch reference, but Delores gets a free pass?" I knew the answer, but wanted to see if Mack had it figured.

"Different deal." Apparently, Mack had it figured precisely.

Chapter Five

Hannibal was glad to see me when Mack let me off back at the apartment. He bounded around the place like a bullet, coming to a stop near the front door. I gave in, "OK, let's go." I headed back out and down the stairs to the weedy strip that masqueraded as a lawn, where Hannibal ripped around the building to make his high-speed inventory of all interesting smells. On the second pass, he added Hannibal smells to the list by anointing every vertical object in sight. I am always amazed at the ability of dogs to meter out urine in precisely the proper quantity so that the maximum number of objects can be defiled. Hannibal's list included four car tires, a concrete bollard, a propane tank, two light posts, and a bicycle, all on a single bladder. The final territorial marking took place after considerable deliberation, by placement of a steaming mound of recycled dog kibble directly in front of Apartment 122. Hannibal looked up with pride after completing this mission. "Nice work, Ace. You're going to be popular in the neighborhood." Apartment 122 belonged to a tattooed and studded punk with blue hair and a very loud stereo system that tended to run at max volume late at night. He parked his 1974 Dodge Dart sideways in the lot taking up at least three spaces, leaving a 'Kirby's Pizza Delivery' sign stuck to the roof like a Mohawk.

Due to Punky the Pizza Boy's stunning contributions to society, I felt pleased to give something back. Or at least Hannibal gave something back. So we left the big steamer piled in front of 122 and headed back up to talk over the day's events. I had to do some serious brainstorming and needed Hannibal's advice to help sort through the options. I had left Mack with the promise to devise a plan that would keep us both walking upright and breathing without mechanical assistance. My baseless confidence left Mack smiling and I had promised to meet him the next afternoon, with a foolproof plan to end the association with Perez. I would need tomorrow evening for my plans with Claudia Auckland, whom I had not forgotten in the turmoil of the day. Whatever else had happened, whatever difficulty I had corkscrewed myself into, I felt better about it all, looking forward to dinner on Saturday night. It seemed like it was all part of the same event... as if the date with Claudia was directly connected to the rest of the day, and without the rest of the craziness, the date would disappear too. I wondered if that was true. Perhaps it really was all part of the same connected series of weird cause-and-effect responses. Take away one chemical component and the rest of the reaction ceases to occur.

Hannibal flopped at my feet as I stretched out on the couch, looking up at the stained ceiling. I had never noticed that the one big water stain looked exactly like Jimmy Hendrix riding a lawn tractor. "Check it out, boy. Jimmie Hendrix is trying to mow our ceiling." Hannibal raised one eye to the stain and lost interest immediately. Not much abstract thinking going on tonight for him. I decided to get back to the issues at hand and let Jimmie go on mowing. Maybe kicking back into Bertrand Chauncey mode would knock loose an idea or two. "How shall the invincible team of Chauncey and Hannibal approach this delicate situation, my astute colleague?"

Hannibal had begun snoring and having dog dreams, because I could see his feet twitching as he sailed after some dreamland squirrel that had encroached on his turf. It had been an exhausting day. I could not force my mind to sort through the avalanche of events since the morning. It seemed like a month ago that Bert Clauster had driven into work, parked his truck, and began stocking inventory in the conduit department. At some point as I lay there on the couch with Hannibal sawing logs by my side, I lost touch with the world and drifted off. I did not join Hannibal in chasing dreamland squirrels, but I remember dreams of being chased, and being caught by Mack, who lifted me off the ground by my arms and said, *'Sorry, Chauncey. Gotta do the right thing this time,'* as he tossed me into the back of a police cruiser. In the back of the cruiser sits Claudia, handcuffed and in tears. She looks utterly defeated and ashamed, and it's my fault. All of it was my damn fault.

It was light outside when I woke up with my head hung over the side of the couch and Hannibal licking my face. It took a second to place the sensation, as there was no dog living there the day before. Right… Hannibal. I checked extremities to be sure he had not returned to his former eating habits. All intact. Good. "Hey pup, let's go out." Hannibal approved of the plan and we ventured down the stairs to repeat the cycle of the previous evening. I glanced over to Apartment 122 and saw a brown gloppy footprint dead center in the pile Hannibal left the night before. The prints repeated themselves in a short sequence toward the door and then disappeared into the apartment. "Nice work, Hannibal. I believe you have endeared yourself to Pizza Boy."

After a round of inspections, Hannibal returned to the scene of the crime, conducted a series of determined sniffs, and proceeded to lay out another Dukey the size of a small cat in close proximity to the 122 door. He smiled back at me during the process, then wrapped up his work and trotted over. "Good job, partner. I think we have delivered the proper message to our acoustically indifferent neighbor." Apparently the message had gotten through, because I saw the curtain part and Punky the Pizza Boy's disheveled face peered out of the grimy front window. A moment later the door burst open and Punky himself spilled out onto the concrete walk, stepping precisely where he had stepped the previous evening.

"Aw shit! Keep your fuckin' dog the fuck off my lawn!" Punky seemed a little cranky about his failure to avoid the new poop pile. He was all puffed up with arms pulled back, fists at the ready, and face red as a beet. Bert Clauster would have apologized, picked up the poop, promised to stay clear of Punky's personal space, and left well enough alone. But Bertrand Chauncey would have none of it.

"Perhaps you would be so kind as to delineate the perimeter of your '*lawn*' as you refer to it. In actuality, there is not a blade of living vegetation within sight, making the term '*lawn*' distinctly inaccurate. And, as you obviously have no lawn, my associate could not have violated something that does not exist. Perhaps the offending material was your own." This statement did nothing to calm Punky down, who got even redder and puffier as he approached me with arms cocked back. Undoubtedly, this body language may have been intended to convey his best "whup-ass" look, but it came across as a bit comical.

"Somebody's fixin' to get their ass whupped!" Punky was screaming in my face now, spitting mad and smelling strongly of freshly smeared dog excrement. His greasy blue hair was flying at half mast, sticking ludicrously out from the side of his head. He must have just rolled out of the sack when he heard us outside his apartment. His eyes were wild and unfocused, but that might have been due to some chemical enhancements rather than lack of sleep.

"Yes, indeed. I believe you have correctly assessed the situation. Congratulations, you are keenly astute at discerning the blatantly obvious." Punky looked back at me with confusion and rage. So I decided to enhance his fury. "Furthermore, may I clarify the exact individual whose ass is in imminent danger of getting '*whupped*', as you so colorfully phrase the deed? As I have no intention of raising so much as a mild sweat in this endeavor, and there is no one else here to receive the measure… that leaves you as the logical recipient. I presume you have substantial healthcare?" At this query, I leaned casually against the closest tree and inspected my nails. "Good heavens, I need a manicure."

I recall the fleeting thought that this charade was destined to fail, and Punky would light into me any second, and fists would fly, noses would break, and testosterone would burst from our veins and everyone would die. I found it intensely interesting that none of this happened as I imagined; actually the sequence of events unfolded quite differently. Punky began to back away, looking at me like I was infected with ebola virus. "You're fuckin' nuts, man. You're a sick fucker. Leave me the fuck alone, man." Punky was back-peddling into his apartment door, hands out in front, in case I charged him, I suppose. On the way backwards, he managed to hit the same smudge of Hannibal mess he had stepped in twice before. The trifecta… the hat trick… three for three. The boy might be an ignorant white-trash punk, but damn, he had a knack for finding the feces.

"Mind your step, Punky," I commented as he backed into his apartment and slammed the door shut. Curious change of attitude, I thought. One second he was coming hard, fists clenched, and the next he was ducking for cover. Maybe he had a morbid fear of fake English accents. Maybe he thought I was Pierce Brosnan. I had no idea this Chauncey thing had such power over people. Just when I had convinced myself of my superhuman powers, someone stepped from just behind me. I had not seen anyone prior to that, and the close proximity made me jump.

"Yo, Chauncey. You havin' problems with that little blue-haired rat?" Mack sidled up. He was in his style of work clothes;

black pants, tight black shirt. He was staring at Punky's closed door and had a look on his face that indicated he was unconcerned about Punky's health care coverage. Now I realized why the little ass-wipe scurried off in such a rush. Must have seen Mack behind me and decided the whup-ass odds were dropping like a stripper's panties at a congressional yacht party.

I recovered from my surprise, "Him? Certainly not. Just passing commentary about the weather."

"Sounded more like he was fixin' to toss a couple of haymakers up side of your head."

"Oh, I think not. He was just a bit put-off by his inability to detect one of Hannibal's land mines." Hannibal trotted over and gave Mack a nudge hello. Mack obliged with a rough head scratch. "What brings you over to my little piece of paradise?" I swept my arm around theatrically to indicate the vast expanse of '*paradise*' I was ensnarled in.

Mack deflated a little. He was worried about something, and not too good at hiding it. "Perez. He catches up with me after I leave your place last night and starts askin' questions. Wants to know '*How's it going, Mack?*' and '*Anything you need, Mack?*' But Perez, he don't give a rats rip how I'm doin'. I just figure he's got some other job for me to do, you know. But then he keeps up with the twenty questions, and I start to sweat. I mean I dunno what the fuck all this is about." Mack's head was down and he was trying to put together the next thought.

"So what's the problem, Mack? Perez send you off to bust up the Pope?"

"Naw, that ain't it. Problem is, Perez asks me if I been making some nice friends in the neighborhood. He even pronounces '*neighborhood*' just like that guy with the sweater on T.V., you know, '*It's a wonderful day in the neighborhood...*'". Mack did a passing impersonation of Mr. Rogers that was horribly incongruous with his bulky frame.

"Well, did he want to talk to Mr. Mailman or take a trip to the Magic Kingdom?" This was intended to humor Mack, but it sounded a little bit insensitive. Mack grimaced and sunk a little deeper into silence. Then it occurred to me what he was talking about. "Oh, shit. Perez knows about our meeting last night? That is disconcerting."

Mack looked up and said flatly, "He wants to know if I been making friends and running my big mouth about the operation."

He waited for my reply. "That's pretty much exactly what you've been doing. But how did he find out so quickly? You think he may have someone watching you, Mack?"

"Perez, he's got little rats on the payroll all over town. My guess is it was that a-hole bartender, Wally, at that dive. Maybe Delores, the waitress at Hauzer's place... although I sure hope it weren't Delores. I kinda liked Delores." Mack smiled at this thought and went quiet for a minute remembering how Delores had called him Sasquatch and a few other cute little pet names, then scribbled her name and number on a card for him.

"Mack, I doubt if Delores would pass out her phone number to some giant guy if she intended to sell you down the river. That would seem a bit counterintuitive."

Mack looked up, still smiling, "Exactly. Counter... whatever. She wouldn'a dunnit. Had to be the a-hole, Wally. Might havta' pay a visit to Wally to have a chat." Mack ground his fist into his hand, but kept smiling.

"Hang onto that for now, Mack. No need to tip your hand just yet. Besides, it could be any number of people we saw last night. Look, Mack, what did you tell Perez? He doesn't know you spilled the beans about his nefarious activities, does he?"

Mack was confused again. "I don't even know if he's got any of those nefariouses. Most of his stuff is just criminal; guns, drugs, fake passports and stuff."

"My mistake. Look, did you tell him about our conversation? Is he sitting inside a van down the street with a laser scope pointed at my skull?" I looked myself over to make sure a bright red dot was not dancing around on my chest somewhere. This news was making me increasingly anxious and I needed some answers.

"Naw... first thing that come to me was the car wreck. I was worryin' anyway about what to say about the fender, and I ain't no damn good at making up lies real quick like them pimps or drug dealers or politicians, so I told him the truth... sort of. Said you smacked into the fender in the parkin' lot and I tracked you down to get a little satisfaction. Perez said I done good not to call the cops and bring attention to ourselves, what with him owning the car and me being his '*employee*' and all. Told him you coughed up five-hundred bucks once I leaned on you a little. He says I should'a' gone for a grand, minimum. Tells me to hit you up for the rest next time I see you. Then he says, '*Watch your fuckin' mouth when you go socializin'. Wouldn't make me happy to hear you been talkin' bout your work.*' And that's that. I just say '*Sure, Mr. Perez,*' and he lets it go."

I could tell that was not the end of Mack's meeting because I could see he was gearing up for the next thought. "So, was that it, Mack? Perez just told you to zip your pie-hole, takes the money and leaves?"

"Naw… I peal some bills outta my wallet. But he tells me, '*Keep it, Mack. Get the fender fixed over at Eddie's Garage. Tell him to do a nice job… and send him my regards.*' So I drop it off this morning, and Eddie says he'll have it out by noon; no charge. I think Eddie knows Perez and he don't want no trouble."

"Perhaps he was simply charmed by your engaging smile."

Mack shook his head. "No, Chauncey, that ain't the bad part. I think I might have done somethin' bad. I'm really sorry about opening my big mouth, it just sort of slipped out, what with me being so nervous with all them questions about who I was meeting with." Mack's head drooped down and he looked at his shoes that scuffled around in the dirt by the edge of the parking area.

I was bracing for the bad news when I detected a slight movement of the filthy curtain behind Punky's window. The piece of cat-crap was spying on us from inside his hole. I doubted if he could hear anything, but I motioned subtly to Mack, indicating the window. Mack picked up on the issue and turned casually back toward me, as if he had not noticed anything out of the ordinary. With remarkable swiftness, Mack bent over and selected a large chunk of brick laying amidst the urban detritus, turned and fired a ninety-mile-an-hour, belt-high strike directly through Punky's window. There was a tremendous explosion of glass as the curtains ripped backward, followed immediately by a sound that indicated the destruction of modern cheap furniture due to the application of excessive human pressure. Technicians in Hollywood have worked for years to design stage furniture that shatters on impact for theatrical effect, but have, as yet, been unable to improve on the engineering currently utilized by commercial furniture manufacturers whose products exhibit the structural integrity of a Styrofoam cup. "A bit inside on that pitch, Mack. I believe you may have struck the batter. Shall we award the lad first base?"

"Yep. I'll go give him the good news," Mack said as he strode over to the imploded window to examine his handiwork. "Hey, Dickweed." Mack was peering into the hole where the brick had passed. Barely audible groans emerged from inside. "If you poke that zit-covered beak of yours into other people's business, it might get ripped off and crammed up your keister. Are you getting this, Asswipe?"

Curiosity got the best of me and I saddled up to the window to inspect the damage. Hannibal took an interest in the commotion and loped over to join us. Punky was sprawled out across the remnants of a splintered coffee table, holding his shoulder, and staring fearfully up at Mack's enormous head that was poking in through the window. "I didn't mean nothin' mister. I never heard nothin' either. Honest to God, I had my stereo on and couldn't hear shit." His eyes were wide and he was trying to inch his way away from the window by crawling backwards with his butt cheeks.

"You lying little turd. If your stereo was on, why don't I hear nothin'?" Mack made a good point. Things were pretty quiet in there.

"I believe he doth protest too much," I commented on Punky's performance.

"You say some weird shit, Chauncey," Mack concluded. Punky the Pizza Boy succeeded in butt crawling in reverse till his head bumped the back wall where he continued to try to retreat from Mack's glare. "Looks like we have a problem with prick-ears here. I think we need to take a ride, boy." This did not seem to cheer Punky up much, but Hannibal got excited about the mention of a possible road trip and barked approval.

"Mack, it might be best to delay any resolution to the issue as we seem to have attracted the attention of a few neighbors." A couple of doors were open and people were looking over to see what the noise had been. I turned to address the onlookers, "Damn kids hit a baseball right through this poor bastard's window. Anybody see them run off?" That resolved the problem nearly instantly as everyone immediately lost interest and returned to their daytime soap operas or their internet porn surfing or whatever occupied the bloated, pasty, collection of human backwash residing in my lovely apartment complex. "Let's find more private quarters, and you can fill me in on rest of that story."

"What about the turd-ball?" The turd-ball peered up expectantly, with a glimmer of hope that he may be allowed to live after all.

"I have a suggestion," I said, addressing Punky through the hole, "We give you one more opportunity to show that you have reformed your attitude. If you make noise to anyone, we cut you up and feed you to Hannibal." Hannibal barked again and wagged his tail. "You see, Punky, Hannibal has a taste for greasy little pizza jockeys like yourself. Perhaps because they are permeated to the bone with the stench of pepperoni. By Monday afternoon you will have fixed this window, cleaned the dog shit off your walk and your carpet, picked up the garbage from around the place, and cut off that ridiculous mop of blue hair. And if you ever mention that you have seen either my associate or me, or if I ever hear your hideous music after nine p.m., all three of us will come by for a little visit. Including Hannibal. Is all this very, very clear to you?"

Visibly relieved, Punky sat up, still clutching his battered shoulder and nodded his head in agreement with the plan, "You bet... no problem. I'm on it right away! And I never seen you guys. Never. And I don't know dick about no car wreck or nothin'."

"Aw, shit," Mack said. We turned and walked away, out of earshot of the pizza punk.

"Let it go, Mack. All we talked about was the wreck. Perez knows about that already. If he gets news of this meeting, just tell him you were working me over for the last $500. It's all legit." We headed around the corner, went up to my apartment and let Hannibal in ahead of us. I thought about my use of the word 'legit'. Maybe too liberal use of poetic license. Mack slumped onto the couch and Hannibal piled up with him for a head scratch.

I took a chair from the kitchen table and straddled it backwards to face Mack. "Maybe you better finish telling me what went down with Perez last night. You said you may have made a mistake with him. What exactly do you mean?"

"Guess I may as well lay it out, Chauncey. I got us in pretty deep."

That sounded ominous. "Us?"

"Well, yeah. That's the bad part I mentioned. So here I am getting grilled by Perez about meeting with you and maybe talking too much, and I'm all in a sweat about what he knows and don't know… and just when I think he's all done giving me the third degree, he lays out this job for me take care of for him. For a couple of weeks I been keepin' watch on this little shit weasel named Darrell over on the south side with a big warehouse where they do a little business now and then, you know." I didn't know, but Mack continued, "Perez tells me this guy is making major jack, and not payin' Perez his cut of the jack, so I offer to go visit him and straighten him out a little, but Perez says, '*No, that ain't gonna work this time; not with this dude, cause he's got some muscle of own, and stays surrounded by about ten guys with hardware.*' So Perez is tryin' to work out some plan to level the turf with this guy, and last night he says, '*Mack, maybe you could get in there and conduct a little transaction with this guy and we can hang him out to dry.*' And I say, '*You mean set him up?*' and Perez gets excited about the idea and says, '*Yeah, sure. We set up a deal, maybe purchase some goods, and leave a little trail of bread crumbs for the cops to follow.*' And I ask what kind of operation we talkin' about here. Perez tells me this guy's got a nice room with furniture inside the warehouse where he has cameras set up to film porn flicks. Then he sells the tapes to big shots and makes a bundle."

"Aw, good old American enterprise! Sounds like the free market economy humming along at its own demented pace," I offered, failing to see any reason for concern.

"You don't get it, Chauncey. These ain't old strippers looking to make a few bucks after working the late shift at the IHOP. This assbite is using high school girls; some even younger. I parked up the block from the joint last week and watched his boys drive in with the girls. Some of them are all bound up with duct-tape when they come in. Word on the street is that Darrell has this one big goon named Barkov, some gigantic Russian gorilla makes me look like the tooth fairy."

Wow. I knew there were some twisted shitheels in the world, but this Darrell guy was right here in town. I was reeling back from the shock of that realization and was struggling to sort out the basic mindset of the business principals. "So Perez, being the civic minded pillar of virtue that he is, decides the whole idea has financial merit and decides to cut himself into the action. Hard to imagine what might go wrong with that prospectus."

"Yeah. This is some bad stuff, Chauncey, and I don't want no part of it."

"OK, but if Antonio Perez puts Scumbag out of business, isn't that a good thing?"

"Perez don't want to shut it down… Perez want to transfer it over. It'll be ten times worse when that son-of-a-bitch takes over. He'll move the location to one of his units, but take Barkov and the rest of those goons with him. He was talkin' about that last night, playing it out in his head and getting' all excited about it. And he wants *us* to set this a-hole up."

"Us?" There was that word again. I did not like the context in which it was being used. "*Us*, Mack?"

Mack looked down, assuming his familiar hang-dog posture, "Well, yeah. That's the bad part I mentioned earlier."

"Oh, and the rest is all good stuff? Well, too bad we finally have to end this fairy tale and get to the depressing part. How exactly did you manage to get me into this bedtime story?" Things were taking a serious turn here and I had the feeling it had not bottomed out yet.

"Sorry, Chauncey, but like I said, Perez had the heat on me and I was flustered, so he keeps thinking out-loud about how to set up the a-hole and rout him out of his operation, when he says, '*What we really need is some rich perv to start throwing cash around, get Darrell frothing for money, then get him to stick his neck in the noose.*' Well, then's when I thought about you." Mack looked up expectantly, like this compliment might smooth everything out.

"Rich perv? And of course, you feel I fit this description perfectly and offered my services to Perez, right?" I took offense to his evaluation of my character… fictitious or not.

"Well, yeah… I mean no. Look, I know you ain't into kiddie porn or nothin' and I can tell by lookin' around this dump you don't got two nickels…"

I was fuming for good reason, "Oh, how comforting, Mack. But you still thought I might be able to pull off a one night stand as a sicko. A little command performance in front of armed thugs. Jeez, I hope the reviews are good. I hate it when murderers and child abusers do not appreciate my talents."

"Sorry, Chauncey," was the best he could muster.

I mulled over the developments, "Well, maybe this provides us with an opportunity… maybe."

Chapter Six

Being a man of few attachments and frugal lifestyle, and despite the outward appearance of my residence, I had horded away a few extra bucks while working diligently for two years at State Electric Supply. So, in keeping with my recent self-promotion to the status of International… (it seemed to be getting closer and closer to International *Fugitive*, but I had been hoping for something a little more… well, legal); I decided to make an impression on Claudia and sweep her off her feet. To practice my sweeping I swept out the pickup and spread an old quilt over the front seat to hide some of the stains and soften the springs that poked up through the upholstery. I even took a first cut at some of the more neglected aspects of my apartment. But it quickly became apparent that a thorough cleaning would take considerable time and perhaps heavy machinery.

Evening attire was even more challenging, as my collection of formal wear was limited to an old paint stained t-shirt that had the imprint of a tuxedo on it. This impressed several girls at a few frat parties years ago; but then again, those girls had been pretty drunk. And the shirt had not aged well. Only one logical solution… had to make a run to the Pick-and-Poke thrift store to shop for duds. So Hannibal and I roared off on a shopping spree.

Bonanza! For five bucks I scored a ruffled blue long-sleeve shirt, a pair of pleated pants that sort of fit, and some snazzy stringless wing-tips that were only one size over par. Piece of cake. Just have to know where to shop. I brought my loot out to the truck to show Hannibal. "Check this out, boy, new rags to impress the lovely Claudia." Hannibal gave the shirt a long sniff and then hung his head out the side window, looking the opposite direction. "Oh, give me a break! The whole outfit only set me back five bucks!" Hannibal gave me a quick look that seemed to translate as '*I rest my case.*'

One quick stop at the hardware to pick up some shoe-strings, and a quick pass through the cemetery on the way home. I could not believe my luck was holding out. Fresh digs in Lawnmere Cemetery. Some poor schmuck had just gotten plugged in the dirt and flowers were stacked up like cordwood. Hannibal and I jumped out and paid our respects to the dearly departed and read the shiny new headstone. '*Arthur P. Grimbley - You Will Be Missed*'

"Damn Arty, just kicked off last week, huh? Sorry about that, old timer. Looks like you hit about ninety-two though. Nice going." Hannibal made his rounds and watered a couple of headstones nearby. "Hey Arty, mind if I borrow a few flowers? Got kind of a hot date tonight." Hannibal came up and gave me the fish-eye. I defended myself, "What? A few flowers for a nice lady... what's wrong with that? Arty's cool with it. Right Arty?" Continued fish-eye. "C'mon! It's not like I'm yanking his fillings out. You're the one who has been pissing on everybody's headstone, and now I get the stare-down for lifting a couple of posies?" Touché. Hannibal took two steps forward toward the fresh mound, hiked up a hind-quarter, and bid Arthur P. Grimbley a fond farewell. It felt good to be partnered with another creature of flexible integrity. Life is far too short to get your tail in a knot over the small stuff. I selected a large bouquet of orange fluffy looking flowers that looked reasonably fresh. Hannibal stopped in his tracks and gave a sharp bark. I swear he was looking right at the orange flowers. "Of course not, partner, just checking your judgment." I replaced the cream-sickle bouquet and studied the remaining selections with care. "Ah, the giant sunflower arrangement with the delicate background fan of maiden-hair fern." Hannibal growled dangerously. "Alright, Martha Stewart, how 'bout a hint here before we get arrested for robbing graves?" Hannibal sat back on his haunches and remained still for a minute, waiting for me to catch on. "Come on! What do I know about flowers, I'm a warehouse Stock Boy!" Hannibal cocked his head sideways. "The Lillies? No?... no, perhaps not. A bit too morbid." With a sudden certainty, I snatched up a small bundle of yellow roses lying atop the headstone and headed back for the truck. "I should have noticed you pointing to those earlier. Not too perceptive this evening, eh?" Hannibal loped on ahead happily. His student had finally gotten the point, and he was a happy dog.

Once back at my slum-dwelling, I began recalling the events of the past two days, and the realization weighed down my mood as I prepared for dinner at Claudia Auckland's place. It was impossible to ignore the gnawing issues that were sure to surface after Mack had suggested casting me as a sexually twisted stuffed-shirt in Perez's con scam. Apparently Perez was thrilled that Mack had come up with an overbearing English bore on a moment's notice. Perez was willing to forgive my 'debt' and sweeten the pot with another five hundred if I pulled off the con. The details were not yet clear, and I doubted if they ever would be. Perez had nothing to lose by the attempt, as he would be safely tucked away. If Mack and I took a bullet, then gee, it was a good try boys, but just not our night. The whole mess was dominating my conscious thoughts, rather than thinking about how lucky I was to be heading to Claudia's for dinner. I knew I couldn't let the craziness ruin the evening. "Bertrand Chauncey does not allow his evenings to be ruined by common thugs... he ruins the evenings of common thugs," I thought out loud. How profound. There's a nice inscription for the head stone. Beats '*He Will Be Missed*' which was all Arthur P. Grimbley got.

I was getting better at switching into Chauncey mode to avoid visualizing scenarios that involve pain and/or incarceration. But it was harder to trivialize the very real possibility that I could be placing other people in harm's way. It was sobering to think of Claudia being dragged into this ugly quagmire. I had to be very careful tonight. Keep my eyes open for Perez and his minions. I also needed to find out what a minion was. And I needed to be able to recognize a minion... or at least recognize Perez. There was a very serious deficit of knowledge here, and it was likely to come back to haunt me. Or get Claudia hurt. Or Mack. Funny... I had begun to worry about Mack; a guy that busts femurs for a living. But there was something decent about Mack that I could not dismiss, even with his violent occupation. I suspected the stories he told were true, and had seen his actions first hand with Punky the Pizza Boy who probably locked himself inside his grandmother's basement with a family-size meat-lover's delight, a 64-ounce Slurpee, and an ice pack on his shoulder. '*Don't tell em' I'm down here Gramma! There's crazy people after me.*' Not a cheerful image.

With these disturbing thoughts bouncing around, I finished preparations for my dinner outing by brushing down Hannibal and giving him a spray of after-shave to mask any latent odors that lingered after his bath. I gave myself a shot too, to mask any of my own lingering odors, and checked out the new outfit in my mirror. My first impression of myself was something between Pee-Wee

Herman and Austin Powers. The blue ruffled shirt was a little too large, and the pleated pants were definitely tight in the crotch. The wingtips were ultra-shiny, and they sort of stood out. Plus they flopped around a little, even with new strings. Too late for fashion phobias, time to make tracks to Claudia's.

Before heading out to the truck, I decided that feeding Hannibal was a good idea. With a full stomach, maybe he would not eat Claudia's transgender Irish setter cat-dog named Cecelia. I loaded up the bowl for Hannibal and popped a beer to pass the time while he woofed down the food. The food was woofed before I had dampened my gullet, but the distraction gave me a few minutes to think through the events of the day and decide what to do about keeping Claudia clear of the impending storm. I checked out my window. No suspicious cars hanging around the lot. No trench-coated characters reading magazines while leaning against the tree across the street. No one casually slipping a magnetic package of C-4 explosives under my truck frame.

Maybe I should call off the date. Or stand her up cold and get her pissed off. She would avoid me like the plague and thereby improve her odds of staying alive. But that would be rude, and I really did not have the heart to do that. Maybe I should just talk to her about what I had gotten into. Maybe she could help me think through it. Of course that would expose me as a dangerous wack-job and she would show me the door and tell me to get lost. Plus, I really wanted to spend a little time with this girl. She seemed like someone I could get excited about, something that hadn't happened for years. I thought about Maggie, my high school sweetheart, who had left me at the prom and gone for a "ride" with Phil Clyatt in his new GTO. She did not come back to the prom, and I was humiliated. I had not gotten serious about anyone since then, just random dates that would last a weekend or two, then find some excuse to cease calling. Why was it so hard to find someone? I had convinced myself it was just bad luck... that the right girl would wander by some day. But I was beginning to wonder if it wasn't more related to me being in a constant state of anger and bitterness at being left at the curb while Maggie pursued more exciting interests. Phil Clyatt was a basketball star in high school. Phil Clyatt had a cool car. Phil Clyatt even had a cool scar up the back of his neck where the dumbshit had tried to do a flip off the top of his backyard barbeque and broke his fucking neck. I did not have a GTO. I did not have a cool scar. Back then I was Bert the Squirt Clauster-Fuck, standing in the cool mist of an April evening, looking at Phil Clyatt's taillights racing down Main Street with my date snuggled up beside him.

This would have ended differently with my new persona. Maggie would surely have chosen Bertrand Chauncey, exciting International … whatever. And ten seconds after he showed up, Phil Clyatt would have had *two* interesting scars to show the girls. I really needed to make time to come up with a solution to this 'International… whatever' issue. It was beginning to bug me.

I began to wonder if, back then, I had been able to pull off a Chauncey maneuver and win the beautiful babe, where would I be now? Married? Maybe. I was sure back then I was in love with Maggie. And maybe if she had come back to the prom with me I would be married to... what? To a woman with the moral integrity of a street hooker. Or possibly far less.

Thanks, Phil. Maybe you did me a favor. I was on the way out the door to meet a truly wonderful young lady, I had a faithful and interesting dog named Hannibal, I had a wonderful new friend the size of a Brahma bull, and there was a drug kingpin trying to track me down and plug me into a hole by the railroad tracks. Doesn't get much better than that. And Phil Clyatt was probably still out there somewhere, working his ass off framing track houses while his wife Maggie was shopping for shoes and meeting Enriche after lunch for a romp.

I was feeling better by then. Fear and anger and bitterness are for losers. I might have been a loser in high school, but I wasn't one anymore. And I didn't give a rip about getting hurt or feeling betrayed. Bertrand Chauncey did not have time for such foolishness. I knew that obsessing about the possible negative consequences of the future is a good way to guarantee negative consequences. "Onward, Hannibal! To the chariot!"

Chapter Seven

We were met at the door of a unique little wooden cabin that was nestled graciously into the surrounding woods like a hobbit house. Despite the urban zip code, Claudia's small cottage was surrounded by old maple and hickory trees, and blended so completely into the foliage that at first I could not see the door. "Bertrand! I'm glad you found me!" Claudia emerged from the Hobbit door to offer a hug as Hannibal shot past me into the house to make acquaintance with whoever might turn up. Claudia looked beautiful. On the drive over I had pictured her wearing an exotic slinky black evening dress, and I wondered if I could maintain my cool. But her simple mid-length skirt and warm smile instantly put me at ease.

I looked over her shoulder into the cabin as Hannibal charged through the living room in hot pursuit of a furry red dog. "Uh oh. Maybe I better restrain the beast."

"Nonsense. They will be fine. Come on... you'll see." We ventured into the most charming little cottage setting I had ever seen. It did not look in the least like the home of a young beautiful woman. It looked like something out of J.R.R. Tolkien's imagination. The early evening green light from the tree canopy filtered through small cross-hatched windows. The walls and floor and ceiling were all golden colored knotty wood, obviously hand crafted and fit together with intricate notches and joints. Here and there, the branch of a tree protruded from the wall with some ancient gadget or interesting carved figure dangling from it. It was hard to tell if you were inside or outside. All the furniture was crafted from the gnarled branches of twisted trees, and expertly joined to fit perfectly into the nooks and alcoves of the cabin, so it was not so much furniture at all, but extensions of the architecture.

Claudia must have noticed my awed expression and said, "It was Granddad's old place. He built it as young man; before he met Grandma, back before the First World War, when this place was half a mile from the nearest neighbor. I used to come here to visit him and he would read me books while I stared into the fire and let my imagination run wild. He knew I loved it here, and he knew I loved him, too; so he left it to me when he passed away a few years ago. I really miss him."

"Do you have a picture of your grandfather? I would like to see him." I was still stunned at the warmth and craftsmanship of the cottage, but I was serious about wanting to see her grandpa.

"Sure. On the bookcase, over by the fireplace. That's us when we were fishing on Willow Lake. I was maybe fifteen then." She led me over to the framed photo of an older fellow in a plaid shirt with a huge smile, arm draped around the shoulder of a skinny girl holding a fat largemouth bass in one hand, fishing pole in the other. Grandpa looked fit to bust.

"Nice catch." I held the frame carefully, knowing it was an important part of her life.

"I thought it was a whale. Granddad had to help me a little, but we got him in after a while. He had my dad take the picture and then bragged about it for years." Claudia was standing close to my side as I looked at the photo. She smelled wonderful. The cabin smelled pretty good, too, like something wonderful was simmering in the kitchen. "Grandma died just before I was born, so I never got to know her, but Granddad would tell me stories about their adventures, so I felt like I knew her a little."

"Sorry to bring up sad memories, with your grandfather, you know." I was starting to stammer and stumble, thinking maybe my inquiries were making her feel nostalgic.

"No sad memories to have… all good ones. I miss him terribly, but I am still really glad to have had him around all those years. He said the sweetest thing to me when he was sick, and knew he was getting close to the end. He said, '*Chipmunk, when I kick off you're goin' to cry for a bit. Then one day you're gonna laugh out loud at some joke one of your friends makes or at some old hound that bumps into an apple tree, and you're gonna feel guilty cause I'm not there to share that laugh. When that happens, I want you to remember one thing…*' and Granddad sat next to me with that big smile you see right there," she said as she pointed to the man's grin in the picture. "He said, '*I did share that laugh with you. People don't disappear when they die, Sugar, they live on inside the hearts of those they love. Is that big fish a part of your life?*' and I told him, '*Sure, Granddad.*' '*And am I part of your life?*' And I told him he was a huge part of my life, and that I didn't want him to leave me. But he just smiled and said, '*Of course you don't want me to leave, Chipmunk. I'm not all that fond of the idea myself, but fact is, I am leaving... want to or not. But that doesn't mean I'm goin' to be completely gone. Nobody can take away the part of me that lives on in you. So I'll still be around, any time you think of me, I'll be right there with you. Same goes for your mom and that little bugger of a brother of yours.*'" Claudia was smiling now, not looking sad at all, and that sort of surprised me.

"Sounds like a pretty cool grandpa to me. I'm glad you told me about him."

"I'm glad you asked. Now come help me in the kitchen, Mr. Chauncey, and tell me where you were able to find such... interesting attire," she said as she led me off toward the marvelous smells wafting through the cabin. Interesting attire? Hmmm. Not exactly the unconditional endorsement I had hoped for.

As we turned from the bookcase, I heard a plaintive wail emanate from the back of the house and I suddenly remembered Hannibal soaring into the cabin, and disappearing from view. Claudia calmly commented, "That would be Cecelia. She must be entertaining Hannibal." Claudia certainly did not seem concerned about her dog, even though it sounded as if Cecelia was caught in a leg trap.

I made a move toward the wailing, "Hannibal. Come here, boy." But Hannibal did not appear. I rounded the corner that led into a cozy, well-lit room where Hannibal was laid out on his back in the center of an old floor rug, with an Irish setter attending to his personal hygiene by applying a liberal tongue bath to his undersides.

"Barrooooff!" came the low wailing again, but it was coming from Hannibal, not Cecelia. Hannibal was wailing away, feet in the air, thoroughly enjoying the bath he was getting from Cecelia, who I was forced to admit, was a remarkably attractive animal, gender confusion notwithstanding.

"That's just wrong, boy." I caught a sideways grin from Hannibal whose upper lip was flopping over his teeth, due to being upside down.

Claudia caught up with me and hooked her arm through mine under the low arch that led into the room, "Told you. Cecelia is very good at entertaining. She is a bit of a slut, though."

"Nonsense! Far be it for me to judge the personal habits of consenting canines." The scene seemed suddenly comical, and we both cracked up and returned to the kitchen to prod along the cooking. "What can I do to assist with the feast?"

"Why, I do believe Bertrand Chauncey has arrived! How splendid! I was secretly hoping you might make an appearance." Claudia had picked up on my sudden switch to the dashing dialogue, and seemed pleased. I had not even intended to do it, it just sort of came out while watching my dog being serviced by an Irish setter who thought it was a gay cat. That sight was enough to knock anyone into a parallel persona.

I seized the opportunity by sweeping an arm around her waist as she stirred the sputtering sauce on the stove and said, "Did either of us happen to mention how breathtaking you look tonight? I fear we have both been remiss."

"Why, I'm sure I would have remembered if either one of you had!" She spun around to face me and wrapped her arms around behind me. A groan of contentment emerged from the next room and Claudia burst out in her delicious laugh.

"Ah, the sound of young misguided love." And I gave her the first of many, many kisses. None of which I ever came to regret.

"This is all lovely, Mr. Chauncey, but we must focus on the task at hand, or the kibble will burn and we will go hungry." She pulled away gently after planting a quick peck on my right cheek.

"Kibble!" I had nearly forgotten the promised menu. "Such delicacies enrage my culinary passions!" I followed close behind, hands raised in mock attack.

"Desist, you rogue. Or you shall feel the sting of my blade!" She waved a wooden spoon at me menacingly. I realized she might be better at this English adventure than I was.

I froze my advance and stared with horror at the spoon, "What devilish misfortune has befallen me? My conquest has been derailed by a common kitchen utensil? I yield to thy mighty spoon and ask your humble mercy." I bowed in submission, arms splayed to the sides with head lowered to accept my fate.

"Mercy is granted on one condition… you must attend to the kibble lest it burn while I prepare the garlic bread." She yielded the spoon to me and indicated the simmering skillet of delicious smelling red sauce. I stirred away happily. Claudia peeked over my shoulder as she sliced French bread, "Time to put on the pasta," and she emptied the pasta noodle box into a large pot of boiling water next to the sauce. "I hope you like simple meals; I'm afraid I have not mastered fine cooking just yet."

"What? No beef Wellington with Crème Brulee? No Peking Duck with asparagus tips garnished with shredded goat cheese?" I had never eaten those particular items, but I thought they sounded delicious.

"Forgive my shortcomings, Mr. Chauncey, but I was never accepted into culinary school."

"Your shortcomings smell fabulous." I spun around and wrapped my arms around her waist. "And we simply must get past this 'Mr. Chauncey' lunacy. Much too formal, don't you see." She was looking right into my eyes, smiling like an angel.

"Looking for something more informal? And what would you have me call you, then?"

I thought for a moment and replied, "Well, you could address me as Sir Bertrand, Defender of the Realm and Befriender of the Beast."

"Oh yes, that would be much more informal… but a bit cumbersome, don't you think? By the time I get that out, the kibble will be burnt to hades." The smile never faded.

"Yes, I suppose it is a bit of a mouthful. Would 'Bertrand' be more appropriate, given our growing familiarity?" But suddenly something sunk into my clouded mental processes that were sailing high above the world and the events of the past days. Before she could reply, I gave her a quick, but purposeful kiss, and pulled away toward the door of her cottage. "My heavens, I am a buffoon. Defend the realm without me for a moment for I shall return with a most important item. Fear not, my dear." She just laughed as she took over the stirring duties and I slipped out the door toward the pickup to retrieve the roses I has swiped from Arthur P. Grimley who was kicking back at Lawnmere Cemetery. He will be missed.

Darkness was settling in by then, so I was walking quickly, but cautiously along the cobblestones that led out to the driveway where the old Ford was waiting patiently with a bundle of yellow roses wrapped in wet paper on the seat. As I picked my way towards the truck I glanced up to see the interior light of a car parked just across from my truck. I might not have seen it at all, but it was dark and the light allowed me to see the form of someone sitting in the driver seat of a new Lincoln Towncar. As I reached through my open window to grab the roses, I realized the light was too dim to be from the overhead bulb, and it had faded out quickly. In its place was the dull red glow of a cigar being stoked into full production. I was close enough to smell it.

The car was not parked in front of another residence; it had no reason to be situated where it was. '*Uh oh. This can't be good*,' I remember thinking to myself. My worst fears were taking shape on the very first night I had driven to Claudia's. Some wingnut had followed me there and was parked out front, waiting for his opportunity to... what? Shoot me? Abduct Claudia? Steal my truck? No, I knew that last one was not likely. The keys were in it, if he was interested.

I snatched the roses from the front seat and moved casually around the pickup to retrieve some imaginary item through the driver side. This put me much closer to the parked Lincoln and the guy stoking the stogie. I caught a quick glance of his profile, not too large, arm out the open window of the Towncar, cigar glowing in the dark night air. Careful Bertrand. Stupid theatrics and false bravado do not repel bullets.

I spun around from the truck and strode casually toward his open window, "Cuban? At first I thought it might be a hand wrapped Montecristo, but I can tell now it must be a Bolivar. But not from Cuba. It smells as if the only thing Cuban about that piece of cat feces you have stuck in your face is the imprint stamped on the box that some greasy Pakistani nose-picker passed off as the real deal. My sincere condolences on your deception." I had moved directly to his window without any hesitation in my step. To his credit, he never moved a muscle during my approach, except a slight turn of his head to peer out at me as he gnawed away at the end of his smoke.

"You got quite the fucking attitude for a warehouse grunt with a piece-of-shit pickup and a fake accent. Still, I gotta hand it to you… not many dipshits like you got the cajones to try some cheap shit like this in my face." With this dubious compliment the man I now was certain was Perez raised the cigar in his left hand to his lips, and raised the semi-automatic pistol in his right hand to the window and directed at my internal organs. I remember thinking how clever I had been to waltz up to within easy firing distance and accuse Perez of smoking a cat-turd. Brilliant. This was working out just as I had hoped.

"Oh, yes. Spot on, mate. But tell me something, Antonio; how does it come to pass that a warehouse grunt with a fake accent puts a big kingpin like yourself in such an awkward position? Losing your edge, eh?" I leaned against his car with complete indifference to the pistol. Perez sat with his cigar hanging forgotten from the corner of his open mouth. I think it was a unique experience for him to have his victims ignore imminent danger of death.

"Look, asshole… first, nobody but family calls me Antonio. Number two, in one second you can get perforated with this nine millimeter if you don't shut the fuck up with this bullshit."

"Oh, sorry. Didn't realize you had something to say. And put the gun away. It wastes both our time and might possibly be mistaken for an act of aggression that would result in that tiny little laser spot on your forehead being used for its intended purpose." What in the hell was I talking about? Laser spots? Perez glanced toward his rear view mirror with a sudden glint of fear. "Paranoid tonight, aren't we. Look, Buckwheat, you drove all this way to poke a gun at me and make me feel all gooey inside and quiver in fear. Looks like that part is not going all that well for you, so maybe we get on with this little chat and spit out whatever ludicrous demands I am supposed to surrender to. I have a date with a lovely young lady waiting inside. No offense, but you're not my idea of a romantic evening."

"OK, smartass, you want the deal, here it is. You play your little English asshole accent and convince a few of my competitors to engage in a little business deal, and I let you live in return." He was smiling now, looking like he had turned the table on me at last. He was in control, just like always, and he sat back to enjoy my certain collapse and agreement.

"Very tempting, Buckwheat. Very tempting. But I have an even better plan… you take your pea-shooter and your flaming Cuban cat-turd, and ram them both up your poop-chute. When I am satisfied you have been successful in this objective, I will consider letting *you* live. Deal?"

At that point, I knew Perez would either shoot me, or counter-offer. I doubted he would sign off on my first request. Instead he began to grin like a Cheshire cat. "Perfect. Just fucking perfect. Mack said he knew the perfect guy for this gig, but I had to see for myself. You got some major huevos, Chauncey; got to hand it to you. You and Mack meet me tomorrow morning at ten and we'll set this thing up. You might just pull it off. Flaming Cuban cat-turd! What a fucking genius!" Perez lowered the gun and laughed.

I suddenly realized he had addressed me by my alter-ego. Mack must have given it to him. Probably better than having him know the real one. "I must have missed the part where I agreed to all this. Did we skip one act of this play, or have I been caught napping?"

"Oh, no, you didn't miss nothing. You run along and enjoy your date. She's a real cute little lady. Be a shame if she was to fall victim to some horrible criminal activity, don't you think?" Perez was still grinning widely, even as he began to roll up his driver window and pull away in the big Lincoln. "See you tomorrow morning, Chauncey." The window zipped to the frame and Perez rolled away from the curb. I had not even responded to his threat. I had not been able to counter with spontaneous witty return volley. It had been an effective shot; more efficient than the nine millimeter, because it was designed to achieve his objective. The gun would not have solved any of Perez's problems, and might have created an extra one or two. He never had any intention of shooting me. He had every intention of using me. The shooting part could wait till later.

I turned toward the cottage and saw the silhouette of Claudia's classy outline backlit by the cottage lights. She was looking out, wondering why I had not returned. I sprinted up the path, roses in hand, into the front room where she waited by the window. "I offer no excuse for my forgetfulness, but I assure you my intentions were honorable." I swept the roses toward Claudia and bowed deeply.

"Oh, how wonderful! I love yellow roses! How did you know that? I'm sure I never mentioned it." She took in the fragrance of the bouquet and hugged the bunch to her chest.

How did I know that? I didn't. Time to give credit where credit was due. "My floral consultant was kind enough to offer advice on the selection. He has impeccable taste."

"Would this consultant be lying on his back in the next room?"

"Actually, yes. That would be Hannibal. Amazing beast." I returned to my assistant cook duties while Claudia drained the pasta and pulled a rack of toasted garlic bread from the oven. But I was thinking hard about Perez and his lightly veiled threats. It was tough to keep up the light banter I had enjoyed with Claudia earlier. She picked up on the change in mood.

"When you went for the roses, I saw a car by the drive. Was that someone you knew?" She asked, looking a little concerned, but trying to keep the question casual.

"Not exactly." I was struggling to develop a cover story that would keep her out of this mess, but reached no solid ground. "Let's enjoy this remarkable feast, and we can sit down and talk about that after dinner and a glass of wine."

"Sure." She looked puzzled, but agreed to the delayed answer, since the dinner items were coming together nicely. "And I have a special treat for you." She reached into a small pantry alcove and produced two large bowls, one filled with dog kibble, the other with Cecelia's cat food mixture. "If you are a good boy, I have dessert!" and laughed. Both dogs heard the rattle of the kibble in the bowls and appeared from the adjoining room to investigate potential feeding opportunities. Claudia set the bowls down in the corner and the pair lined up side by side, to munch away happily. Cecelia even allowed Hannibal to sample the cat food without so much as a growl.

We followed their lead, and sat across from each other at the small table crafted into the corner of the kitchen. The table was made of a thick slab of walnut, with beautiful grain patterns and a natural outer edge that was once the outside of the tree trunk. "Did your grandfather build homes for a living? He must have been very talented," I said as I ran my hand along the smooth table edge and admired all the intricate woodwork around me.

"Granddad worked his whole life at the shipyard, trying to make enough money so my dad could go to school and get a good job. But he learned a lot of things helping Uncle Tony with his construction company. Granddad would work with Tony most of the day, then start his shift at the shipyard at three. Grandma used to tell me how tired and sore he would be once he finally got home late at night. But he would always get up and go again the next morning, trying to make a good life for his family. Whenever there was some problem or family crisis my Granddad would say '*Just go to work, and tell the truth. Everything works out fine if you just tell the truth and go to work.*' And off he would go, lunch pail in hand. He would swing a hammer all day and load cargo all night, and somehow, all those problems would disappear in time. I think he was right about that."

"Sorry I missed meeting him."

"Granddad would say '*You're meeting Claudia. So you're meeting me.*' I think he might be right about that too, in a way. I still think about him a lot, and even catch myself acting like him sometimes."

"Well then, how do you do, sir? You are certainly the loveliest grandfather I have had the pleasure to meet. Somehow I pictured you with more facial hair." She took my hand across the table and smiled back radiantly. I knew any defenses I had built since my last romantic disaster were melting away right in front of me like a snow-cone in a tropical heat wave.

"Thanks for coming over tonight. I don't meet many guys I like. You seem different to me. Maybe because there seems to be two of you in there," she said smiling, and probably only half joking. "Bert is cute and sweet, and Bertrand is dashing and adventurous. I kind of like them both." Wow, she liked Bert too. I thought it was hopeless without Bertrand, but maybe not. After a few seconds she added, "Sorry, but there is just one of me. Kind of boring, huh?"

"How do you know?"

"Know what?" she replied, confused.

"How do you know there is just one of you, in there?" I pointed towards her and then poured two glasses of Cabernet for us. "That's what I thought too, until a few days ago, when I had to rely on Bertrand to get out of a jam that Bert would have muddled up royally. And it was Bertrand that was able to sweet talk his way into dinner here with you. Bert would have tripped on his way to the car, spilled his soda all over you, and then frozen solid with fear."

She leaned over a little closer to me, "So Bertrand is the more recent addition, I take it? I thought maybe you spent your whole life as Bertrand Chauncey, and simply made up the imaginary character of Bert Cluster to impress me."

I leaned back, wine glass in hand and shifted easily into the English dialect, "Possibly… one never knows, now do we?"

"Oh, how simply delightful!" She clapped her hands together once and beamed. She was just as adept at this game as I was.

I was not sure what I was asking here, but it came out nonetheless, "You see, my dear, I needn't be the only one to bounce back and forth like a cricket ball. It would be lovely to have a partner in this adventure. What say you throw your lot in with mine, we'll make a run at it?"

She brightened even more, if that were possible and said, "Oh, could we? It would be ever so much fun. I haven't had a good adventure in ages. Forever, really. I accept, without hesitation." But then she looked down, thinking. "But who shall I be? Claudia seems a bit mundane, don't you think? If we are to be dashing about, doing adventurous things like scaling walls and snaring ne'er-do-wells, then I shall need a more appropriate moniker."

"I see your point… although I am quite fond of Claudia. Auckland is dashing, but I suppose it might be best if we operate under assumed names. More difficult for our enemies to track our movements, I expect."

"Precisely. My middle name is Brigetta, after my Grandmother. I don't think that works either, do you?"

"Perhaps, but Beretta might work beautifully. You know… like the pistol?" I could see the delight in her face. "Now for a first name…. let's see here…" and I pondered something jazzy to go with Beretta. "What was your grandfather's name?"

"Chester Nathan Auckland. Any clues there?"

"What do you think about Cheshire Beretta?"

"You mean like the cat, Cheshire?"

"Why not, with that beautiful smile? Cats love a good adventure; they are quiet and stealthy… and dangerous… at least if you are a mouse."

She mulled over the suggestion for a moment, then did what she should have done before… consult with the authorities, "Hannibal, Cecelia, I need your attention for a moment." The two dogs responded immediately and looked up from half-empty bowls to listen attentively. "I am considering joining forces with the dashing and dangerous Bertrand Chauncey in an effort to right the wrongs of the world through various adventurous endeavors, and I first ask for both your blessing and approval." Hannibal walked over and put his head on her knee and looked up at her. "Thank you, Hannibal. Your acceptance is very important to me." She scratched his head behind the ears and he wagged his tail in delight. Cecelia came over on her opposite side to share the affection.

"Now then, Bertrand has suggested a new name to better fit our alter-ego lifestyle. What do you two think of Cheshire Beretta?" Cecelia left the room and Hannibal turned around to stare at me in disgust.

"No, boy? Cheshire not going to do it? OK then, help me out here. Nathan is out, not much you can do with that… Chester is too rough…" Hannibal barked and came over to me wagging his tail. "Chester? You think Chester is better that Cheshire?" I got the fish eye from Hannibal. Cecelia came back into the room and looked hopeful.

Claudia piped in, "What about Chessie? I like that a lot." Hannibal barked and Cecelia ran around the room. The dogs began an elaborate cat and mouse game around us and Claudia laughed at them. "I think we may have hit on a winner, Bertrand!"

"Chessie Beretta." I liked the sound and rhythm of the name. Very classy. "I hope your Grandfather would have been pleased."

"Correction, Mr. Chauncey. Granddad *is* pleased."

"I wonder what Granddad would have said about your getting into cahoots with such a shady fellow as Bertrand Chauncey?" I sipped my wine and tried to look dashing.

She thought about that and said, "You know, I think he would have been a little worried. But I know what he would have said; '*Go to work, and tell the truth.*' Do you think we can do those two things together?"

"They will be the foundation of the partnership, my dear Chessie." I knew immediately that I was about to get Claudia Auckland… and the newly christened Chessie Beretta into deeper trouble than either one of them had bargained for.

Chapter Eight

Hannibal and I were back in the truck, floating toward home after a very late first date with Claudia Auckland and her new alter-ego, Chessie Beretta. I had done exactly what I had wanted to avoid… told her the whole sordid story. After dinner we refilled the wine glasses and sat on the sofa in a quiet corner of her cabin and observed the first rule of our new friendship (courtship, maybe?); Tell the Truth. We had agreed it would be the foundation of the partnership, whatever we were partnering in. Despite my misgivings about the possibility of getting her in trouble, it meant a chance to see her more often, and I felt like that was good. Even though I was elated with the way the evening went, I had not wanted her involved in this mess with Mack and Perez and the body parts behind the warehouse. But I sat there sipping wine and retold the events of Friday when Hannibal had shown up and I had followed him out to the tracks to discover the pieces of some poor schmuck that probably crossed Perez and gotten himself diced into chunks and plugged into a hole. I told her about the big behemoth named Mack that probably put Mr. Schmuck into that hole, and I told her about crunching Mack's fender to keep him from following her home. (I got a nice reward for that part of the story.)

But I also told her about Mack's inability to hurt dogs or women and his feelings about being trapped in a job he felt badly about. I even told her who I met in front of her cottage and what he wanted. I left out the bit about Perez hoping Claudia didn't meet with any trouble. I told her the truth, just maybe not every sordid detail of the whole truth. I didn't want to scare her, but I did tell her to start watching for anything suspicious near her house, and keep the doors locked. I told her to call me if she saw anyone around her cabin that didn't belong there.

The most interesting part of the story came when I told her about the proposal Mack had made to Perez, in a moment of weakness, that he knew the perfect English stiff to set up the sleaze-bucket who was forcing young girls into filmed porn scenes. This part made her angry, and she had stormed around the room, fuming at the 'piece of trash' that was doing such things to girls. She was even more inflamed at Perez for scheming to take over the racket and make it his own. After her third rotation around the room, venting her fury, she turned to me and said, "I'm in. Let get this piece of crap before he hurts anyone else. Let's nail them both while we're at it."

"How exactly do we do that… and continue staying alive?" I had asked her when she flopped back down beside me.

"This Perez scum wants an answer, right? Well, give him this one, Bertrand Chauncey." And she laid out her ideas as if she had planned the entire set-up for months.

I met Mack the next morning near the coffee shop where he said he usually met Perez to get job descriptions and directions. Perez was nowhere in sight, so I motioned him across the street where we ducked around the corner to a secluded garbage bay behind the bookstore. I had scouted it out earlier and knew no one could approach without me seeing them, and there was a route of escape in either direction. If I was going to be an International Dashing Type Guy, I had better start being more careful. Oh God, I had to figure out what the hell Bertrand Chauncey was before some criminal mastermind asked and I gave them a stupid answer like *International Dashing Type Guy*. Then I could shoot them while they were rolling around laughing.

"Mack, you meeting Perez today?"

"Sure, Chauncey, I meet him in half an hour. You better beat it. He sees you here, and things might go bad for both of us."

"Look, Mack, tell him that you ran into me again and I sent along a message for him. Tell him I think he's a piece of rat droppings, but I am willing to perform a single transaction for him if he agrees to lay off of Claudia." Mack looked pleased to hear his suggestion might be soon a reality, getting him off the hook with Perez. Mack, there's more… tell Perez he is a miserable sack of vomit with the intellectual agility of a hamster. Tell him he doesn't have the mental capacity to plan the birthday party for a two-year old."

"Hey Chauncey, I can't say that stuff to Perez. He'll get sore and cut me or somethin' maybe worse. Besides, I can't remember all that fancy stuff."

A voice boomed from just behind a stack of empty book boxes, "Oh, you don't have to remember all that fancy stuff, Mack. I was takin' notes while this dipshit here gave his little lecture."

"Ah, it's the piece of rat droppings himself. What a dubious pleasure. I was just briefing your esteemed associate here on my firm belief that you couldn't think your way out of wet toilet tissue, so I am understandably reluctant to participate in your little grade school performance, whether you cast me as the Fairy Godmother or not." How in the name of Jumping Jasper had he come up behind me that quickly? Damn… I had some serious practice to do if I was going to survive in this industry. Mack just stood dumbfounded, mouth agape, unable to comprehend the atrocities that might befall someone who spoke to Perez that way.

"You'll do as you're told, chump, or I get rough with cutie-pie. Remember the deal? So, how'd it go last night? You get lucky with the babe, or did you get the boot? Sorry I couldn't stick around to enjoy the show, I had some business to arrange." Perez stepped out with one hand at his side, cocked a strange angle.

"Got the pea-shooter ready, Buckwheat, in case I make a play for my 'piece'? Which low-budget 1970s gangster movie are you living in? Look at yourself, hiding behind a trash heap, eavesdropping on people, ready to pull out your trusty Smith and Wesson and fill me full of lead!" I laughed out loud and slapped my thigh. "How could anyone possibly take you seriously?"

"You better start taking me seriously, or things are goin' to get messy in a hurry." He pulled the same brushed steel automatic pistol I have seen the night before and directed the business end of it towards me.

"Mr. Perez," Mack cut in. "Mr. Chauncey here was just telling me he was willing to make the deal with Darrell for us over at the warehouse." Mack was trying to keep Perez cool. He was also trying to keep me alive. I was moved.

"No, Mack, I've changed my mind. Antonio here seems intent on calling all the shots and mucking up the works beyond any hope of success. If he is unwilling to accept the obvious truth that there are others more capable of orchestrating this deception than he, then I must decline the invitation. Pity… I was beginning to warm up to the idea." I leaned casually against the corner of the building and awaited Perez's next volley. I was not about to get shot. I knew that from yesterday's exchange. Perez wanted Darrell to go down, and he knew he needed help to do it. "Unwilling to even listen to the script for the first act, Buckwheat?"

"OK, Chauncey, you got ten minutes to lay this out. In my car out in front… by yourself."

"Piss off, Perez. I couldn't lay out breakfast cereal in ten minutes. And Mack comes with us because he plays prominently in the production… as does Ms. Beretta, by the way. We'll meet at Hauzer's Brat Haus for lunch around oneish; there's a private room there and I know the owner. Bring a notepad and your credit card. Lunch is on you."

Perez looked on with an amazed expression. "You're a fuckin' piece of work, Chauncey. Shit, I'm startin' to regret this already." Perez lowered the weapon shook his head.

'Not half as much as you're going to regret this', I thought.

Mack looked over to me with a puzzled expression, "Hey Chauncey… who the fug is Buckwheat?"

I stopped at Claudia's at noon to go over the details prior to meeting with Perez. Mack was with me, so I made the introductions and turned Hannibal loose to romp around with Cecelia. Mack watched them tear around the room, bounding over each other and then disappear for unmentionable activities in the next room.

"She is a beautiful dog, ma'am," Mack commented to Claudia.

"Thank you, Mack… but we need to lose the ma'am, if you don't mind. And *she's* a *he*."

Mack looked confused, "Cecelia is a boy dog?"

"Well, sort of. He thinks he is a female cat, I believe. Probably some genetic short circuit in there somewhere. Hannibal certainly seems comfortable with it." Claudia smiled up at Mack.

"OK by me then. Can I just call you Claudia?"

Claudia thought for a minute and then responded, "No, let's get started on the right foot here, since we are getting in this together. I think we should all use the proper names for our roles in this. Bert will be Bertrand Chauncey, and I would like to be Chessie Beretta. Mack, you may call me Chessie and forget the Claudia bit for now. We can catch up on that later."

"How come we changin' our names?" Mack was more confused than ever. I decided to chime in to help out.

"Mack, it has to do with attitude and self-image. Tomorrow Bert Clauster will be stocking electrical parts at the warehouse and Claudia Auckland will be sending out monthly statements in the front office of State Electric Supply. But next Saturday you, Bertrand Chauncey and Chessie Beretta are going to throw an industrial-sized monkey wrench into the gears of two crime rings. Bert and Claudia would get shot on sight... but Chauncey and Beretta, that's a different story."

"OK, I get it. I seen the way you told off Perez; called him a piece of rat shit right to his face. I seen him blast people who just looked at him the wrong way, so I can't figure why he don't give the same to you... but Perez just takes it. That what you mean by attitude, Chauncey?"

"Exactly, Mack. Shifting into the new name helps shift into the new persona, making it possible to stay in the character you need to survive the situation. And the crafty Chessie Beretta can pick a bank lock with a paper clip, charm a Russian diplomat into giving up state secrets, convince White House Security that she works for the president, and be back at the club by noon for tea and crumpets on the veranda."

Claudia slid over beside me and hooked her arm around my waist and planted a kiss on my cheek. "Oh, Mr. Chauncey, you are such a smooth talker."

"Naturally, my dear. But, an accurate description of your talents, nonetheless."

Mack broke up our little trance with a flat statement, "I want a new name too."

I tried to explain, "But Mack, you already have the attitude with 'Mack'. Remember how you make your living? That sort of fits the type of guy we need to pull this thing off." I did not want to lose the '*Mack*' in Mack.

Yeah, I know. That's the point Chauncey, I don't wanta be Mack no more after this. I've had enough bein' Mack. When we get done with this, maybe you two can help me come up with a new name so I don't have to bust people up no more."

Now it was Mack's turn for a reward. Claudia slipped over to him and planted one on his cheek. "We promise, Mack." Mack turned red and shuffled his feet in embarrassment.

"Thanks, Chessie. You tell me what needs to be done. I can't act all fancy like you two, but I can act like Mack for a little longer, I guess, if it gets me outta this mess. You be thinkin' of a new name for me, OK?"

"We will, Mack," I said.

We got to work going over the scheme Claudia had developed the night before, and then gathered ourselves into my truck to pay a visit to Hauzer's Brat Haus for our one p.m. rendezvous with Perez. We let Mack out early so it would not seem like we were too cozy. We did not want Perez to suspect the depth of our new partnership.

Perez, of course, was nowhere to be seen as we pulled up to Hauzer's, but I guessed he was peering out at us from some nearby hole. We went in and met Hauzer coming out of the kitchen. "Ah, my friend Bert! And vit such a beautiful fraulein! Come in!"

"Hauzer, this is…," I hesitated a second and said "Chessie… Chessie Beretta." It was the first time I had used her new name in public. It sounded pretty good I thought.

"Vonderful! Come, sit, I have a little boot' in the corner vor you two."

"Actually, we are meeting with a couple of other folks. Would you mind if we sat in the private room in the back?" I indicated the curtained entry to the small room across from the kitchen.

"Ya, shore, no problem for dat. You go on in dere, and I send Delores in a minute. You bring in dat big fellow today?"

"Mack? Yeah, actually he should be walking up any minute."

"Oh boy, I better put more bratvurst on the grill." Hauzer sauntered off to his kitchen and Delores appeared in the doorway.

"Bert! How are you, honey? This must be your sister, 'cause I know you couldn't get a date with nobody this perty." Delores was beaming with enthusiasm at the chance to berate one of her favorite customers. It was an activity she relished and had perfected to an art form.

This time I took particular pleasure in contradicting Delores, "As a matter of fact, my dear Delores, this is indeed my date, Chessie. Chessie, this is the queen of the greasy spoon, Delores." Delores clasped Chessie's hand and they both smiled at our exchange of insults.

"Don't pay him no mind, Chessie. I know he loves me, but he's way too young fer me. Besides, I kinda took a shine to that big hunk of a body guard he came in with a couple of days ago. Where is that big fella?"

"Your lucky night, Delores. Turn around." Mack had appeared and literally darkened the doorway behind Delores.

Delores spun around to see Mack and exclaimed, "Oh, Sugar Cakes, it's about time you came to see Mamma," as she slid over to Mack and gave him a pat on the chest. "How's about a keg of beer and a half-dozen bratwurst for an appetizer?"

Delores was talking Mack's language. I don't know if that look of Nirvana on his mug came from thoughts about Delores, or about the half-dozen bratwurst. "Yes, ma'am. But not sure I can eat six of them... maybe four." We all laughed and Mack got red, but never quit smiling at the object of his affection. (Delores, I think... not the bratwurst.)

Delores gave Mack another affectionate chest rub and said, "You just plop down here, Stud, and I'll be right back to get everybody's order."

"Actually, Delores, there is one more coming. A greasy little weasel named Perez. He should be slithering in any minute," I added.

"He about five-seven with greasy black hair and an earring?" Delores asked.

"That's the weasel."

Delores started to boil, "Well, jump my stump, that turkey is already here. Said he was with County Health Department and wanted to look at our cook-stove."

I set her straight on Perez's occupational endeavors. "Mr. Perez is no health inspector, Delores, he's just a paranoid loser who thinks the world is out to bugger up his shady business dealings."

Perez appeared in the doorway with a clipboard in hand, acting like he was checking off a list of possible violations. "Can't be too careful about where you eat. Just checking to make sure your venue here was up to my high standards."

Delores turned on Perez and advanced into his face, "I'm about two seconds from jerkin' a knot in your tail, mister. I don't give a dead rats ass about your high standards… you don't come sneakin' in here playin' to be somethin' you ain't!"

Mack cut in before Delores had the chance to jerk that knot, something I was relishing seeing done, "Delores, this here's Mr. Perez. I work for Mr. Perez, so it would be nice if we didn't have no trouble."

"If'n you say so, Cutie-Pie. But I don't abide by that kind of silliness in my place." The doe-eyes she was directing toward Mack turned to daggers as she turned back on Perez, "Mack or no Mack, you pull that 'Health Inspector' crap one more time and *you'll* be in sore need of a gall-dern health inspector!" Perez's scouting methods had touched a nerve and revealed that Delores was apparently a force to be reckoned with.

Perez decided Delores presented a more formidable opponent than he had originally assessed, so he backed off on the B-movie gangster tough-guy routine a bit, "Look, lady, my fault. Take it easy, OK? I just needed to look around to be sure nothin' out the ordinary was going down in here prior to my meeting with your friends here. Everything checks out, so no harm done, right? Put lunch on my tab, and somethin' for yourself while you're at it."

"Humph!" Delores spun around and took her leave. She took no stock in Perez's apology.

I smiled amiably at Perez as he watched Delores retreat toward the kitchen, "How nice that you are making new friends, Buckwheat! I think she is taken with you. Did you see how she lit up when she realized you were a lying slime ball instead of a legitimate member of the human race?"

"Shut the fuck up, Chauncey. Sometimes listenin' to your bullshit gives me a headache. Sit down, all of you, and let's get this little meeting over with. I got shit to do, I don't have time to play Shakespeare with a bunch of losers like you." Perez was intent on establishing his role as Alpha dog. Too late for that, I thought.

"Good call, Perez. Couldn't agree more. Sorry to have wasted your lunch hour." I got up and headed for the doorway where Perez was still standing. "Toodles." I brushed my hand sideways to indicate that Perez was to vacate the passageway so I could depart. Perez didn't move.

"Sit the fuck down, Dickhead."

"Dickhead? I believe that might be anatomically impossible." But I grudgingly returned to the table with Mack and Claudia and slid into one of the chairs. "Mr. Perez, let's summarize this little arrangement. Even though I hold you in lowest esteem, I have been informed by your subordinate, Mack, that it is in our best interest to cooperate with your plans to subvert the enterprises of an individual named Darrell who runs a marvelous little business employing young female actresses. Despite the social benefits offered to these girls by this opportunity, you feel it best to reorganize the management personnel and replace Darrell with someone more apt to expand your financial holdings. How am I doing so far, Buckwheat?"

Perez glared back at me, "One more 'Buckwheat', and you get a cap in your ass."

"That would be a new experience for me. Never had a *cap* in my *ass*. Settle down, Antonio, and let's get through this rehearsal so you can get back to killing a small animal or breaking someone's fingers, or whatever it is you do for a living."

"Look Chauncey, or whatever the fuck you call yourself today, I don't appreciate the attitude. It's wearing a little thin… so lose it. Now get on with this crap so I can get the fuck out of this rathole and get the hell away from you crazy bastards. I swear to God, it's like Monty Fuckin' Python listening to you."

"No it isn't," I countered, recalling one of my favorite old Python skits.

"Yes, it fuckin' is! Now shut the fuck up and let's get on with this before I lose my fuckin' patience!"

"You seem to have an unnatural fondness for that word; fuck. That was three times in your last exchange alone. Have you considered seeing a speech pathologist? "

"I'm warning you for the last fu… for the last time, Chauncey!" I found it amusing that he stumbled over his favorite adjective that time. But, I let it pass without further comment and we went back to the purpose for the meeting and lined out the role of each participant in the scheme to send Darrell to the Federal Penitentiary. Most of that plan seemed relatively straightforward. The tricky part was ensuring Darrell would have Perez for a cellmate. We did not share that portion of the plan with Perez.

Delores brought out orders of bratwurst and beer, and fawned over Mack while casting disapproving looks towards Perez. After an hour or so of diagrams and timing discussions, Perez stood up to leave the room. "You people do what you got to do. I don't got that much to do with this, sounds like. What the fuck, don't you think I can act like a Limey a-hole?"

Claudia took the lead to prevent me from further inflaming Perez, "Mr. Perez, I am sure you could play a convincing character, but do you really want to expose yourself to the risk? There are no guarantees we will not be apprehended for purchase of illegal materials. Maybe this Darrell character is setting us up too, you know."

"Yeah, good point there, Ms. Beretta. You're a pretty sharp cookie. Let me know if you ever want a real job. I could use a hot little personal secretary like you. Be different to have a broad who could spell her own name for a change. 'Course you might have to dump Winchester there." Perez was still standing in the doorway, leering at Claudia.

Claudia seemed repulsed for a moment, but recovered before Perez could catch the look. "Yes, very generous offer, Mr. Perez. At the moment, I am happy with my current position, thank you. And also very happy with 'Winchester' here." She shot a quick smile towards me, and I melted. She was happy with me? Cool.

Mack looked from me to Perez, befuddled. "Who the fug is Winchester?"

Perez laughed and made his exit after dropping a hundred dollar bill on the counter in front of Delores. "Keep the change, Doll."

Delores' grumpy demeanor toward Perez temporarily brightened. "Hell, for a hundred bucks you can come in here and inspect Hauzer's boxer shorts if you want." Delores was staring at the bill like it was the first one she had ever seen.

"He's not my type, but he does make a nice bratwurst." Perez turned from Delores to Mack and added, "Hey, Mack.... don't forget who you work for."

Mack looked up to Perez who was already turning to leave. Mack started to say something, but just sat with mouth agape, watching Perez's retreating figure.

Chapter Nine

We had a week before the plan was to be executed. OK... executed is a bad choice of words. Before the operation was to be staged. We had planned to entice Darrell into a meeting Saturday evening with a wealthy English gentlemen who may or may not be interested in purchasing his original videotapes. We would stipulate that the actresses involved must meet a rather stringent maximum age limit. This information needed to be delivered by someone whom Darrell would not suspect of being associated with prudish law enforcement officers who frown on underage girls being forced into prostitution or sexual slavery. Hence, Mack.

Not only did Mack look like the last person on earth who might be undercover, he had the advantage of field experience working with slime balls like Darrell and Perez, and therefore could 'speak the language'. We pointed this out to Mack during our planning sessions after work. The first day we met at Claudia's, then rotated to my place, then the State Electric warehouse, just to keep Perez guessing. We wanted to send Mack to visit Darrell just before the proposed meeting, to prevent Darrell from sniffing out trouble.

So, on Wednesday evening after work hours we met in the back of the warehouse and Mack came in through the loading doors to sit with us in folding chairs I borrowed from the front office. We avoided the front because we did not want to be seen through the storefront windows, and the lights in the warehouse did not show from outside. Mack sat down heavily across from us and looked a bit dejected. I asked him for an update, "So, Mack... why the long face?"

"Oh, you know... Mr. Perez, he's gettin' jumpy about this gig with Darrell. Keeps showin' up right behind me and scarin' the fuggin' shit out of me. Kind of creepy the way that guy just appears out of the fog. Wants to know all the details about our plans for Darrell." That didn't sound good... even though Mack did not exactly have all the details. Claudia and I had spent a long time considering how much information to give Mack. We both trusted Mack, but we didn't know how well he would hold up if Perez started grilling him about the plan. So, some of the details about how Perez would get picked up in the sweep were kept between Claudia and I.

I tried to comfort Mack, "Look, Perez knows the basics. As long as he keeps his intrusive little snout out of the works, he can know whatever he wants."

"Yeah, I know. But it don't sound like he wants to trust you with all that cash. It don't sound like he trusts me to keep tabs on you, either. I got a feelin' he wants to play it close when this thing goes down." Through Mack, we had requested Perez supply us with the wads of hundreds we would need to successfully entice Darrell and get him to produce the goods. Sounded like he was reluctant to send us off with fifty-grand without keeping a tight rein on the cash.

"Not a problem, Mack. Perez can hang around behind the scenes, as long as he stays out of sight. Please convey our request that he honor the deal to stay out of the mix till Darrell is apprehended. He will get his reward shortly thereafter." I hoped that was true, but the second phase of the plan was trickier than the first. "Just tell Perez to have the cash together by Saturday noon. You are going to try to set up the big purchase that evening. How can you communicate with Darrell to set it up?"

Mack looked up and began to brighten his mood. He smiled and said, "Oh, I got no problem gettin' to that guy. He sends Tommy over to scout the talent over by the high school every Friday afternoon. Word gets around the school that there's this guy with lots of cash in a red Miata sports car. Rumor goes around that he might part with some of it for girls with talent. I heard he sits and lets the girls come to him, beggin' for the cash. If Tommy smells a trap, and it's no deal... he don't know nothin' about nothin'. Tommy ain't stupid, that's why Darrell uses him to scout the girls."

"Just disgusting," Claudia put in, making a face like she had just swallowed a cockroach.

"Yeah. So I can get to Darrell through him, I think. I know the car. Seen it hauling girls to the warehouse where he does his tapes. Tommy can set up a meeting, but I don't think we oughta' sniff around the warehouse. He keeps that place pretty tight, with that big Rooskie goon and security cameras and all.

I considered this issue and thought we might want to set up the meeting elsewhere to minimize the goon factor. It might not eliminate it, but it might thin out the population a bit. "So, Mack...

where do you think we should try to set up the meeting with Darrell? He's not about to invite us into the studio to watch a film session."

"He's probably got some rathole somewheres downtown. Someplace he can see who's comin' and crawl out if he has to. Won't be good to meet him in a place like that. I dunno. Maybe some doughnut shop or somethin'."

Claudia had a thought, "Or... perhaps a Bratwurst shop".

"Why Ms. Beretta, how genuinely brilliant! I knew you were more just a pretty face!" I jibed in my best Bertrand Chauncey lingo.

"Why, thank you Mr. Chauncey. So pleased you finally noticed." She was smiling back at me as she delivered the volley. I could not quite get used to the ease with which she was able to slip into her persona as the beautiful and intriguing Chessie Beretta. But I knew I liked it.

I considered the suggestion and it began to grow on me. "Hauzer's place. Interesting. Think he'll go for it, Mack?"

"Dunno. Worth a shot I s'pose."

"We need a contingency plan in the event Mack is unsuccessful in arranging the meeting at Hauzer's. Any backup locations come to mind?" I asked the others.

The beautiful Ms. Beretta was the first to arrive at the obvious conclusion, "No. No contingencies. We must start acting like our characters in this play. Bertrand... who are you supposed to be?"

"Um... a wealthy English aristocrat with a twisted, deviant sense of entertainment?"

"Precisely. Mack?"

"Uh... s'pose I'm still Mack... right?" Mack looked a little confused.

Claudia put her hand on Mack's arm and smiled up at his huge mug, "Not exactly, Mack. For this job you need to be a ruthless agent of a sick, demented sexual pervert. One that has plenty of cash and is used to getting things done his way. Can you do that?"

"Sounds like what I do now for Perez, sort of."

Claudia continued, "Good. Keep that in mind when you meet this Tommy guy at the high school. No contingencies. No deviations from the plan. Have him arrange for Darrell to meet us at

Hauzer's Brat Haus at seven p.m. sharp. Tell him you don't give a shit if Darrell shows or not. Plenty more action around the corner if he is not interested. And then tell Tommy if he double crosses you, he will find himself strung upside down in the alley being gutted like a pig." That comment coming from Claudia was a bit shocking.

I rocked back in the folding chair and put my hands on top of my head. "Remind me never to double cross you!"

She just smiled back at me pleasantly. "Yes. Remember, I am more than just a pretty face."

"Right. I've heard that somewhere before."

Mack just sat, staring at her as if he had never seen her before. Finally he caught on, "I got it. We call the shots. Act like we don't give a rip about the whole setup."

Claudia smiled at Mack, "Exactly, Mack. I think the whole setup depends on your first contact with Tommy and whether he believes the offer is legitimate. You said he was no fool, so you need to stay in character throughout."

"We all need to stay in character throughout," I added, thinking about the million ways this thing could coming crashing in around us.

On Friday I took Claudia to lunch at a little deli near State Electric. It was so busy and noisy that it seemed private enough. Our plan was set, but we needed to reassure each other it would work. "Did you talk to Hauzer last night?" she asked.

"Sure. I filled him in on the details and he is all in. He has a daughter, you know. Grown now and living somewhere in Bavaria, but he is not fond of scum like Darrell."

Claudia considered this a moment and continued to worry. "Isn't he afraid of getting cross-ways with the wrong guys and ruining his business?"

"Hauzer? You kidding? I think he is actually getting excited about helping with this. I think he has been considering selling the business and going back to Bavaria to spend time with his family, so he's not that worried about the long-term consequences. Besides, I don't think he has ever been afraid of anything since birth. The guy is a three-hundred fifty pound German sausage maker. One time, I saw this guy get rowdy in there, and Hauzer lifted him out of a booth with one arm and pitched him out by the curb. Never said a word, just chucked him out with the trash."

Claudia added, "Probably good he got to that guy before Delores did. She might have done even more damage." We had a good laugh about that, and I couldn't believe my luck to be sitting with Claudia Auckland, alias Chessie Beretta, sharing a turkey sandwich and tomato basil soup, and listening to that delicious laugh.

"Speaking of Delores, she will help us with the back room. No way was she willing to be left out of the deal. Better to have her in the loop, in case things get sideways. At least she can call 911 if the bullets fly."

"Oh, let's hope it doesn't come to that. I have faith in you." And she leaned across the small table and kissed me, and smiled. "We better finish off this soup and head back to State Electric before we're missed. I do hate to start idle rumors." Her last line had all the flair of Chessie Beretta.

"Right you are, love." After polishing off the meal, my alias Bertrand Chauncey slid gracefully out and pulled back the chair for the lovely Chessie Beretta, offering an arm and escorting her through the packed crowd towards the door. On the way out, we passed an adjoining table with a single occupant bent low over his table, sandwich in one hand and newspaper beside his plate. He appeared to be closely examining the paper and paid no attention whatsoever to us as we passed. Something looked familiar, but I was missing the connection. As I got to the door and swung it open for Claudia, I took the opportunity to look back at the man for another clue. He was around sixty; rumpled clothes and nothing remarkable about his appearance. Just some local Joe in for a sandwich. Until he peered up from the paper and met my eye for an instant. He quickly looked away, but I caught it. Big walrus moustache.

Once outside, I turned to Claudia and said, "Notice that chap next to us reading the paper?"

"Well, sort of. Did you know him? He kept looking over towards us and it was starting to creep me out a little."

"Hmm. Interesting coincidence. Got to find Mack and buy him a beer after work. I might have an idea for a bit of insurance." I was grinding away at a new thought and walked right past the truck.

"Woof." A friendly dog face hung out my truck door to remind me about the real world.

"Hannibal! What good fortune! My personal car alarm has alerted me of the location of my vehicle. How convenient."

"Mr. Chauncey... would you mind clueing me in on your musings? We are partners in this you know." Claudia slid into the seat with Hannibal and I rounded the front to take the wheel. Hannibal had fallen for Claudia worse than I had, and he laid on the seat with his head in her lap.

I began to explain about the guy with the moustache, "Remember me telling you about the sleazy little bar called the Palm Frond Saloon where I took Mack after ramming his car at the grocery?"

"The one near the Shop-n-Stuff that looks like a disease distribution center?"

"That's the one." I filled Claudia in on my suspicions that Walt the bartender was on the Perez payroll, or at least trying to curry favors. That would have explained how Perez was able to find out about my first meeting with Mack so quickly. And Walt certainly presided over the exact type of low-brow establishment that Perez would have his sticky fingers into. I remembered urging Mack to resist the temptation of flattening out Walt and tipping our hand. Turned out that Walt might come in handy after all. "Do you think Wally overheard us talking about the setup at Hauzer's?"

Claudia thought about this as we pulled into the lot at State Electric, "No. Way too noisy in there. But he sure was interested in our chat. Do you think he will go back to Perez with this?"

"Absolutely. Perez probably sent him in there to keep track of us. Perez is wound up pretty tight about this meeting with Darrell, and he's probably trying to hedge his bets with a little inside information."

She protested, "But we didn't say anything in there Perez doesn't already know!"

"Yes, but we are going to say some things now that Perez doesn't know." I smiled at Claudia, waiting for her to catch on.

"Ah... I see. You are a sneaky devil, Mr. Chauncey. You wouldn't be having that beer with Mack at the Palm Frond Saloon this evening would you?" She was sporting a devilish grin as we walked back into the office to face our afternoon of electrical enterprises.

"What a capital idea, my dear Chessie!"

Chapter Ten

Hannibal and I had an uneventful afternoon in the warehouse. One Kenworth truck with two pallets driven by Scotty the Pirate. One of my all-time favorites, Scotty came swaggering in from the loading dock like he was Captain Jack Sparrow from the Pirates of the Caribbean. "Harrr tharrr, Bertie, my boy. How's it hangin'?"

"Scotty! Glad you sailed in. What's in the hold for us today?"

"Arrrg, the usual loot. Let's drag 'em out and be done with it!" He was jerking up on the back roll-up of his truck.

"No, Scotty, once we drag them out, *you* are done with it. Then I get to go to work sorting out all the loot, while you toodle off to the nearest strip club."

"Harrrg. I 'spose you're right tharrr, lad." Many of Scotty's words involved multiple "r"s. "And how did yarrr know about the titty barrr?" He didn't wait for an answer, "Marrrvelous place they got over tharrr on the furrr side of the tracks. Yarrr oughta get an eyeful of Marrrge... she kin tie a man's crank in half hitch ferrr a dollarrr."

Now there was a pleasant visual image. "I'll have to pass on Marge, Scotty. She's all yours."

"Harrrg." Scotty the Pirate was lost in a daydream about Marge and unusual configurations of his pirate privates, so I sailed the forklift into the hold and began extracting the two pallets. I wondered if Scotty had ever frequented the Palm Frond Saloon late on the weekends. I could picture him sitting there with the good Reverend Habbersham watching Tiffany and Marge swing around the pole and flash their treasures for dollar bills. A stripper named Marge? Really?

"Hey, Scotty. You sure this chick goes by Marge? In a strip club? That can't be right."

Scotty recovered from his revelry, "Narrr. Marrrge is her real name. She goes by Ethel in the barrr."

"Oh, well, there you go. Ethel makes sense. Tiffany, Candy, Jizelle, and Ethel."

"Yarrr knows Jizelle?"

"No. Never mind. Ever hang out in the Palm Frond Saloon between loads? It's over by the Shop-n-Stuff. Used to be the old 'Pole-n-Hole' strip club."

Scotty turned serious when I mentioned the Palm Frond. "Narrr, lad. Stay away from that one tharrr. You'll not be wantin' the likes of that kinda trouble."

"Rough crowd?"

"Narrr. Not the crowd, laddie. Tharrrs not a man in the world that can hang all night with old Scotty. Just keep yarrrself clear of the Palm Frond Saloon. Darrrs not a place for a free man." Scotty turned away at that, and wouldn't elaborate more on his harsh assessment of the bar. Sure it was a rathole, and probably doing some sleazy business late at night, but to scare off Scotty... there must be some wicked weird business going on. I wondered if all this led back to Perez somehow. One way or the other, I supposed we were about to find out.

I had Mack's cell number, and gave him a call on my way out to the pickup after work. I had a healthy suspicion of saying too much over the phone, as it was Perez that had given it to him. There was probably some way for Perez to eavesdrop on his right-hand enforcer. So, I kept the conversation limited to common knowledge. "Hey, Mack. Chauncey here. Look, I want to go over one or two more details for the gig tomorrow. We need to get this act down pat if we want to be sure that a-hole Darrell goes down." I was playing this up a bit for Perez's sake, in case he was listening.

"Right. Want to meet up at Hauzer's for a beer?" Mack was probably thinking about Delores and another chance to visit.

"Sure... that might work. But hang on... I have to pick up some groceries... so how 'bout that dive by the Shop-n-Stuff?" It was my best casual response, and I hoped Mack would not argue.

Mack hesitated, reluctant to let go of the Delores connection, "OK, Chauncey, meet you there in a half hour. But I might stop by Hauzer's later. I like those sausages they got."

"Sausages... Right, Mack. Can you pick me up at my place? My truck is on the fritz again." My truck was fine, but I needed to prep Mack on the Palm Frond conversation before we got there.

"Sure, Chauncey, whatever."

"I'll leave Hannibal in the apartment." Hannibal followed me out to the truck as I finished the call and he shot me a look after leaping up into the passenger seat. "It's OK, buddy. Got to make a little call on our friends at the Palm Frond." Hannibal shot me another dark look. "But maybe we can go see Cecelia and Claudia later on." That did the trick. Hannibal relaxed and eased up on me a bit. I got the distinct impression he was not thrilled with my plan to return to the Palm Frond. Maybe it was just Scotty's comments earlier that I was projecting onto Hannibal, but I was no longer feeling that comfortable about the Palm Frond Saloon.

We cruised into my apartment lot and piled out. Hannibal shot around the building a couple of rounds, checking for new smells or stray cats. All we found was Punky, hanging out in front of his door, talking on the cell phone. He looked up as Hannibal darted past, and spotted me coming from the truck. I could not resist a quick greeting, "Afternoon, Jeebs. How goes the pizza business?"

Punky made a break for his door and slammed it so hard behind him the cardboard taped to his window fell out onto the sidewalk. I had not really expected him to repair the glass. And it would be years before Francisco Rodriguez Hernandez Shapiro ever got around to fixing it. Hannibal investigated the scene and took aim at the little bush outside Punky's door. It was far short of the love muffin he left last time, but the thought was there. "Good boy. Let's get some kibble before Mack gets here."

We cruised on up to my apartment and I laid out a bowl of liver and lamb, and some fresh water for Hannibal. I was checking through a few days of accumulated mail, when Mack knocked. "Bring it on, big boy... door's open." Mack came on in and parked himself on the couch, giving Hannibal a rough scratch on the head. For some reason, it seemed comforting to have Mack seem so relaxed at my place. The guy kind of grows on you, despite his propensity to split peoples' heads open on occasion.

"So, wassup with the truck, Chauncey."

"Trucks fine, Mack. Sorry about that, but I needed to talk with you before we hit the Palm. We can go over some details of the plan, but there's another reason for the outing."

"You havin' issues with your girl?" Mack looked genuinely concerned.

"No Mack, nothing like that. I think the Palm Frond Saloon might have a big rat inside. May as well make full use of the opportunity."

Mack looked confused. "I don't see how no rat is gonna help us bust Perez."

"This one might. Here's what we need to do." I went over the plan for the Palm Frond with Mack and we bid farewell to Hannibal and headed out to his car for the ride over. We discussed the details on the way, and then slipped into a spot behind the bar. I had forgotten how pleasant the aroma from the dumpster had been, until opening the door to get a full waft.

"Wow. Nice." I nearly collapsed. It smelled like warm recycled beer, bile, and bait. And something far worse mixed in... rotting meat maybe. "Don't they ever dump this thing?"

"Nope. Truck lifts are busted. I see them all over town, just grabbing the top two or three bags outta the bins, and leavin' the rest of the floating goop 'cause the trucks won't lift 'em no more. Too heavy. Guess most of the stuff just floats around forever."

"Remind me not to order the soup in here."

"You don't wanna order nothin' in here. Maybe a beer. And skip the glass. Besides, they haven't served no food in this dive for ten years. Health department made 'em quit."

"Mack, you ever hear of anything weird going down in here? I mean, anything even weirder than usual for the Palm Frond?" I was thinking back to my conversation with Scotty the Pirate who refused to be specific about his warnings.

"No. Forget I said anything. I don't know nothin' about this joint." But it sure seemed like Mack knew something about the Palm. I decided not to press the issue, because Mack seemed a little defensive. We had enough to think about without confusing the issue on the way in. But why would the Palm Frond Saloon dumpster smell like rotting meat if they did not serve food? A very distracting thought as we picked a table across from the bar.

True to form, Wally the Walrus was giving us the stink-eye from behind the bar. He gradually finished his chore and grudgingly trudged out to take our drink order. I had thought about sitting at the bar to be sure he caught our conversation, but that seemed a bit too obvious, so we decided to take a table. Wally finally drug himself over, "What's your pleasure, gentlemen?"

I considered the question a moment, "Our pleasure? Why just being here is pleasure enough, don't you think? However, since you asked, I'll have a Guinness black-and-tan, light head, side shot of Woodford's Reserve, and a copy of the Times, if you please."

The Walrus gave one great puff of his moustache, shook his head, and said, "Bud Lite OK?"

"Of course. That was my next choice."

Mack added, "Make it two." And Wally retreated to his den behind the bar to scrounge up two bottles of Bud.

I started right away with our discussion of the Darrell sting operation. "So, Mack. We need to get this straight before we arrange this thing for Mr. Perez. I'm only agreeing to this folly to protect the young lady, so I will need your assurance that no harm..."

Mack cut in, "You can stick your assurance up your ass, Chauncey. You do what Perez wants or I bust her up good. In fact, you fug this up, Chauncey, and you both get whacked. It don't matter how much dough you got, Perez wants this deal done. You got it?"

Wow. Mack was better at this than I expected. Even *I* believed him. "Take it easy, Mack, we got the deal covered. I just need to go over the money transfer for the goods." I clamped up because Wally was coming over with the beers. He plunked them down along with two greasy glasses that we both bypassed. They may have been washed, but not in recent history. Wally spun around and headed back to the bar, with entirely too much indifference. Bingo. Once he was securely immersed in his duties, we continued our planning session. "All I need is your assurance that the money will be presented as we previously discussed. Once we corner the little shit-weasel Darrell, I give the briefcase and the videotape back to you, just like we talked about. No questions. After all, you'll be right there, right? As for that weasel Darrell, I could care less what happens to him once we are through. The video should put him away for a long time."

"Yeah. A long, long time. But any funny business and *you* get put away for a long time, got it you Limey prick?" Mack picked up his beer and downed it in one long pull, then slammed the bottle down and walked out the door the way he came in.

I looked over toward Wally and commented, "Well that went smoothly, don't you think?"

Wally looked up from the rows of liquor bottles like it was the first time he noticed I was in the empty bar. "Who gives a fuck. Long as you pay the tab." What an endearing fellow.

I extracted my cell and rang Claudia. "It seems I have been left without a ride, my dear. Mind if I impose on you? ...yes, the charming little place behind the Shop-n-Stuff. Bring a respirator and some Raid. ...fine. See you then... toodles, love," and punched off. I couldn't resist one shot to Wally's blindside, just to see if he was paying attention. He was. He knew enough not to let on he was eavesdropping, but he slammed a case of Budweiser into the cooler with enough force to rattle the liquor case. I heard him mutter some unintelligible insult as he shuffled off to the storage room to vent.

When he came back, I decided to continue having fun with my new friend Wally. "Say Wally, be a sport and fetch another one of your finest for me, would you?"

He was still fuming over the Raid comment. "Did you say 'fetch'? I don't do 'fetch'. And you can drop the Wally and stick with Walt like everyone else around here who values their skin."

"Oh come now, Wally, there is no one else around here, and since I'm becoming such a valuable regular customer, I thought you might appreciate the informality." Wally looked like he might grow tusks and come waddling over the bar to gouge me, so I backed off a bit. "But since you ask so sincerely, I will try to remember '*Walt*' is your preference. Say, I have a lady friend expected in a few moments. One more Bud Lite and a cosmopolitan for my friend."

Walt had not yet simmered from the previous volley, so he was a bit reluctant to let bygones be bygones. "We don't sell magazines in here. She want something to drink or not?"

"Oh, I see... my mistake. Would you happen to have cranberry juice back there?"

"Yeah, of course we got fuckin' cranberry juice."

"And I can see you have several very selective bottles of vodka just behind you. Do any of them cost more than five dollars a bottle?" I quickly slid back into dangerous territory.

"They all cost more than five fuckin' dollars, you dipshit. Which fuckin' one do you want?"

I considered the selection carefully while he extracted another bottle of Bud and waited impatiently for my reply. "Oh, let's be adventurous and try that one with the train on the label. Do you recommend that brand?"

"Night Steamer? Yeah, it's the fuckin' best. If it sits on the shelf over a year, we use the leftovers to clean the linoleum. You're gonna fuckin' love it."

"How thrifty of you! Just mix some of that fabulous concoction with some of your cranberry juice in a plastic cup, put a little ice in there to prevent spontaneous combustion, and that will do nicely, I'm sure." I smiled cordially up at Wally the Walrus.

"Why didn't you just say you wanted a vodka-cranberry?" He started to mix up the drink in a plastic beer cup that said 'OPERATION WHOOP-ASS 1998' across the front.

I took a chance at offering an educational tidbit, "Actually, a cosmopolitan is a bit more complicated than that, but in keeping with the colloquial spirit of this establishment, I thought it might be best to keep it simple."

The big bartender finished the mix and brought that and the beer over to the table, "I don't appreciate your smart-ass remarks about my place here. I keep a nice clean bar, and there ain't nothin' colloquitate about it."

"I'm afraid you mistook my comment, sir. Colloquial is quite the compliment... it means charming. I enjoy local establishments such as this. I am, after all, a Londoner, and nothing is as dear to the heart of a true Londoner as the occasional pub crawl through some the town's most colorful taverns, not unlike this in many respects." I had never been on a 'pub crawl' but I assumed those that did so frequently were not overly discerning in their taste. Wally dumped some of the Night Steamer over ice and filled the cup with what I hoped was cranberry juice and brought both the drink and the beer over to the table. I picked up the beer and noticed it was significantly above room temperature. Like it had been stored all day in the trunk of a car in a Las Vegas parking lot. "One moment, Walt. I need a word with you."

Wally looked over his shoulder as he was heading for the back room, "I'm busy... be with you in a minute."

Walt had finally succeeded in locating Bertrand Chauncey's melting point. "NOW... Wally!" I left no room for question in my tone. Bert Clauster would have left some cash for the warm beer and drink and slipped outside while Wally was in the back, but Bertrand Chauncey would have none of it. It would have been horribly out of character to sit in the town's most disgusting dump and be treated like I belonged here. Wally spun on his heels, rage on his face, and came charging back towards my table to resolve the issue with finality.

"I told you once, you foreign fuckin' asswipe, I'm busy and..."

"Cork it, dipshit. When I need to hear your blather, I will ask for it." I kicked the adjacent chair out from under the table and it hit Wally in the shins with considerable force.

"Shit! You asshole! Whadda fuck you think..."

"Sit! NOW! You have two seconds to shut the fuck up, then some very ugly things are going to happen that will require diligent efforts with a pressure washer and a body bag."

That tirade had a surprisingly beneficial effect on Wally's mood. He flopped into the chair, rubbing his shins, but still glaring menacingly at me. He had, however, shut the fuck up. Progress. "First off, I will address you as Wally... or Wally the Walrus... or Assbite... or whatever I choose and you will rejoice in the fact that you are still alive and privileged enough to be allowed to take care of my every need while I grace the premises." Wally took all this in with growing impatience. "In the event you choose to neglect my every need, or those of whomever I happen to be sitting with, you will find yourself honored with a visit from my friends. My friends tend to socialize with two distinct groups; one set is commonly found inside offices at city hall attempting to find ways to make sure I am not unhappy in any way with the manner in which the city is being managed; and the other set of friends are definitely never seen at city hall. Which group would you prefer to deal with, *Wally*?"

Wally was processing this data in a mentally low gear ratio. The pain in his shins suddenly shifted into a lower priority. Wally figured things had taken a drastic turn for the worse and his mental gears were grinding in reverse, trying to find a way to annul the damage. "Look, I don't want no trouble. I run a decent bar here and..."

"Bullshit, Wally. You run a slime-encrusted pit that caters to every sleaze-ball within fifty miles. Every weekend you dangle some strung-out teenage drug queen in a g-string and pasties so your 'decent' local deviates can stuff dollar bills in her butt-crack. So don't give me the 'decent little bar' speech here, Wally. And you and I both know the girls are the least of your little '*indiscretions*'... am I right Wally? In fifteen minutes, I could have ten guys with a police escort, out front screwing plywood across the front door, and none of them would really give a shit if they leave you inside to rot or not. So get off your lazy fat ass, pour out this beer you pulled out of the oven, and fix a vodka-cranberry that does not taste like lighter fluid."

Wally obliged quickly without further comment, cleared away the drinks and limped back around the bar to start over. Much better. Nothing wrong with Wally the Walrus, he just required a brief attitude adjustment. I thought he was now properly tenderized to perform the duties we required him to do. Wally rummaged in a cabinet behind the bar. I was keeping a close watch on his movements in case there was firepower in there I needed to duck. He came up from the cabinet with a bottle of vodka in hand and displayed it across the bar. "Grey Goose OK?" he inquired in a genuinely helpful tone.

"That will do nicely." As I approved of the upgrade, Claudia arrived and cautiously pushed open the door, peering around into the dimly lit interior. "My dear!" I rose to meet her and gave her a hug and quick kiss.

She made a quick assessment of the bar and commented flatly, "Charming."

"Chessie, this is the proprietor of this tavern." I thought about it, but decided to give him a break, "His name is Walt and he was just about to mix you a refreshing frosty adult beverage."

Walt nodded toward Claudia. "Pleased to meet you, ma'am. Vodka-cranberry OK?"

"Yes. Thank you, Walt. Pleased to make your acquaintance."

"Make it two, Walt. The Grey Goose looks delicious." We settled at the table. "My heavens, you look remarkable today." Which was the first honest thing I had said in an hour.

"Well, thank you, Mr. Chauncey. What a lovely thing to say!" Out of the corner of my eye, I actually saw Wally make a note on a bar napkin as Claudia mentioned my name. Subtle. I nodded my head toward Wally who was bent over the bar, taking notes. She glanced over and then shot me a '*What's up with that?*' look. I rolled my hands in front of me to indicate '*Just keep it going.*' She smiled, happy to be in on another adventure.

"Just met with Perez's gorilla... the guy named Mack. We are on for tomorrow's purchase. He will set it up. Hope to complete the transaction and make the switch. Do you have the two briefcases in the car?"

She caught on quickly and confirmed, "Of course. Identical pair."

Wally came around and I changed the conversation with Claudia abruptly. "I'm sure it will be sunny tomorrow. I do hope your shopping trip goes well."

"It always does, Bertrand." Claudia beamed as Wally came up and set the two drinks in front of us and attempted a smile. He was not accustomed to it, and his face looked like it might crack. Claudia directed her radiant smile to Wally, "Why thank you, Walt."

"My pleasure, ma'am. Let me know if you need anything else." Wally hustled off a moderate distance to busy himself with some imaginary chore behind the bar, still within earshot inside the deserted tavern. The two glasses actually looked relatively free of grime, and the drinks were excellent. Amazing what a simple baseless threat can do to improve one's behavior. I wondered if the comment about the strippers had taken Wally aback. I doubted it... everyone in town knew about the late night weekend dancers. I suspected it must have been the other comment, about the girls being the least of his indiscretions. That was about the time he began to droop like a silk flower in a firestorm.

Claudia leaned across the table the table and pretended to speak secretively. "Are you sure Darrell won't suspect the switch?" Wow. She picked up on the theme of the conversation really quickly.

"No way. Darrell will never see it coming, if you do your part."

She smiled at the lead-in, "Oh, you can count on me, Mr. Chauncey. I'm very good at being distracting."

"Yes, I know," I said with a bit of desire in my voice. The desire was not part of the act. It was real enough. "Perhaps later you can practice on me."

Claudia leaned back across the table and took my arm, "Oh, I suppose a little practice wouldn't hurt." And she gave me a quick kiss on the cheek.

"We must be off, my love, I have a meeting with a producer in a half-hour." In a slightly louder voice I called across the room, "Walt, I think it is time we leave your company. We appreciate the hospitality. What do I owe you, my good fellow?"

"Drinks are on the house. You know, professional courtesy. Sorry about the warm beer thing..." Walt was groveling pathetically, but I still found an element of humor in it. I slipped a twenty onto the table anyway and took Claudia in arm as we turned toward the door.

"Thank you, Walt. Excellent drink. We may see you again some time." We moved a little away from the table when I thought about the sudden change in Walt's demeanor. "One piece of advice, if I might. Be careful here, Walt. Small family businesses like this are so hard to come by these days. It would be frightfully sad if some slip on your part were to cause a decline in your enterprise. You do understand, don't you, Walt?"

Back in the parking lot, Claudia needed to have some holes in the story filled in. Despite her amazing ability to ad lib, she had no idea what just happened. "Identical briefcases? Mind if I hear what mischief you are planning?"

"Oh, sorry about that. I would have warned you if I had known. Sort of making it up as I go along. But, I had an idea about how to snare Perez in the process."

Claudia laughed, "Seems like we're always making this up as we go along. It's fine. Sort of fun trying to figure out what you are talking about on the fly. What's this distraction thing?"

I didn't have a complete picture about how to make a quick briefcase switch, but I suspected it would require a distraction from somewhere. "Well... seemed like it sort of went with the briefcase thing."

"Let me see if I have all this straight..." and Claudia did a two-minute drill with the sequence of events we had discussed with Mack earlier. "And then... what happens next? Darrell hands over the videotapes, and we are standing there with Perez's cash in the briefcase... or do we have the empty briefcase? And where's the real briefcase? Are you sure he will bring the tapes to Hauzer's tomorrow night?"

"Whoa, there, Annie Oakley. Give me minute to catch up with you. I guess we are not going to be able to fill in all the variables. You OK with winging it a little?"

She smiled back a devious grin and put her hand in mine on the car seat, "Wouldn't have it any other way, Mr. Chauncey. Now kindly direct me to this infamous apartment of yours. I'm dying to see how an international emissary lives!"

"Ah, yes. A quaint little domicile, really. Have to keep my cover, you know. Take a left by the tracks and follow Seventh about a mile. Lovely little book of flats on the left. Leans a bit to starboard, and the roof leaks, but only when it rains."

"Sounds splendid."

My brain tripped up on her earlier comment. "What did you just say?"

"Your place sounds spectacular, Bertrand."

"No, before that. International something..."

"Emissary. You know... sort of a diplomat or envoy to a foreign nation."

I was still struggling to find the right word for the adventures of Bertrand Chauncey. Emissary was a definite possibility. "I like it. Has a nice ring to it. Should we print that on our business cards, love? Bertrand Chauncey and Chessie Beretta... International Emissaries?"

"Oh, I think not. A bit pretentious don't you think? How about Chauncey and Beretta... Covert Services?"

"Woo! That packs a punch. Sure you want to be associated with covert operations? Might be tough to explain the income on your 1040 form." I gave her hand a squeeze as she mulled over this problem.

"Oh, I don't think that type of income ever finds its way onto a tax form."

"Why Chessie, I had no idea you lived so dangerously!"

She looked over at me and said half-joking, "It looks like I do now." And I was reminded how my recent activities were radically changing her life. I hoped they were not shortening it.

"Look, Claudia, you don't have to do this, you know. It has been a hoot so far, and I love that you are in for the adventure... but in all seriousness, I have no control over how this all comes out. These are not nice people we are about to mess with, and they are not likely to be happy about the outcome, whether we succeed or not. Why don't you let Mack and I deal with Darrell and Perez?"

Claudia did not hesitate with her reply, "Not a chance, Mr. Chauncey. You're stuck with me now. And who is this Claudia person you keep mentioning? Are you seeing another woman?" She had that mischievous look in her eye again, and it was completely irresistible.

"As a matter of fact, I've been meaning to chat with you about that. There is this stunning young woman working at State Electric that has captured my heart. Looks a bit like you, in fact."

She pulled the car suddenly to the curb and skidded to an abrupt halt. Then she planted one across my lips that sent my heartbeat into fibrillation. She pulled back and looked at me with a bright glow, "Tell her to get lost, you're all mine."

Chapter Eleven

As we pulled into the lot beside the apartment complex, Claudia looked dubiously up at the leaning building. "Is it safe to park this close to the building?"

"Perfectly. I have been here for years and the building has not collapsed once."

"Comforting. I think we should spend more time at my place." She had a point. I seldom considered how the apartment appeared to others, it was just a place to crash... maybe make some toast in the morning... store my gear in the closet. Was the place really that bad? I looked up at the building from the parking lot. No... it was worse. She was just being kind.

"I suppose it is a bit of a dump." We proceeded up to my door to the apartment where Hannibal was awaiting my return. He was doubly excited when he saw who was with me, but slightly disappointed that Cecelia was not along for the ride. He bounded out of the door and greeted Claudia with excited dog noises, then tore off to anoint the shrubbery. "Welcome to my humble abode," I said as I swung the apartment door open to reveal a room strewn with the trappings of bachelor life being lived to its fullest. There was an old pizza box on the floor, several articles of clothing in various states of repose, and innumerable empty beer vessels awaiting transport to recycling.

Claudia hesitated at the threshold before entering. "Wow. Who does the decorating?"

"All part of covert operations. International emissaries can't be too careful, you know."

"Were you trying to develop your cover as a common farm animal? Really, Chauncey, you must try to at least maintain your health. Do you own a vacuum?"

"Yes. But he's outside peeing on the bushes right now. See how clean the pizza box is?"

She examined the empty box beside the couch, "Sparkling."

There was a knock at the door and we found Mack outside with Hannibal at his side. "Saw the pooch downstairs and thought he might have gotten loose." Mack squeezed his enormous frame through the door and joined us inside. Hannibal came in and sniffed the pizza box hopefully. Maybe it was time to reload the kibble bucket.

Mack asked for a review of his performance earlier. "So, Chauncey, how'd I do today at the Palm Frond?"

"Mack, it was a command performance. I think Wally went for the whole enchilada. My guess is he went straight to Perez with every word. I even saw him taking notes on a bar napkin."

"So, how'd you get back after I left?" Mack stepped over the pizza box and settled into the couch that produced an audible groan under the load.

"My lovely partner here was kind enough to stop by for a cocktail and offered me a ride."

"Oh, good. You know, I don't think that Wally guy likes you much. I got the feeling he wanted to bust your head open." Hannibal piled up beside Mack and offered his head for Mack's attention.

"Mack, perhaps Wally has had a change of heart. After you left we engaged in a brief chat regarding his attitude, and I believe he has now found a more appropriate approach to customer relations. He then served us complimentary cold drinks!"

Mack looked amazed, "At the Palm? You sure we're talkin' about the same guy? Grumpy old bastard with a walrus moustache?"

"Yes, that would be Walter." I commented flatly.

"Must'a been quite a chat."

"Yep. I think he has seen the light, so to speak. Did you get over to the school?" I was wondering if Mack had made contact with the sack of garbage named Tommy who hustled underage girls for Darrell.

Mack grinned and I knew he was about to tell us he had succeeded. "No problem. Tommy was there, right on cue, tryin' to flag down some tenth grader in a plaid skirt. Man, I wanted to bust his chops right there. I come up behind him and hear him promising this kid the moon if she hops in and goes for a little ride. I walk up real close but he don't know I'm there. This kid sees me, gets scared and takes off runnin' like hell. Tommy hollers, *'Hey Doll, where ya goin'?'* and she just keeps haulin' ass down the sidewalk. Dickface turns around to get back in his car and I'm maybe two inches from his miserable mug. He bounces off me and says *'whadda fug you doin' standin' there? Who the fug you think you are?'* So I says, *'That your daughter you was tryin' to give the money to?'* And he says *'whadda fug business is it of yours?'* And I says *'Oh, she's a cute one. Thought you might want a picture of her, that's all.'* And Tommy wants to know what I'm talkin' about, so I show him what I'm talkin' about." Mack produced a digital camera from his pocket and hit the review button to show us a very high resolution close up of Tommy holding out a wad of cash toward the young girl in the plaid skirt and pointing with the other hand towards his red Miata convertible parked at the curb.

Claudia's eyes narrowed to slits and she was breathing fire. "That piece of crap. The police are going to have fun with that photo."

"Not just yet. Let's sink this ship in deeper water, not just shoot the deck hand. So Mack, what did Tommy do when he saw that shot?"

Mack smiled again, "Oh, he reached for the camera."

"That probably didn't end well for Tommy, did it, Mack?"

"Naw. I had to kinda brush him back a little."

I knew that wasn't good. "Oh, Lord"

"He was still standin' at that point. I didn't hurt him much... just the one arm." Mack seemed almost apologetic that he was not able to do more damage. I looked over at Claudia who seemed to brighten at the prospect of Tommy getting a little justice administered. "Then I give him the message about havin' Darrell at Hauzer's at seven sharp tomorrow night. I told him about the rich English turd... no offense Chauncey... wantin' to buy up some tapes of the kids. Told him we would only deal with the boss, in cash. Then I turn the camera around so he can see the picture again and say *'Sure you don't wanna buy a picture of this nice little girl? Oh, looky... you're in here too... givin' some money to the nice little girl... for makin' good grades, maybe.'* And Tommy, he gets all steamed and comes for me with the one good arm."

"Oh, Lord"

"Yeah, I think that's what he said, too. He hit the ground pretty hard. Might be eatin' his dinner through a straw for a while."

Claudia could not contain herself any longer, "Good! Deserves what he gets! You know, we can't leave it here, or the whole mess will just keep right on building. Mack, I think the way you handled that creep was exemplary."

"Is exemplary good?"

Claudia was pacing back and forth, still furious. "Yes, Mack. Very good. The picture insures that Darrell will get involved personally, because he will know that his operation is in danger of being blown wide open unless he follows through at the meeting at Hauzer's tomorrow." Claudia might have been on a full boil, but she was thinking hard as well. I realized that I had no chance of convincing her to stay in the background now. She was on a mission, and there was fire in her eyes. She became silent, staring ahead without looking at anything, concentrating on her thoughts.

I opened the refrigerator door to check my food stocks. "Strategic planning requires sustenance. Anyone in the mood for a semi-cold cheap beer and some stale pretzels?"

Mack piped in immediately when he saw the can of Old Milwaukee I was holding, "I got a better idea... let's go see Delores."

Claudia came out of her revelry, "I second that motion. All in favor?"

A chorus of 'ayes' were sounded and Hannibal jumped off the couch and barked. He knew Hauzer's Brat Haus meant leftover sausages, even if the sauerkraut gave him dog gas that could melt the seat covers.

We headed out and I followed Claudia to her cabin. She parked her Honda and I pulled alongside in the pickup. I hustled Hannibal out from the front seat and loaded him into the truck bed. Claudia made a dash into her hobbit house and returned to take over Hannibal's spot between me and Mack. She climbed in with a large State Electric box on her lap without making any comment on the contents. Hannibal went riding happily in the back, ears flapping and eyes watering as we cruised through town toward Mack's rendezvous with Delores.

Curiosity finally got the best of me, so I asked, "What's in the State Electric box? Got a new flood light for Hauzer?"

"Sort of. Remember what you told me about your reason for the trip to the Palm Frond Saloon?"

I remembered. "Sure. You mean for insurance?"

"Exactly. You have your insurance policy... and I have mine. You'll see." The girl got more interesting every day. What did she have in there? An M-16 and a case of grenades?

After the short drive from Claudia's, we wheeled into Hauzer's and piled out. Hannibal got back up front to await leftovers, accepting the fact that he was not likely to get into Hauzer's during business hours. Claudia brought along the box and we followed Mack into the restaurant.

Delores was on duty, and obviously happy to see the room darken as Mack entered the front door. "Well, if it ain't Bigfoot and his buddies come to visit!" She came over and planted a nice wet kiss right on Mack's cheek like he had just come home from the crusades. Mack turned red as a hot pepper, but made no move to avoid Delores. In fact he wrapped his huge arms around her waist and lifted her about a foot off the ground.

"Hi there, Sugar." he muttered after Delores had broken away. Claudia and I just looked on in amazement.

Claudia smiled up at Mack, "Sugar? Mack... are you holding something out on your partners?"

Mack's face was a combination of embarrassment and joy. "Well, Delores and me been kinda' seein' each other for the last few nights."

"Mack!" I chimed in. "You old dog. You should've said something!"

"Well, things been kinda' busy, you know, planning the operation and all."

"True, true. But still... congratulations... I guess." I wondered if this was the appropriate salutation for such an occasion.

Hauzer appeared from the kitchen to see who the new guests were. "Ah, Bert, you bring in da lovely lady, ya. Ser gut. Und da big boy is back, too!" Hauzer turned to face me and whispered loudly, "Dat one dere, he come in every night dis veek. I sink he has das Geschlechtsdrang for da fraulein," and he nodded his head toward Delores.

"My Deutche is a little rusty, but maybe he should see a doctor." I ventured.

"Nein, nein. You know, Geschlechtsdrang..." and Hauzer wrapped his big meaty arms around an imaginary partner, made a smoochy face, and added a couple of hip thrusts to be sure we got the translation. Mack went red again and Claudia busted into a fit of giggles.

For Mack's sake, Delores broke up the party by snapping her bar towel at Hauzer and chasing him out of the room. "Don't you got nothin' better to do than irritate my customers? Get your big lumberjack ass back in there where you belong and leave decent people alone!"

Hauzer beat a retreat while Delores snapped away at his backsides. We all flopped into a booth and finished a good laugh as tiny Delores chased the enormous Hauzer back through the swinging kitchen door.

I turned the conversation back to business, "So, how do we think Darrell comes alone tomorrow night?" Both my partners went silent.

Finally, Mack offered, "He'll show up, 'cause there ain't no other choice... 'cause he knows about my pictures and all. But no way he comes alone. We got to watch for that Russian goon named Brokov. Word is he likes to hear people's bones crack. One of the guys works for Perez told me that even Darrell can't stop him once he gets started on somebody. He kinda loses it, I guess, and starts snapping bones and laughin' real loud. I dunno if that's true, but he don't sound too stable to me. I'd justa' soon not have to deal with him tomorrow."

That little tale put a chill in the room. So far, things had been all fun and games. But there was a growing chance that this adventure we had embarked upon could get ugly, and people could get hurt...

or worse. I wondered if there was still time to back out of the whole scheme. Claudia must have read my mind, "Too late for second thoughts, I'm afraid. If we go to the police now, then what happens to Mack? Remember the little scene with Hannibal beside the tracks?"

I had almost forgotten about that. Mack had been the muscle for Perez for a long time, and there was no way we could keep him clear of trouble if Perez decided to implicate Mack to save himself. And if we called off the operation, then Sleazeball Numero Uno, Darrell, would be free to continue his enterprises. I resigned myself to the task at hand and returned my thoughts to the original plan... to hang Darrell out to dry and somehow scoop up Perez in the process. There had to be a way to eliminate both sickos without losing Mack in the process. Getting enough evidence to get them arrested was easy, there seemed to be no limits to their deranged activities. But separating Mack from the fray was going to be tricky.

"Mack, I have a question for you." Mack looked over at me and waited for me to formulate my thoughts. "What happens if we succeed and Perez gets grilled by the cops about his business dealings? How deep are you into this? Would Perez lay everything off on you to save his own skin?"

"I thought about that too. I guess he would, if he thought it would help get him off. But that ain't gonna work. If they get me too, then I tell them all the evil stuff Perez has been into for the past few years, and he gets in even deeper. I keep this little book, with all the rotten stuff Perez makes me do to keep the cash flowing his way. It ain't much, but it won't look good if that little book was to show up in a courtroom. He don't know nothin' about it, 'cause I figure he would get pissed and plug me if he knew I kept notes on him. So I kinda keep it in a safe place, in case things get bad, you know." Mack surprised us both with this information. Maybe we underestimated his savvy.

"Good move, Mack," Claudia said evenly. "Might come in very handy to keep Perez under wraps."

Delores appeared with a pitcher of beer and three glasses. "That cockroach Perez is not hangin' around here is he? I'd like to put a bump on his noggin!" None of us doubted Delores could do just that.

I put her at ease, "We gave him the night off, Delores. But I expect he will be slinking around somewhere close by tomorrow night. He never gets too far from his money."

"Ya'll still plannin' to nail those two suckers to a pine board?" Delores was anxious to help us with whatever came up.

"You bet. Just trying to figure out how to keep Mack here from getting nailed alongside them," I told her.

"Mack? Hell, he ain't done nothin'. Why would he get into trouble?" We could tell that during their brief romance, Mack had not yet had the opportunity to fill Delores in on all the details of his professional services for Perez.

Mack drooped down a bit in the booth and then looked up at Delores sadly, "Sugar, there might be one or two little things that could be a problem if Perez gets mouthy with the cops."

"One or two things like what?" Delores had her hands on her hips now and was looking down at Mack. "You got outstanding parking tickets... or something worse?"

Mack did not look like he was thrilled with an impromptu confession, "Look, Delores, there might be few things I done that are technically against the law."

Delores looked on disapprovingly, "Technically?"

"Well, yeah. But them guys deserved what they got, you know. Guys that was up to some low-life stuff, and needed to get woke up sometimes."

"Delores did not look convinced of Mack's innocence, "So, you're like an alarm clock for criminals. Get their attention with a smack in the head, then tell them to straighten up and get a job at the library, right?"

Mack slumped lower, "Not 'zackly, no. I guess I ain't no better'n Perez when you look at it like that."

"The hell you ain't. Sit up there, stud, and let's get this thing figured out. You're done with that criminal crap, right Mack?"

Mack brightened up a little since Delores decided to ease up on the interrogation, "I sure hope so. I can't keep this up no more. I don't care if they haul me off or not, I can't work for Perez no more. It makes me feel just like him."

Delores came over and wrapped her tiny frame around Mack's shoulders. She looked like a hood ornament on a dump truck. "Darlin', difference is, you know it's wrong, and Perez thinks it's fine. We're gonna get your gigantic butt outta the wringer, one way or the other, so don't you get in a funk about it." She gave him a kiss on the cheek and Mack re-inflated to his former internal air pressure.

"Good." I said, "Let's make this thing happen. Delores... brats and beer for whole team!"

"On the way!" she said as she unwrapped herself from Mack and headed toward the kitchen.

It was the last night we would have for planning our Saturday maneuvers. But the more we talked about all the variables, the more it seemed impossible to control the outcome. After an hour of considering all the pitfalls of the plan, Claudia summed up the progress, "We are never going to figure out what Darrell, or Perez, or even *we* are going to do tomorrow. There's no point in trying to plan all the details. We just have to trust our instincts and trust each other to get through this somehow." We all looked at one another to see our reaction. "It will be fine. You'll see." She had a way of saying things that made you certain it was true.

"OK. Let's try to get some sleep, I guess." That didn't seem too likely, but I knew we all needed it. It was getting late and the empty beer pitchers were stacking up around all the brat baskets, most of which were in front of Mack. There was one with a half brat left over that somehow escaped Mack's attention. "Mind if I take that one out to Hannibal? We ought to go. Hauzer probably wants to close up, and Delores is dead on her feet."

Mack waved us on saying, "You two go on. I got a ride with Delores when she closes."

"I might stay for a few minutes, too," said Claudia. "I asked Delores to help me with that little insurance project before she heads home. You go on home with Hannibal, Bert, and I'll call you in the morning."

"Actually, I was planning on sitting down with Hauzer to make sure he feels comfortable with what we are doing." We all laughed at the three separate plans to hang around the place after hours, all for different reasons. "Just what kind of insurance project are you devising, my dear?" I wondered out loud.

Claudia extracted the State Electric box from under the booth and held it up. "As long as you two are hanging around, you may as well make yourselves useful. Give me a hand with this stuff." With all the other customers gone and the 'closed' sign hung out front, I was able to free Hannibal to come inside, enjoy his snack, and assist in the preparations.

We worked on her 'insurance project' for another hour. Hauzer and Delores pitched in with the finishing touches while we all talked through the plan for the next night. It was nearly midnight before we finished and sent Mack and Delores strolling out to her car, her hand clutched in Mack's giant paw. Claudia looked at me as we bid them good night, "There goes a cute couple."

"Adorable. Looks like Mack is thoroughly twitterpated." I think that was a word from some ancient movie or old kids TV show reruns I used to watch.

"I think it's great." Claudia beamed.

"Me too. Let's head for home." We waved at Hauzer, who was locking up the joint, "See you tomorrow, Hauz," and we headed over to the truck, Hannibal trotting along beside us.

Hauzer called out to us as we opened the truck door for Hannibal, "You kids be careful not to make ze babies! I sinks maybe you caught some of dat big fella's geschlechtsdrang, too!" And he repeated his amorous gyrations on the porch of his Brat Haus. Claudia turned red, but didn't seem to mind too much.

"Is that true, Mr. Chauncey? Did you catch the geschlechtsdrang from Mack and Delores?" she asked playfully as she slipped in beside Hannibal.

"Absolutely not!" I argued. "I had it long before then... scouts honor." I never tired of hearing her laugh. I circled around to the driver side and started to open the door, but pulled up short when I spotted a note under the wiper. "Damn, this is probably not good." She looked at me with hesitation. I pulled the note loose and climbed in beside Hannibal. I unfolded it and read it, "*Nice party. I wasn't invited?*"

She looked over at the note, "Any signature?"

"Nope. But I'll give you three guesses."

"Perez," she said with resignation.

"That's only one guess. But a good one."

"So, he's keeping tabs on us. If he had seen anything new, he would not have left a note to tell us he was here. I think it's a good thing."

"You are certainly the optimist in the group. I like that about you." About that time we both dove for the window cranks and began gasping for air. "Hannibal... good Lord!" Hannibal sat serenely smiling.

Claudia thrust her head out the window and screamed, "Drive! Drive!" And we peeled away from Hauzer's Brat Haus, trying to force fresh air into the truck.

By the time we rolled up in front of Claudia's, we had almost stopped laughing and forgiven the dog for his gastro-intestinal indiscretions. After all, we were the ones that fueled the furnace. The canine digestive system and German sauerkraut are apparently a volatile combination. I parked the truck next to her car and was hoping for a goodnight kiss to end a nice night. Instead, she looked over at me and was silent. I was confused by the look and asked, "What?"

"I was just looking... trying to decide."

"Decide what?"

"Trying to decide whether I should invite you two in."

Oh my. That might be so much better than a goodnight kiss. It was like the slot-machine jackpot of goodnight kisses. I was about a half second from diving out of the truck and pleading for a positive response, but something held me back. In my best Bertrand Chauncey attitude I offered, "I would be a cad to impose. You must be exhausted and I would only make matters worse. I would like nothing on earth more than to spend more time with you, but really, it would..."

She leaned across Hannibal and kissed me hard. Hannibal wiggled beneath us, delighted with the attention. "Shut up, Chauncey, and get out of the truck." She opened her door and let Hannibal bound out. He knew where to go and made a bee-line for her front door to see if Cecelia was home. We could hear her bark and Hannibal vaulted around on the porch, wagging furiously.

"I suppose it wouldn't do to keep the pups apart. Be a pity to raise the ire of the ASPCA." I took her hand and we headed up her rocky walk to the little wooden hobbit house where Cecelia awaited her knight in furry armor.

"Or the LGBT group," she grinned back at me as she took my hand and we headed up the walk to her door.

I considered her comment, "Oh, right. That too."

Chapter Twelve

There was a sudden crush of pressure around my midsection; sharp jabs in rapid succession, followed by an intense feeling that my face was about to be removed by a food processor. Confusion reigned as I fought to gain an advantage over the attacker. I needed to get my bearings, figure out where I was and who was on top of me. Someone else was laughing nearby, and whoever was clawing at me definitely needed mouthwash. I struggled under the sheets and turned to face not one but two attackers, poised to finish me off. Cecelia was between me and Claudia, furiously licking my left ear, while Hannibal was perched atop my chest, spinning in circles to encourage Cecelia.

"Snark... furburn... fribitz..!" but they only worked me over harder, apparently unable to comprehend my simple early morning gibberish.

Claudia was howling madly at the scene, wrapped up in the sheets and quilt that covered her rustic handcrafted wooden poster bed. "Some International Emissary you turned out to be! Good thing they're not the bad guys. I think we would be in deep trouble." I tried to duck under the quilt to reduce the slobber factor.

"Help me, someone!" I yelled from under cover, "I'm being attacked by wolverines." My retreat motivated Cecelia to search out an entry point so the slurping could continue. A wet dog nose shot in beneath a crack in my armor and warm kibble breath found my face. Before I could dig in deeper, the full force of a wet dog slurp caught me across the mouth. "Oh, yuck! Cecelia, that's disgusting!"

I heard Claudia burst out in a fit of giggles again. I knew it was time to make my move. I scooted sideways under the covers to Claudia, wrapped her warm and beautiful body up tightly, and rolled her on top of me for protection. Then I began screaming furiously, "Get her, get her, get her!" to the two mutts.

It worked. Both beasts renewed their attack on the squirming mass under the sheets and began barking and licking Claudia in delicate areas that caused her to writhe around in glorious agony as I held on tight like a bronco buster. Once I was sure my eight seconds were up, I relented my hold and we both dove deep under cover to ward off the dogs. Claudia recovered from her giggles and put her smiling face close to mine as the dogs continued flailing above us, trying to find a passage for entry underneath. "Mr. Chauncey, you are an absolute monster! That was completely uncalled for!"

"Oh, I don't know. I thought it was a splendid tactic, given the situation." I kissed her lips that were inches from mine.

"Really? You don't think that was just a little bit unfair?"

"Not at all. You see, my love, in those first seconds of the attack, I quickly surmised that my attackers must have been encouraged in their assault by someone collaborating with their efforts. Unlikely they could have developed that level of fury without a little assistance from some third party... perhaps someone they know and trust? Would we know anyone like that who might have reason to encourage such activities?" I snuck another kiss while she conjured up a reply.

"Let me see... it could have been Mack, I suppose. Or Delores... did you leave her a tip last night? I'll bet she plotted the whole thing to get even with you for stiffing her on the bill." Both dogs finally tired of the game and bounded off in search of easier prey.

I cautiously raised the blanket a few inches. "Do you suppose it's safe to come out? Or is this part of the plot to assassinate us as we make our escape?"

Claudia pulled the blanket back down around us and grinned, "Who wants to escape?"

Any hesitation I might have had about getting deeply involved romantically had evaporated. There was not much I could do about it now, and I felt myself crash through the fragile protective walls I thought would keep me from getting hurt again. I could barely remember what the point of the walls had been. Something about old whatsherface from a past life. Gone. Forgotten. Nothing had ever come close to this. I was in uncharted waters, and it felt like a true adventure, not just with all our efforts to lock up Perez and Darrell, but with Claudia as well.

After a few heavenly minutes of snuggling in our bunker, we decided it would be in our best interest to let the pups out for a while and greet the day. I piled out and threw on clothes I found strewn across the floor from the night before. I had apparently lacked the patience to fold and store them properly. Hmmm. I snuck covert looks at Claudia as she pulled on grey sweats and a plaid shirt. I felt my heart rate begin to pick up the pace and tried to look away to prevent another delay to the start of the day. We swung into the kitchen and I helped her get some coffee started as the dogs scampered back and forth, anxious for something exciting to do. We filled two mugs and headed for the door with Cecelia and Hannibal vibrating for release.

We were both quiet as we watched them tear around the yard. Despite the fabulous beginning of the morning, there were some serious activities scheduled for later that day, and the weight of the situation settled in as we walked around the cabin. "We have a big day ahead of us, Chessie Beretta. Are you sure you are up for all this?"

Claudia held my arm closer and we wandered around the yard of her little cottage, following the two dogs as they investigated the territory together. "I'm ready. A little worried, I guess, but ready. It hasn't seemed real till now. All of our fun with Bertrand and Chessie keeps the reality of the situation in a sort of drama play. But it's not a drama play, is it?"

"No." The mood was solemn as we both thought about what we had set up for later that night. "Pretty serious stuff. I'm a little worried too. I am starting to have regrets about dragging you into this. When it all began, I didn't... well, I didn't know..."

Claudia was enjoying my dilemma, "Didn't know what, Mr. Chauncey?" She was obviously not going to let me off easy.

"I guess I didn't know that the dashing and independent Bertrand Chauncey would find the alluring Chessie Beretta quite so irresistible."

"Really?" she said with mock surprise. "I had no idea the dashing Bertrand Chauncey was quite so vulnerable! And how does the sweet and handsome Bert Clauster feel about the common store clerk, Claudia Auckland?"

I stopped and turned toward her, held her tightly around the waist with my free arm, and put on my best Bertrand Chauncey voice, "I think the poor chap is in even worse shape. Can't even seem to find his way home at night. It seems that Mr. Clauster can find absolutely nothing common about Ms. Auckland whatsoever." I wondered why we had slipped into the third person. Or was it fourth person. Confusing. For just two bodies, there seemed to be an awful lot of us around lately. If Chessie Beretta and Bertrand Chauncey went undercover with false passports, it would create a hopeless identity snarl that would never come unraveled.

She smiled at me as I held her close. "I think those two make a cute couple. Maybe we can double date sometime." Wow. She was as confused as I was. But she was smiling at the dichotomy, having a little fun with it.

"If they make a cute couple, then what do *we* make, Ms. Beretta?"

"A formidable team, Mr. Chauncey. Darrell and Perez don't stand a chance." She had lost all doubt in her voice, and she smiled confidently.

"To a successful mission?" I raised my coffee mug to hers.

"To a successful mission," She clinked her mug to mine, but then added, "with no regrets."

I nodded agreement and we continued our morning excursion. We encountered the two dogs behind the cottage, in a corner of the yard where a large oak provided shade and cover next to a row of bushes. Cecelia selected this location to process some kibble into a steaming pile, while Hannibal looked on in admiration. On completion, he dutifully took in the aroma, and then followed suit by planting a stink bomb of his own adjacent to Cecelia's.

"Lovely. His and hers land mines," I commented.

"There's a ritual I definitely do not think we need to follow." Claudia looked on with a distasteful look.

"Nothing says love like pinching a morning biscuit together."

"Only in the dog world, Mr. Chauncey." And we laughed together and sipped our mugs. After a minute, we came around to the front again and went inside for coffee refills, leaving the dogs to play outside for bit. Claudia filled our mugs and we settled into the sofa. "I'm glad you stayed last night."

"Me too." I was glad she felt OK about it.

"My 'Chessie' part sort of took over. I don't think Claudia would have had the guts to ask you in," she gleamed that killer smile at me as I crunched up closer to her on the couch.

"And Bert would have fallen off the porch into the hedge and then run for the truck."

"How did those two ever survive without us?" she added playfully.

"Oh, my dear, it was a dreary existence, to be sure. Ever so much more lively now, don't you think?"

"Ever so much," and she again raised her mug to mine in another toast.

I thought about the day ahead, "What time did Mack say to meet with Perez to get the cash?"

"Five sharp. Coffee shop downtown. Mack says Perez will have the cash ready."

"Great. I wonder if our buddy Wally has passed along his napkin notes. I am counting on Perez to stay close to his cash."

Claudia thought about it and said, "I think Perez will stay close regardless. I don't think he trusts us enough to stay too far in the background, with or without info from Walt."

"I guess we will find out tonight. Anything we need to do before the big event?" I was trying to piece together the sequence to determine if there was anything else I had missed.

Claudia looked me over, "Oh, yeah. We've got plenty of work to do on you, Mr. Chauncey."

I was confused, "Wassup? I think I can pull it off, don't you?"

"Nope. Not dressed like that. You sound like Mr. Bertrand Chauncey, rich English aristocrat, but you are dressed more like Captain Kangaroo. You need a new wardrobe. Let's go shopping!" She looked excited about this prospect.

I rose to the occasion, evoking my best Austin Powers, "Smashing, Baby!"

We took her red Accord to a nearby outlet store strip-mall and headed into Zoot's Suits - Men's Warehouse Clothing to peruse their goods. We had only passed the second rack of dinner jackets when we spotted the approach of an impeccably dressed older gentleman, nose thrust firmly into the air, hustling over to make sure we were not touching the inventory. I felt an immediate sense of fashion inferiority just looking at this stiff in his tailored three piece ensemble. I glanced over at Claudia and wondered out loud, "I do believe Peeves is here to address us."

She commented quietly, "Indeed he is."

Peeves made his final approach as his eyes noticeably traveled my length, producing an even more pronounced scowl. "May I help you, sir? Perhaps you are looking for K-Mart... it's just down the block."

Wow. Did I look that shabby? K-Mart? Really? But I recovered quickly, "400 Oak Street... definitely... K-Mart."

"Excuse me sir?" I had Peeves confused. Good.

"400 Oak Street... Cincinnati, Ohio. Boxer shorts. Definitely... 400 Oak Street." I had Peeves completely baffled, but Claudia was looking for a place to hide and burst out laughing.

"Sir, I'm afraid we do not sell boxer shorts here... so if you would be so kind as to... "

"Right you are, Mr. Placer." I had picked up his name from the nametag on his lapel during my 'Rain Man' speech. "Just a brief test to make sure you are in full awareness of your inventory. Well, done. Now, if *you* would be so kind as to..," I indicated the nearest suit rack that was topped with a large sign that read *Yorkshire Collection – Special Sale!* They looked to me like as good a rack of suits as any other. "Visiting some unfortunate cousins here in the states, and have traded my entire wardrobe for theirs as a gesture of good will and support for the indigent souls. I now find myself without proper attire for the return trip and do not wish to waste excessive funds on a product I am certain to wear only once. So, if you would be so kind as to assist in the selection of one of these... um... suits, I will be happy to vacate your premises without further imposition of your valuable time."

Peeves was visibly reeling, not sure whether to kiss my butt, or throw me out. He considered a moment and chose the former. "Certainly, sir. Let me make a few brief measurements." He extracted a hidden tape from his pocket and I assumed the scarecrow position necessary to achieve the task. "It seems you are very nearly an exact 42 long."

"Very nearly? Am I to assume the suit will then 'very nearly' fit?" Claudia was giving me an amused look from behind Peeves. She gave me a thumbs up for spinning Peeves around in record time. I winked at her and addressed the clerk, "Mr. Placer, this is my personal assistant, Ms. Haberdash..." Oh, my god. Haberdash? That just popped out. We are in a suit store and I give Claudia a name like Haberdash? Claudia mouthed the word 'WHAT!' before Peeves turned to nod in her direction. Too late to change course now. Better go with it. "Ms. Haberdash will be in charge of the final selection and color coordination with the accessories. Please give her your full cooperation and I believe you will find her talents to be most educational."

"Of course, sir." He then gave a nod to Claudia who smiled back pleasantly.

I explained, "My line of work does not allow for time to devote to such details, and I would simply be lost without her. I'm sure you understand." Claudia beamed at such high praise.

Peeves ventured a question as he continued with leg measurements, "And what line of work are you engaged in, sir?"

"International Emissary is my official title, but really, the job description is much more mundane." We still needed to improve on the 'Emissary' bit, but it would have to do for now. "Routine meetings, mostly. A formal ball or two, but seldom more than once a week. Fairly similar to being a butcher, but we use blather instead of knives, and dress a bit nicer, of course."

"Of course, sir." I felt Peeves give a perceptible jerk at the butcher analogy, and also noticed Claudia rolling her eyes. I shrugged at her while Peeves looked downward. "Let's see what we can find." He raised up and went over to the rack I had indicated. The suits were arranged by size and he rifled through the 42 section until he located a nice looking fabric, much the same, in my view, as all the other suits on the rack. In fact, nearly every suit in the store looked to be an identical replica of the adjacent ones. Miniscule variations on fabric color perhaps. A pinstripe or two for flair, but basically dark gray, dark brown, or black suits in all directions. Peeves produced a dark grey model with a light grey pinstripe.

I looked it over, having decided on the proper response prior to his selection, "Good God, man... do you take me for a whoremonger?" I looked toward Claudia who was holding back laughter. "Ms. Haberdash?"

"Hideous." It was the first word she had spoken, but it was perfect.

"My mistake. Perhaps something in black." He quickly replaced the suit and selected a plain black model, nearly identical in style to the other.

I stepped over and took the hanger from him and held it up for closer inspection. I decided to find fault with it too, just for fun. "Mr. Placer, did someone die in this suit recently?"

Peeves took a step back, "Excuse me, sir?"

"I detect a distinctive odor of formaldehyde. Either someone was embalmed while wearing this suit, or else..." I looked down at his stooped frame as he recoiled at the thinly veiled insult to the integrity of his business.

"I assure you, sir, no such activities take place here! Our owners, the Frankel family, have been in this business for three generations, and you may rest assured ..." I slipped the jacket on and cut his defense short by extracting a crisp new twenty dollar bill from the inside pocket of the jacket. I raised it slowly to my nose and gave a brief sniff. Peeves sat down on the fitting bench, mouth agape, waiting for my assessment of the mysterious bill.

"Mr. Placer, were you aware that formaldehyde is used extensively in the process of forging currency? Ms. Haberdash, if you would be so kind." I handed the twenty over to Claudia who raised an eyebrow, wondering for a moment what she was supposed to do. I made no move to give her any clues... it was far too much fun to improvise. "Well?"

Calmly, she raised the bill toward the light and examined it closely, rubbing the paper between her fingers, then bending one corner over precisely, bending it back to flat, then tearing the corner away. She then examined the fibers at the edge of the tear. "Quite right, Mr. Chauncey. Fake as the queen's smile at Prince Charles' wedding. Seventeen-weight paper, typical digital lithogram photographic methods, probably printed within the last week or two. Pity they never bothered to properly flush the formaldehyde before going to market, or you might have gotten a twenty-dollar discount on your suit. All-in-all, a passable effort. I've seen worse."

That was an amazing performance. I almost applauded. Instead I put on a bored expression and commented flatly, "Thank you, my dear. Very perceptive, as usual. Now, Mr. Placer, perhaps you can explain how a counterfeit bit of American currency got into the pocket of a suit made in..." I quickly opened the jacket front and checked the label, "...Malaysia. Hmmm. Easier to pass these little trinkets off over there, is it?" I waved the bill in front of him and awaited his response.

"I have no idea, sir... this is most disturbing. Never in all the years..." Peeves was visibly fumbling about now, knocked completely askew by my discovery.

"Perhaps we should call in the police. They may be interested in the origins of this bill, and perhaps even the import practices of the owners... the Frankels, did you say? Ms. Haberdash, who is it that deals with such international issues here in the States? The FBI?"

"Claudia smiled pleasantly and corrected me, "That would be the CIA; the FBI mainly prosecutes internal criminal activity. The CIA tends to apply more severe tactics for international racketeering, money laundering, that sort of thing. Pity, really." She turned toward poor Peeves and gave him a very convincing sympathetic look. "And you seemed like such a nice man." Nice touch with the past tense.

Peeves was dumbstruck. He sat slumped on his fitting bench, head in hands, trying to come to grips with his crumbling world. "I must try to reach Mr. Frankel somehow. There must be some explanation for all this. I simply cannot believe there is anything illegal..."

I cut him off before he could finish, "I'm sure everything is fine. You must be right, my good man. Can't let outward appearances lead you astray. Ring up your man Frankel and have him jaunt down to straighten all this out. Probably some innocent prank, I'm sure. Nothing more. I'll just pop off a quick call to your CIA lads and we'll have this all straightened out in a flash. What say? None of my business, of course, really. I should just be off and leave it to you blokes to worry about. But, I suppose that would make me an accessory of sorts, now that we know the just of it. You too, I suppose, Mr. Placer. Sorry. Never should have told you... might have spared you the bother."

But Peeves was definitely bothered. Actually nearing collapse by the look of it. Claudia shot me a glance that indicated she was having some trouble inflicting any more stress on this poor suit salesman. She offered a suggestion to give Peeves a way out of his predicament, "Mr. Placer, perhaps the proprietor would be so kind as to negotiate a compromise that would be mutually beneficial."

Peeves did not look relieved. "But you see, Mr. Frankel is on a buying trip, and I don't think he can be reached at the moment."

I ventured a guess. "A buying trip? To Malaysia perhaps?" It was a shot in the dark.

"I'm afraid so." Peeves slumped further.

This was too good to pass up. "Oh my, that is unfortunate. And I suppose you do not have the latitude necessary to resolve this in his absence. Ordinarily, I would be willing to overlook such an indiscretion, but you see, this incident puts us in a position of some risk. If the authorities were to question our involvement..."

"Sir, you may rest assured that I have sufficient authority to resolve any matters in Mr. Frankel's absence." Peeves inflated himself a little to demonstrate his clout but lowered his voice,

"Please, take the suit, compliments of the store. We would be most appreciative if this whole matter could be kept on the Q.T. It would be most problematic if Mr. Frankel were to come home to an investigation... I'm afraid it would look as if I had bungled matters."

I frowned at Peeves, then looked over to my lovely co-conspirator, "Ms. Haberdash, do you feel this is an appropriate solution?"

Peeves looked up to her hopefully as she considered the dilemma, "I think this good fellow is innocent in this matter. I cannot speak for Mr. Frankel, that is his business, and I am afraid if we delay ourselves we will miss your London flight. Perhaps Mr. Placer is making a wise management decision. I recommend you accept his offer."

"Very well, then, Mr. Placer. I will keep this under wraps for now, but I suggest you take a careful evaluation of your employment with this firm." I handed the dark suit back to Peeves, who hurriedly wrapped it in a garment bag and returned it to me. I tucked the twenty dollar bill into my shirt pocket as we turned to go. "I will see to it that this bill is disposed of. Good day to you, sir." I offered an arm to Claudia and we strode purposefully out of Zoot's Suits - Men's Warehouse Clothing, leaving Peeves sitting in stunned silence, contemplating his career, and wondering how his daily routine had so suddenly imploded.

On the broad busy sidewalk we headed back towards the Honda. Claudia chastised me, "Mr. Chauncey, was it really necessary to completely destroy that poor fellow's faith in his employer?"

I was not feeling nearly so charitable, "K-Mart? Remember that little zinger?"

She smiled back at me and said in a flat monotone, "400 Oak Street... definitely K-Mart." We laughed and continued strolling down the block. "I don't think he had seen the movie. He looked a little confused when you suddenly became autistic."

It was my turn to offer a compliment, "Nice work analyzing the twenty, by the way. What was that process? Digital litho... photo... something?"

"Digital lithogram photographic methods, to be precise."

I was impressed, "And what, exactly, is that?"

She turned her face to mine and gave me a quick peck on the cheek, "I have no idea." We got to the small lot on the next corner and located her car, hung the new suit onto the hook in the back seat and climbed aboard, Claudia driving. She was still piecing together the suit scenario. "So, how did you know there was a twenty in the jacket pocket, Sherlock?" she teased.

"Oh, I was quite certain, my dear Holmes. Simple deduction really... it stood to reason that if I had just placed it there moments before, while our dear Mr. Peeves was distracted, then it was a logical conclusion that it would still be there when I looked a few moments later."

She smiled a devilish grin at me, "Not counterfeit, huh?"

I extracted the bill from my shirt pocket and handed it over to her, "Well, not sure really. You seem to be the expert in that department!"

She laughed and held the bill up for examination as she negotiated a right turn out of the lot, "Difficult to tell, really. Perhaps we should test the authenticity of this currency at the nearest deli?"

"Capital idea, Holmes!" And we cruised on along the avenue in search of Rueben sandwiches.

Chapter Thirteen

The afternoon with Claudia passed far too quickly. We lunched and walked and laughed like we did not have a care. But the laughter was a little forced... from us both. I could tell the weight of the evening's prospects were a dark cloud behind the brave front we both presented. Still, I was not going to let it ruin the mood, and we continued along together, sharing our false bravado, and each being genuinely happy to have the other to bolster our confidence.

By five we were at the coffee shop where we were supposed to meet with Perez and Mack to get the cash. We found a table out on the sidewalk with a Cinzano umbrella. The Bistro Etienne was trying desperately to look French. But they overshot the runway. If they wanted French, all they needed to do was ask the customers to bring in useless noisy dogs and smoke cigarettes. Then we could all sit around, blow smoke on each other's dogs, and pay twelve dollars for a small green bottle of toilet water. Que c'est beau la vie.

Mack and Perez were not anywhere to be seen, so we sat in the sun and enjoyed the city scene wandering past us on the avenue. We began to play a little game with the people we saw approaching. "See this guy coming towards us? The one with the plaid shirt and high-water pants?" I asked as she spotted the target.

"Got him. Looks like an encyclopedia salesman from Duluth. Hasn't sold a set in two years. Drives a 1968 Country Squire station wagon with mis-matched tires and a bad cylinder. Wife's name is old Betty Lou Thelma Liz."

Something rang a bell. "Hey, that's out of an old Jerry Jeff Walker tune, I think."

"Up Against the Wall, Redneck Mother." She smiled at me, impressed that I had made the connection. "I had no idea Mr. Chauncey's musical portfolio cast such a wide net."

"We simply must get together over tea and compare our collections some time!" Anyone who could rattle lyrics out of a Jerry Jeff tune had my undying admiration... as if she needed any more of my admiration. This girl kept coming up with the most pleasant surprises.

Claudia spotted another one and leaned in to me, "There's a challenge... the older lady with the little dog in her purse waiting to cross at the corner."

I saw the large woman with the dog immediately. "Oh, that one is obvious, love. That's Mrs. Flubbersquat, the old witch who raises Pekinese puppies in a dark apartment over the Chinese restaurant. She trains the dogs to steal fresh fish from the market and bring them upstairs to her room so she can boil them into a stew that she keeps in mason jars on a shelf."

Claudia was delighted with the description and began to search for another victim of our imaginary judgments. But a moment later, as she scanned the walk for a colorful character, her face darkened and the smile disappeared. I followed her gaze to an approaching man, looking furtively from side to side, but making his way along the walk toward our cafe. Not Perez, I realized. As he came near, I saw him cast his intense gaze across the cafe patrons, but he gave us no more attention than anyone else. He passed by without slowing and continued to the corner where the large woman with the Pekinese was stepping off the curb to cross.

I assessed the situation quickly, "I believe the chap is off to Mrs Flubbersquat's for a nip of fish stew."

Claudia's dark mood did not brighten. "No. That's probably one of Perez's ferrets."

I turned to look at her face for some hint, but it remained focused on the man's back as he stepped onto the far sidewalk and turned to walk across the street from us, in the same direction as he had just come. "What makes you think that guy works for Perez? No sign of Mack. Maybe it's just some guy heading home from work."

"Watch him, he's pretending to check out cracks in the pavement." Claudia   He just looked our way again from across the street. Remember what Mack told us about Perez, he never shows up anywhere till he has checked out every angle. I bet he checks in with his boss to give him a report."

It seemed like an awfully strong reaction to a nervous guy in a cheap suit, but true to her instincts, the guy pulled up at the newsstand down the block, picked up a copy of the Kansas City

Tribune, and pulled a cell phone from his pocket to make a call. I was once again amazed. "Ms. Beretta, your powers of observation are most impressive. My apologies for ever doubting you."

She responded to my compliment with a bright impish smile, "See that you never doubt me again, my love."

"You two got room for me?" Mack gave us both a start when we realized his mammoth frame was inches away from us.

I recovered first and offered him one of the four seats around our little outdoor table. "I'm not sure there is room for you inside city limits, Mack."

Mack squeezed into the seat and a young fake Parisian waiter sidled up with pad in hand, "Monsieur, may I take your ordaire?"

Mack did not look thrilled with the kid's flakey French accent. "Sure, Skippy. Cuppa' coffee and an English muffin."

The kid looked injured, "Perhaps you would prefer a French croissant? They are baked fresh every morning by our pastry chef, Jean-Pierre."

Skippy seemed to suddenly regret having made the suggestion when Mack hesitated a moment, then turned very slowly to the kid with the order pad, "Perhaps I could accompany you to the kitchen and shove your little head up Jean-Pierre's ass while he cooks my fuggin' English muffin." The kid took a few steps back, and a couple of older ladies within earshot at the adjoining table nearly choked on their cappuccinos, got up quickly, and shuffled over one table to increase their buffer zone. They resettled in and gave us all glaring looks of disapproval.

"It will be just a few minutes, sir," and Skippy pivoted around and headed for safety behind the recoiling ladies.

I smiled at Mack as he sat placidly beside us, "Good afternoon, Mack. How goes your day so far?"

"Oh, OK, I s'pose." He looked a little tired, but still dangerous. I assumed the kid went back to the bathroom to clean out his drawers. Probably the last time he would ever lay the French croissant sales pitch on anyone larger than a walk-in cooler. "Perez will be along in a few. He has to sniff around a little first, like usual."

Claudia pointed out the nervous looking character on the far corner, still fidgeting with his paper while scanning the street. "Mack, have you ever seen that guy on the corner before? Something seems a bit odd with him."

Mack checked quickly, but did not bother with more than a passing glance. "Sure. That's Finnegan the Weasel. Perez's little sneak. He'll give word to Perez in a few that the coast is clear, unless he sees somebody he don't trust... then he calls off the deal till we check it out."

"He just made a call a few minutes ago," Claudia added.

"Yeah. That was to me. Gave me the go ahead to move in. I gotta give him the sign before he calls Perez."

We both looked at Mack, waiting to see if he made some wave or signal to Finnegan, but he just sat watching the rest of the restless city life scurry around on the street.

I had to ask, "So when do you give him the signal, Mack?"

"Oh, I already did. Perez should be along in a few. Looks like the place is clear except for those two old bitties." He indicated the two elderly ladies that had scuttled off to the next table.

Claudia seemed surprised by the suspicion of the ladies. "Why worry about those two, Mack? Did you rough up that poor boy just to scare off the customers?"

Mack looked a little embarrassed. "Well, not 'zackly. But I don't much like the way that antennae is stickin' up out of her big ol' handbag there under the table. I seen her scoot the bag over closer to you two before I sat down. Maybe somethin'... maybe not. So I figure, let's see how bad these old bags want their muffins and tea. If they stick around, then we have to move. If they run for cover, then we're good to go."

"Wow! You really do your homework, Mack. I didn't even notice the bag thing." I was genuinely impressed with his attention to detail.

"Yeah, well, you make a few mistakes and it costs you a bundle. Might cost you a few years in the pokey, if one of them little wires gets shoved a little too close to you while business is bein' conducted, you know?" Mack sounded like he might have had a few close calls with that sort of thing.

Skippy returned from the cafe and cautiously approached our table, Mack's English muffin in one hand and his coffee in the other. With a constant watch on Mack for any sign of quick movement, he stretched out to slip the saucers onto the table at a position where he could leap away to safety if the need arose. "Here you are sir, sorry for the wait." The French act had disappeared completely. He quickly retreated to a safe distance before adding, "Anything else you need?" Mack raised his enormous head and gave him a hard stare. The kid was about to pee his pants. "Very well then, I'll just be inside... if you need anything... I mean, I can check back."

Mack just stared. Claudia's more gentle nature prevailed and she interceded, "We will be fine, thank you."

The kid looked relieved, but instead of making his exit, he began to dig into his pocket to retrieve a folded slip of paper. "One more thing, I believe this is for you, sir." He was addressing me and holding the paper out a full ten feet from my reach, unwilling to risk another venture into Mack's range. "Are you Mr. Chauncey?"

"Indeed. Bring it here, lad, Mack won't bite you." The petrified boy shuffled cautiously back toward the table, trying to keep the maximum distance possible between himself and Mack. I could not bear to pass up the opportunity. "Mind you, he might twist your head off like a grape, but he seldom bites." Claudia shot me a glance that said, *'Was that really necessary?'* as Skippy flung the note the final foot or so, and then scampered awkwardly back into the cafe.

Claudia chastised us both, "Really, you two. I don't know which one of you is worse. The poor kid is going to have nightmares for a month."

Mack looked up apologetically. "Sorry, Chessie. When some punk kid puts on a show like he's better'n me, with all that 'Mon-Sewer' stuff, well I only got one way of bringin' him down a peg or two."

"It's OK, Mack. I understand. But we really must try to be nicer to the help. They are just doing their job, you know." She put a hand on Mack's shoulder to let him know she was not really upset with him.

I could not pass up the opportunity, "Oh, Mack's very nice to people, sometimes, aren't you Mack? Just ask Delores how nice Mack can be." Mack turned red, but smiled, obviously pleased with his recent Delores related activities.

Claudia turned her attention to me. "It wouldn't hurt you to be a little lower profile, either, Mr. Chauncey. Now see what's in the note."

I picked the note up and began to unfold it, while trying to defend Mack, "Well, I'm with Mack. Never did like snotty little Frenchmen." I spread out the note and read the message, written with a marking pen across a packing slip labeled for delivery of a dozen cases of Columbian dark-roasted coffee beans. *"Silver Lincoln Towncar. Third Avenue and Frederick.* That's all it says. Looks like our friend Mr. Perez wants to relocate the meeting."

Mack absorbed the English muffin in one swallow and tilted his cup of coffee up to follow behind it. I left a bill on the table to cover the '*ordaire*' and a little extra to make up for psychological damage to Skippy. Claudia noticed the twenty and smiled at me... all forgiven, I hoped. I was certain that Skippy's mental health issues were not worth more than fifteen bucks. "We are one block over from Frederick Street. Sounds like Perez is close by, waiting on clearance from the Weasel over there." We looked up, but Finnegan was gone. "Hmmm."

On the way out we passed by the two ladies that Mack had displaced earlier, having resumed their conversation over tea and pastries. They silenced themselves as Mack's shadow darkened their party. I thought Mack would pass on by without an issue, having been reprimanded by Claudia five minutes earlier, but I was wrong. As quick as a cat snatching a mouse, Mack's meaty arm shot into the lady's handbag and extracted whatever was attached to that small antennae that protruded from the top. He did not bother to bring it up for inspection but let it drop to the floor as soon as it had cleared the bag. Without missing a step, his size-fourteen foot rolled across the small tape machine that ground to a stop as it collapsed under Mack's weight. It gave a sad little hiss and a wisp of smoke rose up from the wreckage.

The two ladies gasped and threw their hands to their face in horror as they watched their property being destroyed. "You animal! That was my book on tape!"

Mack kept moving and barely turned his head to comment, "Yep. And I'm Mother Teresa. Have a nice day, ladies."

When we hit the street, Mack turned to Claudia, "How was that? I tried to be nice that time."

"Much better, Mack. Very gentlemanly. Now we need to work on Bertrand." She took my arm and smiled at me as we headed for the crossing that would lead us around the block to Frederick Street. "Mack, do you think Perez will hold up his end of the deal? What if he gets us in the car and shoots us all?"

"Naw. That don't sound like Perez much. He don't mind shooting you, but he needs to get some profit out of it first. He prob'ly won't shoot you two till later, after you get Darrell out of the way for him. You might want to keep a look out after that."

Claudia frowned. "Oh, how comforting."

'Indeed', I thought.

We came to the next corner and turned toward Third Avenue on Frederick and began looking along the curb for a silver Lincoln Towncar. When we got to Third, there was still no car in sight, but the front passenger window of a black Cadillac Seville parked near us lowered halfway and a shadowed voice said, "Get in... now." The three of us hesitantly packed into the rear seat. It was wide enough for four, but Mack covered about two and a half spaces. Perez was in the front passenger seat and the driver was our friend Finnegan the Weasel.

I decided to break the ice with a little bit of Bertrand Chauncey's famous insolence. "So, Perez, nice silver Towncar. Had an eye exam lately?"

"Jesus, Chauncey you make me sick. You might be the dumbest asshole on earth, you know that?"

"Oh, please, Antonio, you're making me blush."

"First you two parade all over town, till you get picked up by the Feds... then you plop down next to them in the coffee shop and start spilling your guts. And then you sit there waiting for me to waltz in with a case full of cash and announce to the audience that the deal is about to go down... in the event any of the public would like to participate in the festivities. It's a good fuckin' thing you two don't do this shit for a living, cause you're outta fuckin' business in about two hours." Perez was fuming mad and spitting bits of saliva across the headrest toward Finnegan who was doing his best to stay out of the line of fire.

I was struggling to keep up with the assault from Perez. "Wait a minute... those dried up old hags were Feds? Good heavens, my mistake. I thought they were KGB. I thought the waiter was the Fed. I must speak to them about recruiting."

"Shut the fuck up, Chauncey. This whole deal has stunk from the start. No way I'm going to trust you with fifty grand. You might walk in to precinct headquarters and ask them to watch it for you while you take a leak." On some unseen signal, Finnegan the Weasel put the Caddy in drive and pulled out into traffic heading down Frederick Street. We were not given the opportunity to protest, and I doubted the doors would open, even if I tried.

Mack offered up a fig leaf for Perez, "You know, boss, I seen that wire the old bitty had in her bag. I took care of that on the way out."

"Sure, Mack. I know you did. You done good back there," Perez pointed at Claudia and me, "but how do we know these two didn't set up the wire in the first place, huh? Ever think about that one, moron?" Perez took a swing towards Mack with an open hand, but Mack dodged it easily. "Ever stop for one second and wonder how those two agents got seated right next to our friends here? Huh, Mack?"

"I dunno, boss. Look, I'm sorry, OK? You told me to meet them at the coffee place, and keep my eyes open, so I done that. I done what you said, OK?" I knew Mack was playing dumb to keep Perez from venting his anger on him. "But I don't think they set us up, either."

Perez turned to face Mack directly now. I wondered if Mack was painting himself into a corner. "So, you think your friends here are playing it straight?" He jerked a thumb towards Claudia and me.

"Just a couple of honest citizens out to help us roll some porno schmuck in the interest of society, right Mack?"

Mack ignored the sarcasm dripping from Perez's accusations and continued, "Naw. They don't know nothin' about that wire, Mr. Perez. Don't make no sense for Chauncey here to get himself in trouble after helpin' cover up that hole behind the tracks. Now he's gotten his girl into it with him, so they're both on the hook. Way I see it... we go down... they go down. Not to mention what might happen if they try somethin' stupid like settin' us up."

Perez inspected us both for any sign of weakness. I was feeling intensely uncomfortable, and wondered if Claudia was in the same condition. I did not wonder long, as she addressed Perez first, "How do we know it wasn't you that set up that wire to get the goods on us?"

Perez looked a little shocked at having the tables turned on him. "Right, I called the Feds in to bust myself. You're on to something, there Ms. Beretta." Perez gave a chuckle to punctuate his amusement.

But Claudia persisted, "What Feds? Those two old bags were no more Feds that you are! Maybe it was your old wrinkled up granny and her quilting buddy who you sent in with your tape recorder to pick up any juicy tidbits you might be able to use to either blackmail us or make sure we weren't going to double cross you. Too bad Mack here was too sharp to miss the antennae sticking up. And what was in the bag with the recorder, Perez? I'm guessing a compact directional microphone with a battery booster. Still got the receipt from Radio Shack, you cheap piece of trash! Maybe they will take it back on warranty, if you lean on them a little with Mack here."

Holy cow, this girl had some chutzpah. She was right up in Perez's face and giving him every bit of abuse she could think of. Perez sat and took in the whole tirade before responding calmly, "My Aunt Juanita, actually... talked her old bridge partner into helping her out. I send her out once in a while because she likes to think she's being useful. I tell her she's helping catch the bad guys who want to cheat us. She don't know no better." Now I was completely in awe. Claudia had pinned the whole operation on Perez. I guess it made perfect sense. Why else would two old ladies be taping our conversation out of the clear blue? Perez continued, "I didn't think Mack would actually spot them. They look like Mother fuckin' Goose, for crissakes."

Claudia kept up the barrage, unabated, "You want to pull the plug on this deal, Perez? Be my guest... make my day. We take our time to set up a transaction that pegs Darrell to the kiddy porn operation, and all you do is sic your decrepit old auntie on us with a wire. In fact, tell your rodent chauffer to pull it over. Time for us to part company, you pathetic backstabbing little turd!"

Talk about turning the tables. Perez was back-peddling like a drunk at a church social. "Take it easy, sister, don't get your undies in a bunch. No harm, no foul. I was just tryin' to make sure nobody set me up, OK? Guy's gotta look after his interests in this business, you know. You passed the test, so relax, will you? Sheesh, Chauncey, you got your hands full with this one."

"Oh, I quite agree. Pleasantly so, to be sure." I was smiling away, feeling very much like I was being taken on an interesting carnival ride. I had underestimated my partner again. What on earth could she do to top that performance?

She quickly obliged my interest. "Perez, I am sick of this whole deal, and we haven't even started. You've got one minute flat to jerk this whale off the road, hand us the cash, and get the fuck out of my sight. And if you show up at our meeting tonight and screw the pooch, I'm gonna make life miserable for you for the next ten years."

"Look, Toots, ten years is long time. How you think you gonna make me miserable for that long?"

"You call me Toots, or Sister, or anything but Ms. Beretta one more time and you're gonna find how just how miserable you can get."

Finnegan the Weasel gave a little nervous laugh in support of his boss. He had never heard anybody talk like that to Mr. Perez. He chimed in, "Hey, nobody messes with..."

Finnegan's banter was cut short when Claudia let loose a roundhouse open-hand slap to the back side of his head. Bap. "Anybody ask you to speak up, Ferret-face?" She popped him again one more time for effect and added, "Find a place to park, rodent. The stink in here is killing me... Perez!" She turned back and fixed a glare at Perez, who visibly jumped. "Make up your miniature little mind! Have you got the cash, or do we have to apply for a security clearance in some phone booth in New Jersey?" Mack huddled down between us and tried to make himself invisible. Not a feasible task, if you're Mack. We were both sure that Claudia was about to get us all killed.

"I got the cash right here. Calm down, sis... er, Ms. Beretta!" Perez now had both hands up to fend off any potential smacks to his head, and he cautiously reached down to the floorboard and raised a green zippered deposit bag high enough for Claudia to see. "Right here, Lizzie Borden, don't kill Finnegan, OK?" Claudia let the Lizzie Borden reference slide as he passed the deposit bag back to me. Perez then cautiously raised a large brown paper bag and handed it over to Claudia. "This bag has all the newspaper wads to put in the second case. I made a lot of 'em."

I checked the green pouch with the cash, and Claudia inspected the larger paper bag with stacks of paper. The sight of fifty large did not evoke quite the thrill I had hoped for. It looked more like a few hundred. "That's it? Fifty grand in here? Looks more like lunch money."

Perez looked back over the seat, "Yeah, it's fifty all right. Big bills... all hundreds. Would'a looked a little fatter if we used twenties. I didn't have enough twenties, so we used the hundreds. Anyway, it's easier to count. Go ahead, check it out."

I did a quick count of one bundle, multiplied times the number of bundles and came up close enough. "OK. Looks like we got the cash right. You know Darrell is going to want to count every dime."

"Yeah, I figure he will look pretty close, so I used the real stuff this time. Coulda' passed the hot stuff off on the moron, but I figure I'm gonna get it back anyway, so why take the chance, right?" Perez was looking pleased with himself again, now that Claudia had quit beating on them and was busy checking the newspaper bundles.

"Why so many paper bundles? There has to be three times the volume of the actual cash. And Mr. Perez, is this your idea of humor?" Claudia held up a note attached to one of the paper bundles. She read the note to us, "*Thanks for videos, dickhead. You can use these to wipe your ass in prison.*"

Perez smiled back, "Yeah... pretty good, huh? I did that myself. Little love note from me to Darrell. Hope that rat-fucker gets reamed in the can. Ha! Get it? Reamed in the can... that's rich!" Perez was absorbed in self-admiration as we settled back into the soft upholstery of the caddy.

Claudia seemed to be in charge, so I just went with the flow to see where the carnival ride would end. She directed a request at Perez. "Tell your pet rat to drop us off at my car. Wait till I have the trunk open before you pull away. It's up here on Fourth Avenue, about two blocks ahead, red Honda."

"Yeah. I know." Perez nodded, and the rodent directed the Caddy onward toward the Honda. I gave a raised eyebrow to Claudia after her tirade, she winked discretely, and it stayed fairly quiet for the next minute until we pulled alongside Claudia's car. She jumped out and popped the trunk, then motioned calmly for me to hand her the bag and the deposit envelope with the cash that she slipped in between a box of old books and a blue laundry basket.

She slammed the lid as I got out beside her and waited to see what Mack was going to do. He sat tight for a second, but Perez quickly sent him along with us. "Mack here is your new best friend. Where the cash goes, Mack goes. Got it?"

Claudia leaned in close to Perez's open passenger window, put on the smile that had melted my heart a few days ago, and told him sweetly, "If you so much as look in the direction we go after this, or if I see any of your pet ferrets sniffing around for crumbs, I'll tie a rope around your nuts and string your carcass up from the nearest light pole so Kansas City urchins can take turns playing piñata."

Perez smiled back, "...and how do you propose to keep from getting shot in the process, Missy?"

Claudia's right fist shot out at the exact instant Perez finished pronouncing the word 'Missy', catching him completely off-guard, right in the lips. It made a delicious little 'POP' and Perez jolted back into his seat, in shock. "I told you about that 'Sister, Toots, Missy' business a little while ago, but you don't listen too well, do you Shitheal?" Perez just looked out, mouth open and puffing up, staring at her like she was Bitchzilla. Claudia reloaded her right hook, "Get your retarded ass out of my sight." And she calmly spun around and got in behind the driver seat of the Honda, then fired up the ignition. Her window came down and she smiled out serenely at Mack and me, "You two coming along?" Mack and I looked at each other, wondering what just happened.

We recovered a bit, got into the car, and watched Finnegan the Weasel chauffeur Perez and his fat lip down Fourth Avenue. The three of us watched quietly as the black Caddy disappeared into traffic. The moment the car faded from sight Claudia began to bust up in a fit of giggles that quickly spread to Mack and I, and all of us ended up howling like spider monkeys for five minutes.

"Remind me never to piss you off!" I chided her as we all struggled to recover.

Mack was the last to emerge from his laughing fit and looked over to Claudia. "That was the scariest thing I ever seen!"

She grinned back at him, "So, how come we're laughing so hard, Mack?"

"I dunno!" Mack blurted, and we all got caught up in another bout of laughter.

Chapter Fourteen

D-day... zero hour... time to face the music... show time… never take wooden nickels… etc., etc. The curtain was set to go up on our little troupe, and the first act was about to commence. Mack, Claudia and I were arranged around the same table in the back room at Hauzer's Brat Haus where we had met with Perez earlier in the week. We were quickly reviewing the plan to upset Darrell's little kiddie-porn teacart. Darrell was supposed to meet us at the Brat Haus, according to the schedule Mack had arranged with Darrell's recruiter, Tommy, the punk who Mack had photographed hustling the girls at the local high school.

We had parked our three vehicles out front and moved the two bags from Claudia's trunk to Mack's sedan so he could load up the two briefcases… one case with fifty-thousand dollars, and the other with cut stacks of newspaper. We sat with Mack in the sedan as he completed the task of balancing out the two cases. Perez had given us more newspaper than we needed, so Mack left half of it in the bag. I commented on Mack's job, "OK, looks like we have a balanced pair. But what happens if *we* get them screwed up? Could be an expensive mistake."

Claudia thought a moment, then reached into her purse for something. "Hand me the real one, please, Mack." Mack obliged her and she withdrew the cap from a small bottle of nail polish and placed a very small red dot on the handle of the briefcase. "There we go." We both smiled at Claudia's ingenuity, then piled out to nestle the two cases into the trunk of the sedan, and headed into Hauzer's to await our meeting with Darrell.

None of us really expected Darrell to come stomping up Hauzer's steps without casing out the scene, so we were not surprised to see Tommy pass outside the back window, making a full circle outside the restaurant before cautiously coming through the front entrance and looking around. Delores met him at the front and asked, "You eatin' dinner, or lookin' for your dog?"

Tommy was easily confused, "Looking for what?"

"You need a table for one, honey... or are you meetin' a few more?"

"Oh. No, actually, meeting a guy named Mack. Might be a few others, eventually."

Delores thought she realized who he was, being in on the basics of the setup. But it was not Darrell, as she suspected. She fought back the urge to stomp his shins, and showed him to the back room, where we were all seated.

Mack stood up as Tommy appeared with one arm in a sling and his left eye swollen shut. Mack stepped over to face him and greeted him with false warmth, "Well, if it ain't Cousin Tommy. Ridin' point for your boss, Tommy? Makin' sure we didn't plant any cops in the back yard of Hauzer's? What you doin' out back there, Tommy? Takin' a dump? Some of these nice places got indoor toilets now, you know. You don't got to poop out back, like you do at your house."

Tommy was turning red and clenching his one good fist in the doorway, but Mack knew that Tommy was no threat. He was a greasy little fuck-weasel, but he was not dumb enough to evoke Mack's wrath again. "Shut up, a-hole. You do the same crap I do, so you got no cause to sit all high and mighty."

"Tommy, barnyard shit-maggots sit all high and mighty next to you. But enough with the compliments. Go fetch your boss-hole so we can get this over with. These are the two buyers I promised, and they don't got time to sit here and watch you twitch around like you got bugs up your crack. Hey, Tommy… you don't got no bugs up your crack, do you?" Tommy started to make a move toward Mack, who smiled broadly, hoping in vain that Tommy might actually snap and come for him. Tommy pulled up short, just out of Mack's arm reach.

I decided to calm the waters, "Tommy, my name is Bertrand Chauncey, and this is my associate, Ms. Chessie Beretta. Pleasure to make your acquaintance. Frightfully sorry about the rush, but I am afraid we do have a rather busy schedule." I dropped the hard 'k' sound and pronounced the word '*shed-ule*' the way I had often heard it used by people who were either English, or trying very hard to sound like it. "I believe we are to meet with an individual named Darrell? Is that correct?"

Tommy continued to scan the room and look out the window nervously. He acted like he had spent a few hours tossing back double espressos at Starbucks. He made Finnegan the Weasel look like the Prozac Prince. "He'll be along. Sit tight." Tommy spun around and headed back out the way he had come in, pulling his cell from his pocket as he went. We all knew the drill, Tommy had to scout the room, assess the players, check out access and escape routes, and report in when he finished his sweep. He was about to do just that, when Delores stopped him at the front door. "Honey, I cain't take your order if you don't sit down!"

"Sorry, Chickadee. Gotta make a quick call." The connection engaged and Tommy started giving Darrell the low-down as he passed out the front door towards his car to finish the call.

"Delores, could you keep an eye on the front and let us know when you see a large car arrive at the curb?" I asked. Delores was definitely up for the task, and hustled off to spy on the front street for us while we considered what might happen next. "Looks like we cleared the first hurdle. Should be seeing Steven Schoolyard Spielberg any minute now."

But after we had finished a pitcher of Hefeweisen, there was still no sign of Darrell. Delores told us that Tommy had finished his call and driven off. We were contemplating our next move when Delores shuffled back into the room with a cordless phone in hand. "If you start gettin' your business calls in here, big boy, you need to pay me secretary wages," and handed the handset over to Mack, who looked at us in confusion.

"Hullo?" Mack sat listening intently. "Thought we were s'pose to meet here, at Hauzer's." This did not bode well. "Yeah, course they do..," there was a pause where Mack's face turned toward us with concern. "Right now? Shit, I don't know... hang on…" Mack covered the phone and asked, "Darrell's still up for the meeting, but not here. Says you will want to see the operation first hand anyway, so we may as well meet at the warehouse for a tour. What do I tell him?"

I looked over to Claudia who shrugged. I couldn't think of any way to force Darrell to come to us, so I repeated Claudia's gesture for Mack. Mack nodded and spoke to someone we assumed was either Darrell or Tommy, "OK. Yeah, I know the spot. Give us fifteen." Mack clicked off, handed the phone back to Delores, and slumped back into his seat at our table.

I tried to sound optimistic, "So much for plan A. Anyone for Plan B?" I got up and pulled on my jacket.

"Bertrand, dear?" Claudia asked quietly.

"Yes, my love."

"We have no Plan B." She had a good point there.

"Ah, I see. Well, then, we best be off. We can have a bit of a chat on the ride over, eh?" Now it was Mack's turn to shrug, and we all prepared to head across town. We settled up with Delores as Hauzer came out of his kitchen to see why our meeting had not materialized as planned. "No dice tonight, Hauzer. We're off to meet in the Devil's Den, so to speak."

"Ah, Bert, you be careful vit dees guys. I sink day be zum nasty characters, dees guys."

I stayed in character, afraid of what Bert the Stock Boy might be thinking. "Not to worry, my friend. Just a walk in the park for the likes of us... deal with these types on a daily basis. This lot is a bit dimmer than most, in fact. See you back here in a shake."

Delores headed Mack off at the pass, and sidled up to him for a quick word. "You keep out of the line of fire, you hear me?"

Mack smiled at his new sweetheart, and said, "Aw, heck, you worried about me?"

She shoved him back about a quarter of an inch, an effort that required her entire weight, and said, "Worried about a big lug like you? Hell, no I ain't worried. Just that Hauzer here ground up a new batch of bratwurst last week and I'm worried they might go to waste if'n you're not here to woof 'em down."

We laughed, and Claudia added, "That's true love if I've ever seen it." Mack turned red, and we finally got out the door and headed to our rigs. We had all driven in separate cars; Claudia's red Honda was parked in Hauzer's tiny parking lot, my truck with Hannibal in the front was at the curb, and Mack had parked just down the street, probably out of habits formed from years of trying to dodge trouble. I let Hannibal out of the truck and he made the rounds to greet Mack and Claudia, who both scratched his head to return the greeting.

Mack looked at the three vehicles and considered the decision, "I s'pose we ought'a take 'em all, case we need to jump in the closest rig. Might confuse Darrell tryin' to figure out which one to shoot at."

"Your optimism is inspiring, Mack," I deadpanned. "Claudia, follow in behind Mack and park where you can head out fast, if things get weird. Mack, try to park where you can cut off the others if they come after her. I'll try to angle the truck from the opposite direction... for some reason, not precisely sure... seems appropriate. If everything goes bad, get out to the cars and go like mad. Claudia, keep going no matter what. We'll get out of there. We can all meet back at Hauzer's if we get split up. But let's try to keep together, if we can. If we have to make a break, don't forget the backup plan; let's stick to it."

"Chauncey?" Mack questioned.

"Yeah, Mack?"

"We don't got no backup plan."

"Oh, yeah. I keep forgetting. Improvise, Mack. It's our strong suit."

Mack nodded, "Got it."

I turned to Claudia, "You OK? Pretty quiet over there." I thought about offering one last chance to call off the caper.

"Let's go. I'm ready." She had a look of absolute resolution on her face. I decided to let the thought pass. And so we went.

We drove in a loose pack over to the south side of town, into the industrial district filled with large manufacturing and distribution warehouses lined up along the tracks for a couple of miles. Even though trucking had since taken over as the primary means of shipment, the warehouses remained clustered along the rail lines, as they had originally been constructed, to take advantage of cheap rail shipping. It was not the most picturesque part of town, nor the healthiest place to hang out after dark. The district was infested with vermin of several species, both human and rodent, all of which kept watch for the large yard dogs that occupied almost every complex.

There seemed to be an unofficial contest among the warehouse owners to produce the most psychotic, evil watch dog on the planet. The competition was apparently as fierce as the dogs.

Mack's directions led us to an unmarked warehouse that was set apart from most of the others, with roll-up doors and loading bays, much the same as all the others in the district. There was nothing other than the large numerals 413 above the entry door to identify this corrugated metal structure from any of the others. I assumed that Darrell realized billboard advertisement for underage sex videos might be counterproductive to his operation. Still, I wondered how he managed to keep a lid on his greasy little scheme without some big burly dad kicking in his door and putting a fist through his face.

I saw Mack pull into the fenced yard first, with the Honda right behind, and they hesitated for a minute as they considered the best way to arrange the vehicles. Claudia jockeyed hers around, facing out toward the gate, and Mack pulled in perpendicular, behind her. I swung past them and parked around the corner of the building, having absolutely no idea what advantage this configuration might provide.

True to form, just as I emerged from the truck, a behemoth dog of questionable lineage, came shooting out from behind a storage container and would have likely torn one of my legs off, but the chain came taught and he nearly flipped over backwards. The dog, some sort of genetically enhanced Rottweiler cross-breed, regained his footing and strained at the chain, snapping his teeth like an irate tusk-hog, barking wildly, and sending a spray of dog-spit flying in all directions. "Nice little poochie." He was not buying it. Over the snarling I could also hear Hannibal behind me going berserk in the truck seat. I was glad the window was high enough to prevent him getting out. I doubted if he would survive long against Fang.

I caught up to Mack and Claudia. No words were exchanged outside the little metal door, we just exchanged a long look and turned to go in. Before I could try the door, it opened, and Tommy stood grinning at us from inside. "Just in time. See you met security!"

We could hear the dog just around the corner of the building, still madly fighting the restraining chain, trying to break a link so he could track me down and rip a piece of my leg off. "Lovely animal. Seems to have taken a fancy to me."

"Oh, right. He fancies almost everybody... for *dinner.*" Tommy yucked it up over his own joke, but he was the only one amused. Tommy did not seem to be the sharpest shovel in the shed. "Come on in. Mr. Hatfield is in his office. He wants to give you the grand tour."

Hatfield? That was a new name. Up to that point, all we had heard was Darrell. "We were to meet with an individual named Darrell, I believe. Are we to assume Mr. Hatfield is actually Darrel Hatfield?" I ventured.

"You got it... Darrell Hatfield. Say, where the fuck you from, Boston?" Tommy continued to impress us with his intellectual agility.

"Precisely. How perceptive of you. Now, if you please..." I gestured toward the interior to prompt Tommy into action. He turned to lead us along a featureless hallway lined with unmarked windowless doors. I wondered what went on behind those doors, but figured we were all about to find out. At the end of the hall was another blank door that Tommy rapped on twice, then announced our arrival. "That bunch from Boston here to see you, Boss." What a dolt.

"Bring it on," came a backwoods drawl from behind the door. Tommy swung open the door and we peered in to find a thin man of about thirty, dressed in jeans and a Budweiser logo t-shirt standing next to his desk. He had a NASCAR ball-cap skewed sideways across his head, with what appeared to be a mullet haircut spilling out behind. "Hey, y'all! Come on in. Anybody need a beer?" Darrell stepped over to a mini-fridge in the corner of the office and opened the door to reveal the fully stocked contents. "Y'all drink light or reg'lar?" He pulled out one of each and stretched the two Budweiser cans out towards us as we entered the room. I wondered if he knew Wally at the Palm Frond.

None of the three of us had said a word since the office door had opened. Whatever we had each envisioned Darrell to be, this was not it. This was not the ringleader of an underground child pornography syndicate. This was Goober from Mayberry RFD.

Mack accepted the beer, while Claudia and I declined. I stepped forward and offered a hand, "Bertrand Chauncey, Mr. Hatfield. Pleased to finally make your acquaintance. This is Ms. Chessie Beretta, my associate, and our friend Mack, who was kind enough to arrange this meeting with you."

Darrell shook my hand, gave Mack a little salute gesture, and then turned to examine Claudia with far too much interest. "My gracious sakes, Babycakes, you are cute as a speckled pup! You can star in one of my movies any time you want!"

I felt the heat rise in my face as he took Claudia by the hand and gave it an awkward kiss. I watched this scene expecting to hear Claudia give him a sharp rebuke for being such a lecherous ass, but she continued to amaze me with her instantaneous response. "Why Mr. Hatfield, what a marvelously tempting offer. I have often wondered if making one of those films would be fun, but no one ever offered me the opportunity. Perhaps we can talk later." Here she gave him a coy little wiggle and a wink that left Mack and I speechless.

I recovered a bit and decided to explain our roles. "Ms. Beretta and I might have some interest in your production. I think we have identified a discreet market interest and we are willing to make a cash transaction if, of course, the product lives up to the billing." I walked to the bookshelf opposite the mini-fridge, feigning indifference, and began examining the stunning array of literature collected in the shelves. A full series of Camouflage Monthly, a dozen editions of Bowhunter's Guide, a five-foot wide section of old Hustler magazines, and a smaller series of well-worn magazines titled "Ass-Jockeys on Parade!". We were in the presence of brilliance. How in hell did this hillbilly manage to dress himself in the morning? This was our big business contact? Darrell Hatfield made Perez look like the president of Rotary.

"I can flat out *guar-on-tee* that the flicks comin' out of this shack will curl your short-hairs. Make your pecker stand up and salute, too. Nothin' but the best lookin' babes workin' fer me. What you say your name was, buddy? Bertroid?"

"Bertrand, if you please."

"Right. Good enough. Well, let's go have a look at the set-up. You folks might want to see behind the scenes." Darrell, Tommy, and the three of us prepared to exit the office, but Darrell stopped us before opening the door, "Just a sec there, Bart." He stepped in front of me with a long wand device and made a pass in front and behind me with the wand. He had completed the sweep before I could object. "Sorry about this, won't take a minute." He continued to sweep Claudia and Mack in turn, then set the wand down on the desk and smiled broadly.

Mack was the first to comment. He stepped in front of Darrell menacingly, "You think I'm gonna bring these guys in here wired up? That what you think?"

Darrell, surprisingly, did not fluster. "Easy there, Tarzan. Business is business. You don't go bustin' heads every time they pass you through security at the airport, do you? Just takin' the standard precautions, nothin' more. Don't get all butt-hurt about it."

Darrell had satisfied Mack with this explanation, and I disturbingly found myself agreeing with the logic. Business is business. He led us back out into the hall and then passed a couple of blank doors before opening one that led into a large open bay with a high ceiling. It was obviously part of the main warehouse, but the inside was constructed an elaborate bedroom set, Hollywood style, with three walls, but no ceiling. The bed sat in the center, a lavish king-size unit decorated with a red satin bedspread and a dozen matching pillows. A sound boom hung precariously over the bed, and light standards stood to either side of the open room. It was disturbing to think of how many teenage girls lost their self-respect in this room. How many young promising lives had been undermined by Darrell and his enterprises?

Claudia bounced over to the bed and flopped across it, sending pillows flying. "Nice bed, Darrell. Is this where we get to make my first porno?" She again gave him such a convincing little smile, that I was beginning to wonder... was she really enjoying this scene?

"Could be... could be! Course, there's more to making a good porno than layin' flat on your fanny and wailin' like Aunt Bessie's brood mare." The mental images that Darrell could conjure with his analogies were truly disquieting.

Claudia got up from the bed, plucked one of the "adult toys" from the nightstand, sashayed over to Darrell, took him by the collar of his Budweiser t-shirt, and leaned in close to him, "Oh, I think you'll find I can do a whole lot more than whinney like a horse. Especially if I get the right stud." Darrell looked like he might roll the cameras right there, if he could. I suddenly realized what Claudia was up to, and was astounded to watch the sweetest girl I had ever met work over Darrell Hatfield like Rev. Jerry Fallwell works over a rich widow. Come to Jesus. Bring your checkbook. It was an awesome performance.

Skinny-ass Darrell puffed his chest out to its full potential and spoke into the latex wanker like a microphone, "I have been known to bring out the best in a few buddin' young beauties, my own self. Maybe it's time I got back in the saddle."

Claudia gave a not-so-discreet glance down to Darrell's Levi's and whispered, "May-be." Oh my. Darrell was toast. Mack and I were star-struck. Claudia was having a blast.

I broke the spell, "My good fellow... all this is well and good. Might even be a bonus in it if it all works out, but the matter at hand has yet to be determined. Perhaps we should proceed with the tour? I must assume there is a bit more to this operation than satin sheets and vibrating sausages." I thought of Hauzer's, and how we had failed to lure Darrell there to make the deal. While I was still unclear on how to corner the little worm, the skies were definitely brightening.

Reluctantly, Darrell led us back out to the hall, and set a hand on the next door beyond the set for the Red Satin Motor Lodge. "Y'all gonna wanna check this out. You into the kinky stuff, Bartrum?"

"Bertrand. And yes, I do occasionally have a mild interest in the more unusual styles of sexual amusement." I decided to follow Claudia's lead and immerse myself in the moment. "I once deflowered a comely young African woman while we sat atop a basket on the back of a bull elephant in Tanzania." Claudia gave me a clandestine look of shock, then smiled subtly.

Darrell swung open the door, strode inside the large room, and spread his arms wide apart dramatically to highlight the inner workings of his positively twisted imagination. The room was filled with an intricate collection of what first appeared to be work-out equipment. On closer inspection, it resembled more of a jungle-gym arrangement, but with randomly placed padded seats and stirrups. Handcuffs hung from various metal bars, and leather whips were arranged by size along a rack by the wall. More video equipment and lighting stands surrounded the steel framework, all silent and awaiting the next scene.

Claudia surveyed the intricate setup and sidled close to Darrell, who threw his arm around her waist, now completely at ease with her advances. "Oh Darrell, I do hope we get to spend a little time in this room. What fun!"

"Sugar, we could spend a little time in every goddamn room. Wait till you see what we got next!" His eyes were alight with a special glow, shared only by those gifted few with the vision and determination to destroy the lives of others. Darrell took us to the next room, and proved to all three of us that the human race was capable of producing some truly perverse minds. In the next room was a row of stalls, complete with live miniature stud horses, placidly munching away at their alfalfa.

I turned to address Darrell with as much calm as I could muster. "Really, Mr. Hatfield. Is there much of a market for this type of thing?"

"You got no idea, Burney. Folks'll pay for anything. Make half my profits right here in this stall. Little Secretariat there can get it up for two or three girls a night. And all it costs me is a bale of hay a week!" Darrell laughed out loud at this outrageous hilarity, and I caught a look of abject horror on the faces of both Claudia and Mack. I saw Mack moving across the room to get in position behind Darrell. As Darrell looked into Secretariat's stall in admiration, I motioned to Mack and mouthed the words, '*No! Wait for Perez.*' Mack got my meaning, and held his ground.

Claudia once again positioned herself close to Darrell and put a hand on his arm, "Aren't you the naughty little farmer, Darrell."

Darrell's eyes lit up at the attention, "You like them ponies, Honey? We can fix you up with a hot date if that's your style."

Claudia purred into his ear, "Not for me, Lover Boy. I'm more into the younger scene, if you know what I mean." Darrell looked confused for a minute, as did I. "We didn't come here to look at livestock. Bertrand and I were hoping to see what you can do with the younger set. Capiche?"

I was catching up quickly. Claudia knew, as weird and deviant as all this stuff was, it did not pose any particularly damning evidence against Darrell in a court of law. He could simply testify that whatever had happened was done among consenting adults (and livestock), produce some phony documentation that 'proved' the girls were all of age, and off he goes to prey on the next playground. I was supposed to be the 'buyer' so I added, "Impressive operation here Mr. Hatfield, but pretty standard stuff, it seems. I'm sure you will have no problem pedaling your videos at the local flea market, but my investors are interested in a little younger age bracket than you seem to employ here. Don't get me wrong, monkey bars and Shetland ponies are all fun and games, but unless you can produce a product that satisfies the needs of our target audience... well, perhaps we have wasted your time."

Claudia nodded her agreement, pleased that I had picked up the direction. She turned to face Darrell and continued to hold on to his arm, "Pity... I was so looking forward to working with you." She pouted beautifully.

Darrell saw an opportunity slipping away, "Now hang on, folks. I saved the best for last. One more room to see before you go off in a huff. I think I got 'zackly what you're hintin' at." Darrell looked anxious to please, desperate not to lose the opportunity to continue his plans for a scene with Claudia.

"We've come all this way, may as well see it through." I resigned myself to the next scene, unable to imagine how Darrell could sink any further into his own depraved nightmare. "One final room, is it? Very well, then."

On the way out of Green Acres I ventured a question I later regretted, "So, tell me, Mr. Hatfield… how did you come to be in the… entertainment business? Take over from an uncle, perhaps?" I was envisioning generations of Hatfields gathered for a family photo under a huge sign that read '*Hatfield Humpers. Proudly producing quality filth since 1962.*'

"Ah, hell no. Uncle Cletis was a homo. We used to call him Uncle Clitoris. Ha! Get it? Uncle Clitoris… the Turd Burglar!" We got it. Darrell should have gone with a career in stand-up. "Naw, not Uncle Cletis. It was actually this squirrely little creep in polyester pants who shows up at our mobile home one day. I reckon I was about fifteen by then, and meaner'n snake spit. We lived way the hell'n gone up this holler in Arkansas, so when this fancy little shitbird comes saunterin' up, holdin' out a handful of pamphlets, and tellin' us he's worried about our souls, I figure I'll really give him somethin' to fret about. So I come up behind him real quiet like, while he's a puttin' on the dog fer my sister Beula Mae, a'tellin her all about her rewards waitin' up in heaven. 'Bout the time he breaks the news that he needs a small donation to cover the costs of them pamphlets, I take a roundhouse swing with the manure shovel and lay one up side his head that damn near knocks him clean out of them fancy polyester pants. Funniest fuckin' thing you ever saw."

"Yes, I can certainly see how that would be amusing, Mr. Hatfield." We had progressed into the hallway at that point, awaiting the dreadful conclusion of Darrell's childhood antics. "I assume the fellow ran for his life once he recovered from your blow?"

"Run? Ah, hell no. Don't nobody run after I bust 'em with a shovel. Naw. We just plugged him in a hole out by the orchard and then ransacked the fucker's car he had stuck in the mud down the road."

Claudia gave me look of shock, but managed to stifle it before Darrell could see. "Tell me Darrell, how did any of that get you into the pornography business? Wasn't that where we started this lovely tale?"

"Yeah, well, guess what we found in that bible-thumpin' asshole's trunk? It was stocked up with a whole shitload of porno tapes and an old VCR tape recorder. He had lights in there too, and everything. The little cornhole was coming across like some kind of high-and-mighty preacher dude, while the whole time he's back in Daisy's Roadside Motel pokin' the church secretary and sellin' the video to the adult book stores back in Little Rock."

"I see." I did not see. "So you took over for the dead preacher?"

"Ah, hell no." If he said that one more time I was going to have to find my own manure shovel and see if I could knock his mullet out from under that NASCAR cap. "Naw, me and Beula Mae stayed up late watchin' all that diddlin' he had on them VCR tapes. Hell, he was a'pokin' anybody and anything what wasn't buried in the damn ground. We both kinda ended up getting' pretty worked up, and, well… you know..." Darrell was smiling broadly, waiting for us to catch on. He opened the next door and we entered a darkened room with rows of thickly padded seats facing a huge projection screen. Could it get any worse than what we had already heard? Yes, it could. Yes, it did. Much worse.

"Please, go on," Claudia prompted Darrell to finish the story as we took seats along the back row of chairs.

"Hell, we rigged up the lights, stuck that fuckin' recorder on a tripod, shucked our shorts, and I took Beula Mae for a rodeo ride right thar in the mobile home! Ma and Pa were out getting' hammered, as usual, so we figured we was safe. Hell, we made a half-dozen tapes that first week alone. Soon as we could, Beula and me hauled ass down to Little Rock and hit every adult book store and quarter peep show dive in town. End of the week we had eight hundert dollars! All that money, and all I had to do was screw sis! Shit, I'd a'done that fer nuthin'!" Darrell turned to face a small projection room behind us and hollered, "Hey Beula, you in there?"

We heard a rustle and a groan, "Fuck off, Darrell, I'm tryin' to jam in a crammer. I hate dealin' with this shit every month." Beula Mae Hatfield emerged from the cubicle, pulling her shorts back up and giving us the once over.

"Beula, these here folks come by for a tour of our little love nest. Might be interested in making a major purchase, if we got the right stuff. Why don't you warm 'em up with one of our old videos from the mobile home." Claudia shot me a look of panic.

Mack was the first to respond. His voice startled both Claudia and I, because he had been silent ever since we first met Darrell. I had almost forgotten he was there… as if it were possible to forget that a man the size of a small eastern state is present. "Save the home videos, Darrell. I don't think that's the type of stuff my friends here are lookin' for. They made it pretty clear on the way over they got no interest in crap like that. They come in here ready to pay top dollar for tapes you don't find nowhere else… not some horse show." Mack motioned back toward the stalls.

"Got it!" Darrell showed no sign of being offended that his first choice for our cinematic enjoyment had been rejected out of hand by a three-hundred pound primate. "Beula Mae, why don't you slap in one of them tapes we shot last week with them two cute little schoolgirls."

Beula Mae looked positively mortified. "Darrell, you goddamn ignert fuckweed… you know we ain't got no tapes of no little girls. That would be illegal, and you KNOW we don't do no illegal shit around here!" Beula might have been about twenty eight, but looked like she had been doing laundry in the sun by hand for about forty years. There was also something genetically improbable about the way her features fit together… or rather did not quite fit together. Hard to pinpoint, but very disturbing. Even though she was essentially normal, proportionally, Beula reminded me of an old toy from my childhood, Mr. Potato Head. If you could stick the eyes in the ear-hole, put the nose on sideways, and peg the mouth up around the eyebrows, the final creation would give a rough impression of Beula Mae, sister of Darrell, niece of Uncle Clitoris, first cousins to the entire state of Arkansas and probably a half-dozen domestic sheep.

Darrell turned toward his sister, and we saw his amiable hillbilly demeanor turn dark, "Girl, I said put that tape on, now! You got one minute till I bust a welt on your noggin'! Now git!" Darrell resumed his friendly tone with us as Beula retreated to the projection room to do Darrell's bidding. "Sorry for the wait, folks. Won't be but a minute till we get you 'zackly what you come in here fer. You're gonna love this... got us a couple of hot little honeys that don't know a pecker from a pickle. But they shore is about to find out! Har!" Darrell had another self-induced fit of laughter, equally amused with child abuse as he had been previously with shovel-murder. Diverse sense of humor, I supposed.

We could hear Beula Mae in the back, still roundly cursing Darrell while firing up the computer projector and focusing the big blue 'no signal' square on the screen in front of us. The three of us looked at one another with the silent message, *'Are we ready for this?'* The answer written across each face was unconvincing. But choices were limited, so we turned our attention to the flashing computer image that Beula was manipulating to select a file from a frightfully long list of titles that included '*Little Debbie's First Donkey*', '*Junior Pageant Dressing Room*', and '*Fun with Dick and Jane*'. Beula Mae drifted the mouse pointer over '*Leena and Teena Lose Their Lunch Money*' and clicked the file into view on the screen.

Leena and Teena flashed to life, walking along the sidewalk in front of the Eleanor Roosevelt Middle School campus. I recognized the setting from an east side school in a middle-class neighborhood. Leena and Teena looked like they did indeed qualify for enrollment in that level, although their faces were both slathered with rouge and lipstick to mimic the makeup artistry of a New Orleans hooker. Predictably, they both were adorned with short plaid skirts, and had their hair braided into two adorable little pigtails that stuck out sideways from their heads. They clutched their books as they strolled along the sidewalk, talking excitedly about the trouble they were in. 'Ohmygosh, Teena, I can't believe I lost our lunch money again! That's the third time this week! Dad is going to be like super mad... and you know how he gets when he's super mad.'

Leena glanced toward the camera nervously, then turned back to Teena and delivered her first line, 'Jeez, I know, Teena. He gets so weird when we screw up like this. He's like really scary sometimes. What are we going to do?'

The general direction of the production was now transparent. I supposed the assbags that produced this trash could not be bothered with nuances like creativity or originality. True to our low expectations, the two teenaged girls just happened to pass a parked van, windows down, with two sleaze-balls leering out at them. 'Hey, Cutie Pie. What's the trouble?' The camera panned around to view both jerkwads, grinning fiercely in anticipation of destroying two young lives. We recognized the two assholes. They were both in the room with us.

On the big screen, Tommy stole a glance at the camera operator before turning stiffly toward the girls, clearing his throat, and spewing his line far too loudly, like a third grader in his first school play. 'YOU TWO SURE ARE CUTE! HOW BOUT WE HELP YOU GET YOUR LUNCH MONEY BACK!'

165

I turned to Tommy, who stood near the door at the back of the room, grinning. "Impressive!" I gave him a thumbs up gesture. He missed the sarcasm, and stood transfixed by the performance he had had probably witnessed fifty times. The scene continued to unfold with painful predictability.

'Golly, mister, I don't know. Like, we don't even know you guys. But we sure could use some money for lunch so we don't get in trouble again. I guess it would be OK. C'mon Teena, let's go.' At this cue, Darrell leaps out of the passenger door and slides the van side door open, and the three of them duck inside the back of the van while the unseen cameraman awkwardly clambers into the passenger seat vacated by Darrell, then turns the camera around to view the scene in the back of the van.

Claudia gave me look of complete disgust that also conveyed and additional meaning. '*I can't take this anymore. We have to do something.*' Even though I understood the look, she beat me to the punch, and spoke up in her best Chessie Beretta dialect, "Splendid, Darrell! Simply beautiful! How ever did you manage to find such delightful girls? And so talented! You would think they had been doing this sort of thing for years."

Darrell beamed, "Ah, hell, probably some of 'em has! Just the first time they ever got paid fer it, I recon."

I decided to try to avoid subjecting Claudia to any more of Darrell's artistry. "Could we ask your sister to pause the video a moment while we discuss business?"

Darrell looked hurt, "Ah, hell. I s'pose. Don't ya'll want to see the rest of the video? It gets real good in a minute when they commence to earnin' their lunch money."

Claudia slid over to where Darrell was seated, slipped her arm through his and whispered loudly enough for me to hear, "Maybe later, stud. Right now I'm not sure how much more of this I can stand." That was probably very true, but I doubt if Darrell got the picture, because he looked like he might melt into his seat.

"Oh, Baby. You got a hot one here, Baldwin! We could make some money with her! Might be fun, too!" I wanted to castrate him right there, but struggled not to expose the act that Claudia was performing with convincing style. "Beula, shut 'er down a minute while we talk business. Go feed the fuckin' horses or somethin'. Har!" Darrell fell into another of his irritating self-induced humor fits. "Get it, Barnum? Fuckin' horses? Har!"

"Brilliant, Mr. Hatfield." Mercifully, Teena and Leena faded to black just as their outer garments had begun to fly off in the back of the van. "Tell me, how many productions have you made with girls like this?"

Darrell looked suspicious for a moment, and I realized the question might sound like a trap. Claudia picked up on his expression and added quickly, "Oh, I think we could find a market for say fifty or so, don't you think, Mr. Chauncey?"

I really hoped Darrell did not have the chance to make fifty of these videos, but I followed Claudia's lead, "No doubt, no doubt... of course, we would need assurances that all the other girls meet the age criteria."

Darrell lit up like Cindy Loo Who on Christmas morning, "Fifty tapes! Ah, hell, I only got maybe thirty with the young ones, but I could prob'ly step up the recruitin'... right Tommy? Course, I might have to get the boy some help..."

Tommy was still leaning against the wall in back, but had lost his stupid grin, "I don't need no help." Sounded like Tommy had turf issues.

I considered slowly, "Well, I don't know... we still haven't seen the 'actresses' in the other videos. How do we know they meet the client's preferences?" I was doing my best '*Let's mull this over*' act, but Darrell was not about to let this deal slip away.

"You got my personal *guar–on–tee* they ain't a single one over fifteen. Ah hell, I got five or six about twelve, if you like that stuff. Course, they's kinda rough in the actin' department. Always bawlin' fer their mommas and that shit. Gawd, it's like listenin' to a bunch of babies a'sqwualin' sometimes." He shook his head in disbelief at the immaturity of twelve year old girls being abused by grown men. Darrell was one sensitive human being. "Course, Beula Mae could run through 'em all and you can take a look. I got the time if'n ya'll do!"

I pondered the situation with deliberate concentration, knowing that there was no need to scrutinize any more of Darrell's handiwork. Regardless, I felt sure he would supply us with ample material for prosecution. The fact that he was stupid enough to incriminate himself in the videos was a bonus. "No, that won't do. Bit short on the schedule, you see. What do you think, Chessie?"

She was equally deliberate, as she studied Darrell like he was up for bid at an auction. "Well, I suppose we could take Mr. Hatfield at his word. No sense doing business with someone you can't trust. Besides, I don't think Darrell here would double-cross us, now that he has his heart set on making a Chessie Beretta video. Right, Sugar?" Claudia nuzzled up to Darrell's ear and purred. It was hard to watch.

"Good gaddamn deal, then! Let's talk money, Chauncey. Whadda you got in mind? These are top-shelf productions, now. You seen that. Got a shitload of overhead with all this setup, so I cain't turn 'em over fer nothin'." Darrell was putting on the hard sell. He sensed the buyer was hooked, and he was setting me up for a fleecing.

"Oh, I'm sorry, Mr. Hatfield, I assumed you were aware of the fee. Industry standards, so to speak. No bother, perhaps the negotiation process will be to my benefit. Haven't had the opportunity to close a deal that way in years! How delightful."

"Industry standard? What kind of 'standard' we talkin' about here? I mostly deal with truck-stop video rooms and adult porn palaces... shit like that. I don't usually get into the 'industry standard' type deals." Darrell was clearly off-guard now, trying to figure out a way back to his original financial position, fearful of missing out on a deal that could launch his operation into the bigtime.

I considered this for a moment, then turned to Mack and Claudia. "Perhaps you two could be so kind as to bring in the compensation for Mr. Hatfield's efforts, while we continue our chat?"

Mack got up without hesitation and headed toward the door at the back where Tommy was still leaning against the wall. Claudia shot me a quick glance of concern, not certain whether it was a good idea to leave me alone with Psycho Stud. I tried to reassure her, "Bring in two units, in case Mr. Hatfield has more of his marvelous video than he anticipates." I then turned to Darrell, "And perhaps your personal assistant would escort my associates? We wouldn't want anything 'unusual' to happen when we are so close to closing this arrangement." Darrell nodded to Tommy who joined Mack and Claudia as they headed out to retrieve the two briefcases from the trunk of Mack's black sedan.

I returned my attention to Scumbag, who was nearly drooling. I resumed negotiations, "Where were we? Ah, yes... compensation for your talented efforts. Always best to keep these little negotiations private, don't you think?" I was glad that Beula Mae was still out entertaining the ponies next door.

"Oh, yeah. Got it. Good move sendin' 'em all out for the loot." He actually used the word loot. Hadn't heard that in a while.

"Let me bring you up to speed on the typical transaction in this scenario. I look over the product... as we just did... and if satisfied... which I am... a sum of two-thousand dollars per original video is then transferred into your hands at approximately the same time as the videos transfer to mine. Of course, if this sum is not acceptable, I completely understand. You do have 'overhead' to consider, I'm sure."

At the first mention of the price Darrell's eyes widened and he slid forward in his seat. Poker would not be his strongest game. "Well, I dunno. I 'spect that would work OK. 'Course, you're gonna buy the whole lot, right?" His genetically impaired mental gear-works were grinding away, probably trying to calculate the windfall.

"And what quantity would that entail, precisely? Remember, the videos must meet my client criteria to be acceptable."

Darrell got up and hustled over to the projection room and began sorting through racks of DVD cases. In a minute he had counted out thirty-two disks that featured underage girls lured into his warehouse and videotaped. "Looks like we got about thirty-two." Good Lord, he could count higher than I expected. Never even had to take off his shoes.

"Very well. Twenty-five then." I replied in a flat tone.

"'Scuse me? We got thirty-two."

"Yes, I heard. Pull seven of the tapes with the 'older' girls out, if you please. Keep the youngest ones for me. You see, I like to conduct business in standard units. Fifty-thousand for twenty-five videos. When you have managed to produce another twenty-five, I will consider another unit of transaction. That's the protocol. Acceptable, Mr. Hatfield?"

He grumbled a bit, summing up the cash he was about to lose out on from the sale of the additional seven disks, but decided not the push his luck. "I 'spect that'll be fine." He finished sorting out seven of the 'elder actresses', set them back in the rack, and placed the twenty-five remaining videos in a small black zippered bag. "Twenty-five of the finest teenage poon-tang tapes ever made!" he said proudly as he zipped the pouch shut and set it in front of himself, not yet willing to hand over the goods till the cash appeared.

"Excellent. Now, prior to payment, we must be absolutely clear on the terms of this agreement. As I see your business runs in different social circles, I will clarify the requirements, so there can be no misunderstandings." Mack, Claudia, and Tommy returned to the room with the two briefcases as I spoke. Beula had finished her pony duties and slid into the room just behind them, eyeing the briefcases as she sidled toward the office wall. Mack set both cases on the table, with the handles facing me. We had arranged earlier for the money-filled case to be set on my right side. I double checked to make sure I spotted the little red dot.

Mack stood back with Claudia to allow the conversation to continue. "Two units, Mr. Chauncey. No problems in the parking lot." By this I assumed he meant no sign of any unusual vehicles or people hanging around. I doubted anyone was going to jump Mack, even if they did know he was carrying around fifty-thousand in cash. Some things are just not worth fifty grand. But still, I wondered why the big thug they called Brokov was nowhere to be seen.

Tommy added, "Yeah, like he said... coast is clear." Tommy apparently decided that his role as Mack's counterpart on Darrell's behalf needed to be supported by mimicking Mack's diligence to check the surrounding area before committing to questionable business dealings.

I glanced at Claudia and caught her nearly imperceptible nod as I lowered the left-hand briefcase to the floor at the side of the table, centered the other one with the tiny red dot on the handle and clicked open the latches. I did not have to spin the small locking dial mechanism, as we had set this one to remain open. The twin briefcase on the floor was locked. I looked over the cash for a moment without expression, then spun the case backwards for Darrell to inspect. "Well, Mr. Hatfield?"

Darrell Hatfield stood with his mouth open, tobacco stained teeth in danger of plinking out onto the floor. "Whoa!"

"Mr. Hatfield?"

"Huh?" Darrell stood transfixed by the stacks of hundreds.

"This is the part of our little play where you pull out whichever bundles you choose, count the bills, then multiply be the number of bundles to arrive at fifty-thousand dollars. It's all part of the dance, so don't miss your cue. Chop-chop. Time is money."

Darrell gradually fought through his stupor, but kept his eyes fixed without blinking at the bundles of hundred dollar bills stacked neatly inside the briefcase. Beula moved forward to see what had captured her brother's attention and peered over his shoulder, "Hole - ee - shit, look at all that money, Darrell! There must be five hundert fuckin' dollars in there!" Beula was one sharp cookie.

Darrell looked up at his sister and a devious smile crossed his lips. "That's right, Beula, honey, and half of it is gonna be yours. But now I need you to go into the projector room and look around for that one tape I forgot."

Beula looked confused. "What tape you talkin' about, Darrell. Git it yer own damn self."

"Ah, hell no, I gotta close this deal here and count your money, Sugar. You remember, the one in the blue case. Git in thar and fetch it fer Bartholomew here."

Once Beula stormed her way safely out of earshot, Darrell began flipping through one of the wads, counting bills. He needed to count out loud to keep track, and the effort got him completely lost and he had to restart the count twice. He flipped one bundle to Tommy to help and restarted again. Darrell waited for Tommy to catch up and then said, "I got two-thousand, Tommy. Whaddya get?"

Tommy scratched his head. Counting was difficult for Tommy, especially with only one good hand and one eye swollen shut. "Really, boss? You count fast. I only got twenty in mine."

"Wow... really, dipshit? Twenty hundred-dollar bills, right? Whassat add up to, Numbnuts?"

Tommy looked confused, then worked on the math for a while. "Two-thousand bucks! Oh, you was talkin' about the total. I get it."

Darrell hung his head and shook it, "Jesus Christ, Tommy, you're a fuckin' moron." Darrell quickly stacked the bundles into five piles of five bundles each. Darrell's intellectual agility was only marginally above Tommy's, but his financial interests were at stake, so he was motivated to perform the task accurately. "Fifty large as promised. Pleasure doin' business with you, Bernard." Darrell replaced the stacks in the case and shut the lid. I saw him eyeing the other case sitting on the floor. "So, what's with the second one?"

"Ah, well, you see, my sources told me you were a major producer. It had been my hope to secure fifty videos on this excursion. Another unit, you see. We do all our business in units; makes bookkeeping so much simpler." Darrell looked sad to lose the other briefcase. One hundred thousand was much nicer than fifty thousand. A brief look came across his face that send a chill through me. I think Claudia may have caught it too, because I saw her move closer to Mack at that instant. I knew the look. Predatory. Greedy. Darrell was undoubtedly weighing his options and considering how to neutralize the three of us, take both briefcases, resell the video disks, and live happily ever after. He was not a hard man to read.

Then he looked up at Mack. The passing look of devious plotting turned to a mixture of disappointment and fear. Mack definitely presented a very 'clear and present danger' to his aspirations for both 'units' as I had designated the briefcases.

"As I was saying, Mr. Hatfield, as you know, the videos themselves have nowhere near this value. It's the original we are willing to pay for. The *exclusive* rights, of course. I'm sure you understand, if my clients are to profit from this investment, we can't have competition from the producer, now can we?" I waited for Darrell to catch up. He was not as quick to catch on as it might have been with more intelligent life forms.

"Oh, yeah. No, we don't never do none of that. Them is all yours now."

"And just to be sure we do not find our property floating around on someone else's website, please do me the favor of deleting these twenty-five files from your computer memory. Now, Mr. Hatfield?" I looked expectantly, to judge his response. I guess it was overkill, but I really did not want these poor girls to suffer any more humiliation than they already had faced. I knew that if we missed nailing Darrell, he would copy the videos from some back-up drive, and then make another deal for the same material.

Darrell turned toward the open office door and shouted at his sister, "Beula, while yer in there, make a list of them disks, and delete them from the backup drive next to the computer." Beula just stood, mouth open, looking confused. Darrell explained to us, "We ain't got enough room to keep 'em on the main computer, so we store 'em all on a bigass backup drive."

Beula appeared in the doorway, but made no move to delete anything. "Darrell, you ignert fuckwad, I don't know how to do that shit. I don't even know how to find that damn backup thing. Is that the black box thingy next to the screen?"

Darrell stood up like he was about to belt her across the face. "How in the hell do you dress yourself in the morning? You're dumber 'n dog dirt, Beula." Nothing like a warm family conversation. Beula stormed into the adjoining office to monkey with the computer. The office windows were made of one-way mirror glass, like that used for a police lineup room, but we could still see Beula through the doorway, fumbling with a keyboard. After a minute she screeched back at Darrell, "I got all them videos up on the list thing, Darrell. You want me to hit deplete?"

"Leave it be, Beula, before you injure yourself." Darrell jumped up and headed into the office to assist his intellectually and morally challenged sibling, and we followed behind to ensure that the list was completely 'depleted' as Beula suggested, and the recycle bin erased for good.

Mack led the way toward the office, pausing for just a moment in the doorway before stepping aside, allowing me to enter, and then Claudia bringing up the rear… no more than five seconds behind.

Mack stayed put in the doorway, looking distracted. I slid up next to Claudia. I looked at her smiling face and could tell without a word that she was pleased.

Beula stormed out around us, pissed at Darrell for being Darrell. "Do it yer own dang self, then, smartass."

Darrell highlighted the twenty-five titles we selected and turned the screen toward us to show his next move. "There they are! Twenty-five of my very best pieces of work. Sure hate to see them go down the drain, so to speak."

I spoke up quickly, "No need to hit delete, Mr. Hatfield, if you feel you would prefer to retain your creative efforts instead of the briefcase there," I motioned out to the desk top where Beula stood staring at the briefcase.

"Oh, no, no. Deals a deal. Just took a lot of time to build up that collection. Kinda gotta sedimental attachment to 'em, that's all."

"Yes, well, I can certainly understand such 'sediments', but you will always have your memories. And in the end, isn't that what really matters?" I reached across Darrell and punched the delete button. A note came up on screen, 'ARE YOU SURE YOU WANT TO DELETE THESE FILES?' Darrell made no move to stop me from confirming the final touch and the computer whirred into action as the video files were deleted. He just gave a little wistful sigh and stared at the blank space where the file names had been a second before. I thought, *'That's life, Asshole.'*

Darrell stood up and added, "Well, that's that! Pleasure doing business with you folks."

Claudia saw the move and interceded by stepping into the narrow space between Darrell and the keyboard. "Just a moment more of your time Mr. Hatfield," she said as she bent over to the keyboard, quickly navigated to the recycle bin, and repeated the delete process to permanently erase the files from Darrell's grasp.

Darrell looked distraught, but did not stop her. "You folks sure cover yer tracks, don't you?"

I stepped back from the computer and gave Claudia a nod of approval, "Thank you, Chessie. Efficient as always."

We all followed Darrell back into the main theater room where he stepped quickly back to the desk, eyeing the other briefcase like a starving dog. "Hey Tommy. When is Brokov due back from his rounds at the projects?" That rang an alarm bell. I recalled Mack's story about the brutal tactics of the gigantic Russian goon that worked for Darrell, but hadn't seen any sign of anyone but Tommy, who would have difficulty frightening a squirrel.

"Due back around now. Had to deal with that little buttwipe that owns all them dumpy-ass apartment complexes, wassisname... Julio Fernandez Shapino, or some such shit like that."

Uh oh. That little buttwipe owned my dumpy-ass apartment complex. "I believe you mean Francisco Rodriguez Hernandez Shapiro." Not sure why I corrected Tommy. Was not even sure how to get out of it now that I had.

Darrell looked up quickly, immediately on alert. "You know the turd?"

"The *turd* and I are acquainted, yes."

Darrell's suspicions deepened rapidly, "And just how would a fern feller like yerself happen to know a local creep like Shapiro?" He was staring hard at me now, trying to make sense of my association with the hometown real estate rat.

"Simple matter of business, Mr. Hatfield. I'm sure you are aware of your local competition in the adult entertainment industry?" Oh boy. Where was this going? May as go with it. Darrell was standing there in shock now... wheels spinning in place... trying to add up the new info. I tried to take advantage of his shaky mental foothold, "Good heavens, you don't know, do you?" I gave an amused chuckle and smiled at Claudia.

Darrell hit mental paydirt finally, "So that's who's been undercutting us at the truck stops! That little shit-bird has been making his own tapes!" Darrell pounded his fist on the desk. "I'll kill that goat fucker!"

"Now Mr. Hatfield, I never said that Mr. Shapiro was in the porn video business. However could you imagine such a thing? But just so you know, if he did happen to indulge in the fine art of teenage filmmaking, he would likely be very prolific at such an endeavor. In fact, I believe Mr. Shapiro could produce three times our recent transaction every year. So, I would be most upset if someone with such high potential were to be eliminated. Just business, you understand." I motioned to Mack and Claudia, and we prepared to exit the scene. Mack bent over and picked up the briefcase resting on the floor beside the desk, and I retrieved the bag of twenty-five DVD disks. I pointed to the briefcase in Mack's hand and replied, "Pity we were not able to leave that one with you as well. Ah well, perhaps next time."

Darrell was still fuming over the probability that Francisco Rodriguez Hernandez Shapiro was cutting into his market as Claudia saddled up to him and ran her fingers along the small of his back. "Mr. Hatfield? Don't forget about that video session you promised me." She led him easily by the hand into the hallway leading to the exit door and then clapped him playfully across the buttocks.

"Ah, hell no." There was Darrell's favorite chant again. "I ain't gonna forget about that promise till you get back here and show me your stuff!" If Claudia's act was meant as a distraction to keep Darrell from thinking too much about the lost briefcase, it certainly seemed to be effective. He was so distracted he could barely walk.

We spilled out into the darkness of the lot, letting the warehouse door close before looking around nervously. I decided the place was ominously quiet. "It would appear that we have passed the first hurdle. Let's not dawdle about. Might be in our best interest to make haste to the rendezvous." Earlier, we had settled on a return to Hauzer's if we managed to get out of the warehouse without being perforated. We split off and headed for our three cars. Mack jumped into his black sedan with the briefcase and I still had the DVD bag as I turned the corner of the building to my truck. Once again, I had to step back as a frothing mass of dog muscle came ripping at me. Thank God for good chain links… it held fast and Fang again back-flipped himself into a heap of spit, fur and noise, only a few feet from my truck door. But Fang did not frighten me half as much as the hulking human figure leaning casually on the building corner opposite my truck. Hannibal was inside the truck waiting, staring intensely at the massive man, with his upper lip slipping up over his canines in response. Hannibal's alarm bells were ringing as loudly as mine.

As I stepped up to my truck, the behemoth moved quickly to keep me from joining Hannibal, blocking my door. Fang continued on his rampage a few feet away, unabated. "I zee you are going zom vere. Vere might you go vit such a nice bag? Hmmm?" Russian sounding thug. Must be that Brokov fellow everybody has been worrying about. This guy made Mack look like Tiny Tim. And something told me Brokov did not want to tiptoe through the tulips with me.

I had to think of something quick, knowing that time was not my friend. Come on Chauncey, kick it into high gear and get the hell out of this… pronto. "Where I go with this bag is none of your business, Bustoff. It is the business of your employer, who has secured my professional services to deliver this little present to one of his trusted associates. He apparently lacks similar confidence in your services, and felt compelled to employ someone who has an intellectual capacity above that of a small house plant." Uh oh. That might have been over the top.

Brokov advanced to within breath-smelling range. "Maybe I zee vat you have in bag. Make zure you not ripping off boss." I knew this was taking far too much time for my own good. I was hoping Mack had seen Brokov lurking around and was circling around the warehouse for a backup. But I doubted either one of my cohorts had noticed him concealed around the corner from their cars. And that noisy damn dog would have covered up any conversation they might have picked up on. So they were likely speeding off according to plan, headed for Hauzer's Brat Haus to regroup and deal with Perez. Dickhead Darrell was undoubtedly inside fumbling with the locked briefcase that Claudia had so deftly switched with the loaded one while Mack had blocked their view at the office door for a few seconds. Darrell had no combo, but briefcase locks were not exactly bank safes. Even for a stupid dipshit like Darrell, I probably only had another minute or two to live before he came storming out of the warehouse with a wad of newspaper slips in one hand and a shotgun in the other. I was also sure the little note from Perez would not lighten his mood. No time for further sweet talk with Godzilla.

"Just Peachy, Bustoff… you win. Let's have a look at Mr. Hatfield's shipment for your approval." With that I thrust the bag toward the hulking mass, but let it drop to the pavement just as he reached for it. "How clumsy of me." Brokov bent down to retrieve the bag and I shoved his shoulders backward with all my might. It would never have worked had he been standing upright, but his stooped position put him at a disadvantage and he toppled backward a couple of staggering steps and went down in a heap. The second phase of the chain reaction kicked in on cue, and Fang was on him instantly, now that someone had finally fallen into his circle of influence. For all of Fang's former frothing madness, it did not compare to his current explosion of psychotic fury as he leaped onto the fallen thug and began playing Texas Chainsaw Massacre with Brokov's facial features.

I grabbed the bag of tapes and dove for the truck door. Hannibal was genuinely smiling as I piled in, very pleased with my maneuver. "How did we do, boy?"

"Woof." The truck actually agreed to fire up in record time, but I could see a bloody Brokov in the rear view mirror frantically extracting his truck-sized frame from the attacking dog. He lunged forward to grab the truck door, and might have gotten to it before I could peal out of the parking area, but Fang came back at him as he charged up, and the chain caught around one ankle and jerked him off his feet again… back into snapping teeth and flying dog spit.

"Zon of beetch!! Geet da fug off me!" Brokov was clawing away at the dog who was clawing away at Brokov. Heartwarming scene.

"See you, Bustoff! Have fun playing with your puppy!" Not sure that was necessary, but it was hard to resist. Good doggy.

Chapter Fifteen

Back at Hauzer's the team had beaten me to the back room, and Claudia rose to wrap me up with a tight hug and kiss as I entered. "Why, Ms. Beretta, what a pleasure to see you again."

She looked a little concerned as she let me loose, "So what happened back there? Why weren't you behind us pulling out?"

I smiled, thinking of Fang ripping away at Brokov, "Oh, I met a nice little dog and introduced him to a new friend. I think they hit it off immediately."

Claudia was not amused. "What? You were making social calls while Darrell was checking his payoff? Don't you think that was cutting it a little close?" She was upset with my cavalier attitude, which betrayed the fact that she must be getting used to having me around.

I kept up the attitude a bit longer just for fun, "No worries, my love. Could have had tea and a buttered scone, read the paper, and walked the dog before that imbecile Darrell found a way to pop the briefcase lock. Still, wish I could have seen his face when he finally succeeded. Must have been amusing. My only regret is not being able to erase all the videos, instead of just our lot. There must have been quite a few we left behind."

Claudia beamed back at me despite our failure to secure all the tapes, "My dear Mr. Chauncey, how little faith you have in the resourcefulness of your colleagues!" With that she pulled a small external computer drive out from behind her back and displayed it for my inspection.

"Well now, isn't that curious. You seem to have a computer component very similar to one I recently saw in the office of a fellow named Hatfield. Remarkable coincidence." I had seriously underestimated her again. "I see that all that schmoozing with Darrell about making a video with him had a most nefarious intent. Risky... but effective. I am duly impressed."

"As you should be. And how about Mack here blocking the doorway at the perfect time so I could switch the cases? Nice bit of timing, wouldn't you say?" Mack blushed at her compliment. "All things considered, I believe we make a most formidable team."

As much fun as this little self-promotion party was, I needed to get us back to reality quickly. "Look, that was an amazing run of luck back there, but let's not lose track of the goal here. We still have to deal with Perez… and we are probably going to have to deal with Darrell and his Russian goon sooner or later."

Mack had his head down now, at the mention of Perez. "Mr. Perez ain't too far away. I know him. He ain't gonna let that money get out of his reach. We better have our ducks lined up, 'cause Perez can be a tough character."

Almost on cue, Finnegan the Weasel shot around outside the back window, ferreting out anything suspicious, so we knew Perez's grand entrance was not far behind. We all caught the movement outside, despite the dark, and did not need to discuss the certain sequence that would follow. Mack leaned in close to me and lowered his voice, "Chauncey, there's something I need to tell you before Perez gets here…"

I smiled at Mack, "Are you keeping secrets? I am overwrought with intrigue!"

A familiar voice boomed from the hallway behind us, "Yeah, me too. What secrets you got there, Mack?" Shit, Perez was in the doorway before we knew it. Must have slipped in while we were watching Finnegan snooping around out back. Claudia jumped up from the booth to face Perez who continued, "Hiya, Sis. Nice to see you again."

But Claudia remained in Chessie Beretta mode and was unflustered. She moved an inch from Perez and stared directly into his eyes. "Unless you would like to add another welt to your lip to match the one you received earlier, you may wish to reconsider that 'Sis' business."

Perez stepped back to dodge any potential assault from Claudia and defended himself, "No offense, Ms. Beretta. Old habits die hard, you know."

"Claudia did not relent, "I would certainly *not* know. So save your pet names like '*Sis*' or '*Toots*' or '*Sugar Pants*' for your trailer trash relatives. Now sit down so we can get this over with."

Perez complied with her orders, sat in the adjacent seat, but was in the path of Delores as she lugged in a heavy tray with two pitchers of beer and a stack of frosted glasses. "Make some room, Jacko, got a load here." She slid the tray onto our table beside the briefcase and distributed the glasses around the four of us. "Givva holler when you get ready for feed." She gave Mack a wink and quick squeeze on the shoulder on her way out. We filled the glasses and all took a long pull. I was scrambling my brain to figure out what Mack might have meant about '*something I need to tell you*'. It had sounded important, but the early entrance by Perez had interrupted the conversation and I was left to guess what had changed. Too late to ask now, with Perez waiting for his big payoff.

Perez spread his hands apart and gave us the universal '*So, what happened?*' signal. I began, "Like clockwork, of course. Goods secured as promised. Briefcase switched without a hitch." Mack slid the loaded case over in front of him. I produced the bag of twenty-five DVD disks and slid them alongside the briefcase.

He selected one from the batch and held it up to read the title. "'Kimmie and Krissy Kiss a Klown'. Not that's a new one on me. Very creative." Perez pulled anther one out of the batch and inspected the title, "'Little Sis Gets a Big Surprise'. Oh, another good one… not too original, but definitely interesting." He was enjoying himself far too much for Claudia's taste.

People like Darrell Hatfield and Antonio Perez constituted the worst sort of decay of human integrity and Claudia lacked much patience in dealing with them. "Mr. Perez, if you are through arousing yourself at the expense of these children, perhaps you might explain what you intend to do with these videos?" She was in a dangerous mood, I could tell by her tone. But she seemed to have a plan, even if I had no idea how she would pull it off.

Perez responded to the inquiry with a casual shrug, "I think you can guess what happens next. I turn these little gems into a nice return on my investment. And that's the funny part! I don't got no investment!" He pulled the closed briefcase close, popped the two latches, and lost the smirk instantly. "You fuckin' losers!" Just wads of newspaper, looking very much the same as the dummy box we switched with Darrell. "Whadda fug is this shit? Somebody tryin' to get funny? Well I ain't laughin'. I ain't even smilin'. You was s'pose to drop this one on that dumbass Darrell!"

I glanced over at Claudia and she looked back at me with a bewildered expression. I asked her in confusion, "What happened? I thought you made the switch while Mack was blocking Darrell's view."

She opened her hands in front of her, perplexed as I was, "I did make the switch! I pulled up the case from the floor and swung that one down in its place before Darrell could see. I don't get it."

Everybody looked at me. I quickly went over the scene from the warehouse in my head. "I think I get it. Mack had Darrell's view blocked, but not Ms. Potato Head. Beula might have seen the switch from the office window. Remember? She stormed out of the office while we were busy deleting the videos of her and Darrell cross-pollenating themselves. Darrell's little mutant sibling was smarter than she looked. I think we are the victims of a hillbilly highjack."

Perez was fuming, "Goddamn amateurs... never should have left you bunch of losers alone with my $50K! Somebody gonna have to get my cash back by tonight. I ain't losin' no fifty grand to no inbred hillbillies."

Mack got up to address Perez. "I'll go back. My fault, boss. Should'da kept an eye on that girl. Somethin' was not right about her slinkin' around there."

I thought about that plan of action a moment. "Ummm, Mack... you forgetting one miniscule detail? There happens to be a particularly large irate Russian fellow named Brokov back there who, when finished placing duct tape on numerous open wounds, will not be particularly happy to see us again. I could imagine he will not offer complete hospitality when you go cruising back over there to inquire about why Darrell ended up getting cash instead of cannon fodder. I can hear the conversation now... *'Sorry for the mix-up Darrell... if we could just swap out your fifty thou' for these worthless stacks of newspaper, then I'll be on my way.'* No, Mack, a frontal assault is not wise. I'm afraid Mr. Perez is simply out of luck on this one. At least you have some very nice videos." I swept my arm dramatically across the bag of tapes, like Carol Merrill showing off door number three on Let's Make a Deal.

"Mr. Perez ain't out of shit, assbite. You gotta get that cash back tonight or I even the score. You got somethin' nice of mine... now I got somethin' nice of yours..," and with that, Perez swiftly withdrew an automatic pistol from his jacket and pressed the muzzle against Claudia's side. He pulled her by the arm out of the booth and let us all see the gun while keeping it aimed at her ribs. My stomach lurched.

Mack made a move toward Perez with hatred boiling out of his ears, but Perez shifted his aim to Mack while pulling Claudia toward the door. "Hold it, lover boy. I thought you were getting a little too close to these two. Now I'm startin' to get the whole picture." Perez had the gun aimed at Mack's forehead now, and Mack was frozen in mid-step, knowing Perez would not hesitate to shoot. We were having what might be described as a tense moment.

"*PING!*" What a melodious ring that a cast-iron skillet makes as it bounces off the human head. What an interesting look of utter and complete incomprehension passed across Perez's face, as his final split second of conscious awareness faded into fog, and he hit the floor in front of our booth with a dull thud, gun clattering noisily toward us.

I picked up the gun and addressed the only person left standing in the doorway. "Splendid timing Delores. Remind me never to stiff you on the gratuity. Seems you have a bit of a testy side."

"Gall dang right I got a testy side." She moved over to Mack and slipped an arm through his massive biceps and snuggled up close. Anybody point a pistol at my man, and they best check I ain't in reach of cast-iron first. Never did like that little weasel in the first place." Mack beamed back at Delores in complete admiration.

Hauzer appeared at the doorway beside Delores, surveyed her handiwork, then glanced down at the skillet still hanging at her side. "Zo, Delores, you kalunk dat fellow on da noggin?"

"You bet your wienerschnitzel I did! I knew that ratbag was no dang good when he first come in here posin' as a health inspector. Then he tries to pull his pea-shooter out and wave it around like he was some kinda gangster in a Humphrey Bogart movie. I ain't gonna tolerate that kinda bullcrap in my wheelhouse, cops or no cops."

Cops? Who said anything about cops? "Delores. Perhaps you should elaborate on your last comment." I asked her calmly.

"You know... ain't you ever seen a Humphrey Bogart movie, like Key Largo, with all them guys blasting away like they was at the shootin' range?"

I rephrased the question, "Delores, I meant the part about the police. What police?" Perez was stirring around now, trying to get a grip on reality.

Them two out in the front room. I know you said to hold off till I got the signal, but I know these two guys and promised them a free bratwurst if they would stop by. Guess I better round them up before I have to give this turkey another knot on his bean."

She spun around and disappeared into the front leaving Hauzer in the doorway. "I zure hope you got vat you need to keep dis one from coming back to get even. I don't sink he can take too much more from dat skillet."

Claudia rose up to address the two officers who scuttled into the room, wiping mustard from their faces and looking perplexed at the scene. The bigger of the two was an amiable looking character with a nametag that read Rodgers. The second one was a smaller officer was named Kirkland. They both appeared to be relatively calm... no guns drawn or nightsticks at the ready. "Gentlemen, my name is Claudia Auckland. These are my two very best friends, Mack and Chaunc... er, Bert. This groggy fellow at your feet..."

Kirkland chimed in, "…is Antonio Perez. One the filthiest scumbuckets in the state. We've been trying to pin this dirtbag down for two years. Delores says you got something might help us keep this creep on ice for a while?" As Perez wormed around to pull up on one knee, the big cop reached casually down to jerk his arms out from under him, pin them behind his back, and apply a set of handcuffs. Perez groaned and collapsed back into a heap.

"We do indeed. Just a moment gentlemen." Claudia slipped by to enter the kitchen, leaving us all smiling at each other awkwardly. The smaller cop named Kirkland looked up to Mack and gave him a long stare, then nudged his partner to get his assessment.

"Ain't that big guy familiar, Frank?" Before the cops could shift their focus to Mack, Claudia returned with a small green thumb-drive, handing it over to Officer Rodgers with a brilliant smile.

"I promise you will find the security video on this to be most helpful in your case. It was taken from that camera." She pointed at the houseplant on the corner shelf. "With a secondary angle from that camera," and pointed to a row of German beer steins along a high shelf along the opposite wall. It was still tough to spot the miniature lenses, even with directions. "I tested the audio and video quality after we installed the system, and found it to be adequate."

The cops looked intrigued. "So, whaddya got here?"

I let her roll on without interruption. She did not seem to be in any need of help from either of us. Delores and Hauzer looked on with pride from the doorway. "I believe you will find that Mr. Perez has implicated himself in an attempt to purchase a large quantity of child pornography. Fifty-thousand dollars' worth to be exact. The tapes are sitting here in this bag. We acted as purchasing agents with Mack's help, in order to put Mr. Perez out of business."

Officer Kirkland picked out one of the tapes and whistled, "Sarah's Sexy Sleepover. Wow, these kids on the cover don't look to be more'n about fifteen! What a douchebag!" Then Kirkland realized his language was a little rough and glanced at Claudia, "Sorry, ma'am." I wondered if Kansas City had purchased Kirkland at Costco. Did they have to purchase a four-pack? Were there three more Officer Kirklands out there fighting crime?

Claudia was unfazed by the officer's salty terminology and continued, "But you may be even more interested in Mr. Perez's other business dealings around town. It seems he has been a busy little boy with drug trafficking, money laundering, and loan sharking."

She most definitely had their interest now. The big cop, Frank Rodgers, moved over to our table, "We know about some of that, but have not been able to get anything substantial to put him away. You have anything we can use for the other stuff, besides the pornography tapes?"

Claudia considered this, "Possibly. I just may know one of his former employees that would be willing to supply a wealth of testimony in exchange for immunity from prosecution. Would those conditions interest you gentlemen?"

"Those conditions would most definitely interest us gentlemen... and another gentlemen known as the District Attorney, we believe. And who might this former employee be?" They looked over at Mack, but Mack remained impassive. Cops usually have pretty good instincts, and they probably suspected we could never have gotten Perez in this position without an inside man.

"Check with the DA and get back to me. For now, you will find that video in your hand to be sufficient to hold Mr. Perez, especially after he attempted to kidnap me at gunpoint. I do hope the cameras caught my good side." She pivoted dramatically to show us her right side, and we all laughed, despite the tense situation. I gave her a wink and gently held out Perez's pistol by the trigger guard for Officer Kirkland.

The cops struggled visibly to gain complete understanding of the recent events. It was not to our advantage to divulge too much, too soon, so Claudia was taking her time with full disclosure. It was a thing of beauty to behold. And I was amazed with every surprise she presented. She seemed very much in her element as she led the two officers through just enough detail to convince them they stood on the brink of a gold mine in the law enforcement business. But never stumbled into implicating any of the three of us in the process. Simply brilliant.

Big Frank was busy taking notes while his partner hauled the groggy Perez out to the squad car. "So, what we would also love to know, is who got the fifty grand? Seems like this Darrell Hatfield guy is an even bigger loser than Perez. If he is producing this garbage on that scale, then we need to crack his nut ASAP. I got two daughters myself, and this kinda crap makes me wanta puke."

"We may be able to help with that too. But you have to help us first. Call the DA." She folded her arms across her chest and waited for his response.

"What? Now?" Rodgers seemed less than enthusiastic about calling the DA at the late hour.

"Yes, officer, now. Or else let the feds take over and take all the credit. You know they will come screeching over here as soon as they catch wind of a child pornography syndicate. Think they will wait for you to follow up on these leads? No, more like, *'Thank you Officer Rodgers, you have been most helpful. Run along now and let the real agents do their job.'* Is that the way you want this to go down, Frank? Call the DA, Frank. Let's get my guy immunity first. Then I give you the porn prince on a silver platter.

Officer Frank relented, "OK, OK. I'm calling, I'm calling. But if he's out to dinner with his wife I'm gonna get my balls busted."

"And if you hand him two of the town's biggest sleaze balls in one night, do you think he minds a little dinner interruption?" Touché, Claudia.

Frank and Kirkland left us for a few minutes, presumably to make the call. The whole scenario must have begun to catch up with Mack, as he looked up with tears in his eyes. "Nobody ever done nuthin' like this for me before. I don't know whether it's gonna work, and don't even care. Feels good to be done with it all now, whatever happens. Thanks you guys for tryin'. Maybe I can get off with a year or two, if I give 'em the goods on Perez."

Claudia reached across to give Mack's enormous hand a squeeze. "Don't worry Mack. I think we can do better than that, don't you Mr. Chauncey?"

"Oh, immeasurably better. I'm sure of it. Have we ever failed you before?" I smiled and slung an arm around about half of his shoulder width. It's as far as my arm would reach. It was like hugging a mini-van.

"No, you two are the best. I dunno how to thank you for what you done."

"Mack, when the Boys in Blue get back, maybe we should leave out certain details about what Hannibal found out by the tracks. No sense giving them more information than they can handle. Get my drift?" I was envisioning Officer Frank Rodgers knocking on my door at midnight with a warrant in hand. A little matter about concealing evidence in a murder.

"Got it." As Mack responded, Frank returned to the room and sat down.

Claudia smiled brightly and addressed him with complete confidence, "Let me guess... the DA says to make sure the evidence is solid and then threaten to arrest us all if we don't hand it over immediately." She continued to smile at Frank as if she had heard the whole conversation and found it deeply amusing.

Frank frowned, "Well, yeah. Pretty good summary. Sorry I couldn't get your guy immunity. Did my best, but the DA took a hard line and..."

Mack looked up at Claudia, clearly nearing panic mode, but Claudia stepped up to where Frank had plopped down at the table and placed a soft hand on his shoulder, continuing to look amused. "Let's skip that part and cut to the chase, OK Frank? The longer we stall with meaningless gibberish, the more likely it will be that I might forget the name of our guy who worked for Perez... or where Hatfield is making those videos. Arresting us will get you nowhere and we all know it. We called you, remember?"

Frank looked up and smiled, thought about it a second, then gave up. "Well, he told me to try. I had to give it a shot."

"Of course you did. We understand, it's your job. Now... immunity for our friend?"

Frank resigned himself to being outmaneuvered and gave in without any further fluster. "Yeah, DA's good with that... providing, of course, your guy has the goods on Perez and the security tape backs up your story. And there's that issue with the sleaze bucket that is making this crap. Might go a long way if we were to nail him in the process."

I had remained silent for a long time, happy to sit back and enjoy watching Claudia conduct the inquiry like a concert maestro. But she glanced over to me as if to say, *'Jump in here any time, Chauncey. No sense in me having all the fun.'*

I took the hint, "Officer Rodgers.... let me assure you that we would all like to see the producer of this depravity put behind bars so he can experience the 'receiving' end of his endeavors. But after our actions earlier this evening, my guess would be that Darrell Hatfield and his cross-bred associates are in the process of relocating their enterprises."

Officer Rodgers became immediately attentive. "And what would give you that impression?"

"Judging by our failed attempt to double-cross the little rodent by switching the payoff briefcase, I would imagine he now realizes that we were less than upstanding business associates, and is very likely putting the pieces of the puzzle together. Even with his severely limited mental capacity, our dear friend Darrell is bound to conclude that the jig is up, so to speak."

Frank mulled this over. "That means he's likely to pull up roots and run before the next shoe falls."

I agreed, "Yes, before the next shoe falls across his throat, I would imagine."

Frank continued to contemplate the potential loss of half the prize. "You know where this creep Darrell is working?"

"Why, we just happen to have come from there. It would be an honor to serve as your tour guide." I bowed graciously and swept my hand toward the door. "Your limo or mine?"

"Mine is a little packed with your buddy Perez right now. I can call for a backup car to pick you up while we move out."

"Brilliant. But you may want to watch out for a large, badly chewed Russian named Brokov. I believe you will find him to be in ill-humor. Oh, and a large guard dog with a bad disposition toward visitors."

Frank was now lost again, just when he thought he was getting the full picture. "Who the fuck is Brokov? I thought this guy was a skinny punk named Darrell."

"Yes, well, Darrell seems to have employed a rather large Russian primate to guard his interests. Never mind, you might find it useful if we just led you in. We can point out the various pitfalls as they appear. I think it wise to move now and talk later, unless you want to start from scratch to find Darrell Hatfield." Claudia, Mack and I got up to go.

Frank just shrugged and went with the flow. "OK. You three lead us in. But stay back in your vehicle once we get at the scene. I'll give you a walkie-talkie on my channel, if you see anybody run, or see that fucking guard dog, or the big Russian, you let me know. Got it?" He pulled a hand-held radio from his vest, set the frequency, and handed it to me. He keyed the microphone on his unit and mine let out a static bark that indicated they were linked up.

"Oh, goody. Do we get a badge?" I smiled despite being a little apprehensive about returning to the warehouse; police escort or not.

Officer Frank grinned and replied, "Badges? You don't need no stinking badges!" He barked out a big laugh at his own joke and headed out past Delores and Hauzer who were watching the whole proceedings from the next room.

Delores blocked Mack as he went by and put a hand up to his face. "You take care of yourself, Fred Flintstone. No heroics out there, OK? I'll have something warm ready for you when you get back." I doubted she was talking bratwurst. Mack gave her a quick smooch and hug and we went out the front door to the street.

There in my pickup was my buddy Hannibal, head stuck out the window, waiting patiently for us to conclude our business so we could start our next adventure. He would not have to wait long. "Let's take the pickup. Hannibal is ready for action."

"Woof," he responded. Well said.

So, we piled into the front seat, with Claudia squeezing in the middle. Hannibal perched himself atop Mack's lap and stuck his head out the passenger door window. I glanced back at the squad car and gave the thumbs up to Officer Frank and his partner Kirkland. In response to my thumbs up I saw Perez snarl at us from the back seat. He might have wanted to flip us off, but that would have been difficult with his hands cuffed behind his back. After all we had been through together, I blew him a kiss and waved as we pulled away from the curb.

Chapter 16

On the way to the warehouse our caravan was joined by an impressive number of conspicuously non-descript cars with multiple antennae and government issued license plates. Must be a slow crime evening in Kansas City. Everybody wanted to get in on the fun. A few marked patrol cars merged into the lineup as well, so the final tally as we wheeled into the warehouse parking lot looked a funeral procession for the mayor. As we approached the site, I picked up the radio Officer Rodgers had supplied and keyed the mike, "This is the warehouse, Frank. The door will be locked, I suspect. I do not know where the other exits might be. You will want to avoid that dog around the left corner of the building, he has anger management issues. There should be three or four people inside... and a pony."

Frank came back immediately, "A what?!"

"A small horse, Frank. As far as we know, it is not dangerous." Poor Frank.

"Jesus!"

"There may a large person in there too, significantly larger than the small horse. His name is Brokov, but he prefers to be called Asswipe. Now *he* is definitely dangerous. You can probably identify him by the large quantity of bloody gauze bandages he likes to wear." Possibly too much information for Frank to assimilate, but it was difficult to resist.

"Copy. Sit tight." With three people and a dog in the front seat of my old Ford, we were most definitely sitting very tight. The squad car regatta sailed off in alternate sequence, one screeching around the right side of the warehouse, the next going left, until a more or less continuous line of police vehicles encircled the entire building. We remained in front, just outside the circle, while watching Officer Costco back their car up to the front door. Frank jumped out, looped a chain around the door handle, and Kirkland quickly pulled away with the large metal door clanging noisily behind him.

A dozen officers drew their weapons, gushed into the opening left by the door, and began shouting unintelligible commands to whoever might care to abide by their instructions. We kept a look-out for any activity from around the far sides of the building, but despite a great deal of strategic positioning and expertly aimed weaponry, no one killed anyone else, not even by friendly fire. After a long while, Officer Frank Rodgers, Kansas City's finest, came dragging himself out of the doorway, looking dejected. He came up to our rig and leaned in.

"Looks like we missed the party. Nobody home and place is more or less cleaned out. They must'a worked fast. We got the pony, but I doubt if he will tell us much. Computers, tapes, everything is gone. Good chance your friend Darrell Hatfield and his crew cleared out of town entirely, now that we tipped our hand. Maybe we should have held back. Damn!"

I felt badly for Frank. He had rolled the dice on the chance that he could wrap up the sweep with two miserable pieces of scum in one night. But, it looked like it was not to be in the cards. "Officer Rodgers, I am truly sorry. You did the right thing. Darrell would have cleared out anyway. He probably moves every few months just to stay ahead of the game." It was getting a little warm and stinky inside the truck with Hannibal fidgeting to get out. "Mind if we get out for a minute? I think my four-legged associate may need to mark some territory."

"Huh? Oh... yeah. Sure. Looks like the scene is secure enough." Frank barked orders into his radio and all the parade contestants began to grudgingly break down their positions and pack away their toys.

The three of us popped open the doors and Hannibal burst out to conduct his own Crime Scene Investigation. Mack, Claudia and I ambled around aimlessly to stretch out, without much energy in our step. Mack was thinking about missing out on Darrell. "You know, Chauncey, I'm glad to see Perez in cuffs, but I don't feel too hot bout that other punk getting out of the net. I sure would like to bust his chops for all that shit he's been doin' to them kids. It ain't right."

Claudia put an arm through his arm and tried to cheer him up. "Mack, you did a great thing back there, getting Perez off the street. You can't solve all the problems of the world in one day. Maybe we will get another chance at Darrell if we keep our eyes open."

"Naw, I don't think so. He's gonna bolt. It's not like he won't get wind of this little tea party here." Mack swept his arm around to indicate the Kansas City law enforcement spectacle. "Hell, he might be watchin' the whole scene right now." We all automatically looked around to see if Darrell and his mis-aligned sister were peering at us from behind some nearby curtained window. No such luck. Not much chance Darrell would take the fifty-thousand and move into the warehouse next door.

Hannibal was indeed busy marking territory, primarily tires of police cars, much to the displeasure of their occupants. But I grew a little concerned when he disappeared around the left side of the building, in the general direction of Fang. I had not heard any noise from the dog when the police set up positions around the corner, so I was guessing he had gone the way of Darrell and crew. Still, I felt compelled to follow along and be sure Hannibal did not cross paths with the canine rototiller. Brokov would have also advised against it, I imagine.

"Be right back. Better check on Hannibal." I left the team and strode off around the left corner and found Hannibal sniffing around the spot where I had shoved Brokov backward into the teeth of Fang. The chain was no longer around the metal pipe where it had been fixed earlier. There were specks of blood and shredded clothes in a wide circle. It looked like something had exploded. Or someone had exploded. Hannibal lost interest in the spot and continued on around the warehouse where he cut through the circle of cop cars and wandered out toward the tracks. "C'mon, boy. Let's head for home."

Hannibal turned back for a second, but calmly walked on toward the tracks without regarding my request. Might need to consider doggy school for this guy. Definitely the independent type. "C'mon buddy. Let's go see Cecelia." I knew this would do the trick. But all I got was another disdainful glance, and onward he trudged, nose to the ground. Hmmm. I followed along now, ceasing to interrupt him. I had done it again. Begun to think of Hannibal as an ordinary dog. This was one of my new partners here, and I was treating him like some brainless mutt. Bad call, Chauncey. Get it right. "Sorry, boy. Lead on." I got a more tolerant glance, and on he went. No one from the police force paid us the slightest attention. The show was over and the adrenaline level was falling back under the Chernobyl levels, so they were all busy packing their anti-tank artillery back into camouflaged foam-lined cases.

Hannibal cut across the first set of tracks and wandered behind long rows of boxcars that sat idly waiting for their next assignments. Their graffiti coated doors stood wide open, showing potential thieves that there was nothing there to steal. Hannibal turned left between two long lines of boxcars, all standing quiet and empty, and kept moving up the line between the tracks until he stopped at one particular boxcar that looked exactly like all the other boxcars. Except for one detail that was easy to spot... this one had the doors closed tightly. Interesting. Hannibal looked up at the closed door. "Woof." I began to get a queasy feeling. The queasy feeling got considerably worse when a very large man covered in blood-soaked bandages stepped out from behind the adjacent boxcar and pointed a very large automatic handgun at me.

"Zhut dog up now or I blast to hell!" He shifted the gun to Hannibal who sat down quietly and waited my response.

It had gotten me this far, so Chauncey kicked in despite my reservations. "Bustoff! What a pleasure! All this time I thought you were out looking for Moose and Squirrel! Cut yourself shaving?"

"Maybe now I zhoot you before I zhoot dog." He shifted his aim to me as Hannibal waited silently.

I leaned against the boxcar and continued, "There are two essential flaws in your logic, Bustoff. Allow me to illuminate you. First, my associate here has already 'zhut up' making any action to silence him superfluous. Your second error occurred when you assumed I was stupid enough to believe you would discharge a rather large firearm within earshot of the entire Kansas City police force. I assume you noticed the Macy's Day Parade over there?" I pointed in the direction of the warehouse, hidden behind the row of train cars. I shoved my hands into my pockets and waited for Brokov to make his next move. It did not take long. Despite heavy gauze wraps, he quickly holstered the pistol, reached for his belt, and withdrew a formidable hunting knife that he wielded in my face to make his point.

"Knife more quiet. Brokov cut off head of stupid English pig!" He moved dangerously close with knife at the ready. Hannibal sat tight but let out a low guttural growl. I reached up casually and rapped a few times on the boxcar door. "Darrell? You home, Sweetheart? It's me, Chauncey. Be a love and come out here for a moment. You need to collar your gorilla."

The door slid sideways and revealed a boxcar full of the warehouse's former contents, along with Beula Mae the Hillbilly Hose Queen. Darrell stood in the doorway, "Chauncey, you gotta have mush fer brains, rolling back out here with all your law buddies. You miserable piece of shit, stealing my best movies and makin' off with the money to boot. Now I gotta clear out just when business was startin' to peak. You rat fucker!" Gee, not at all the reunion hug I was expecting. And why is he pissed about losing the money? I thought he had the money after all. Darrell motioned to his goon, "Brokov!" and with one swift motion I was launched into the boxcar next to beautiful Beula who was picking her nose and examining the results. I landed with a thud and Brokov followed up next to me with one giant leap. He was still wielding the knife as he stood over me.

"Boss, you want I zhud kill pig now?" There was gleam in his eyes that was disturbing, but Hannibal had resumed barking outside, giving Darrell a choice of which problem to dispatch first.

"Brokov! Shut that mutt up before he brings the whole world running to rescue this a-hole." With that command Brokov turned to leap back down to the tracks with knife in hand, ready to deal with what he assumed was an ordinary medium-sized noisy brown dog. Bad call, Brokov. Just as he squatted down to make the jump, I placed my foot squarely in the center of his butt cheeks and shoved with all my might. For the first time, I was glad that there was another train car on the opposite track.

Brokov launched headfirst into the solid steel side of the adjacent boxcar and plummeted to the gravel by the rail. In a split second Hannibal had him by the crotch and was vigorously trying to rip a chunk of tender flesh loose. The knife had flown clear after initial impact of Brokov's cranium to Pittsburgh steel, so Hannibal seemed to be enjoying a distinct advantage of dealing in close quarters with a semi-conscious unarmed man who, despite the collision, was becoming increasing aware of the immediate danger of becoming a soprano in the church choir. He punched wildly and kicked at Hannibal, making repeated contact with various railway components such as boxcar ladders, railroad rails, and creosote-soaked ties. But as nearly as I could tell, he was having limited success at preventing Hannibal from his appointed duty to separate Brokov from his jewels.

"My word, Mr. Hatfield, it seems as if your man Bustoff there has met with some difficulty. He may need our assistance." I rose to my knees but came up short when Darrell pulled a short-nosed pistol from his belt and pointed it at my head.

"Sit down, asshole. Nobody's gonna pay any attention to a little pop coming from inside a boxcar. Screw that Russian asshole."

"Really, Darrell we must work on vocabulary. That was two 'assholes' in one paragraph. Three, counting you."

Darrell seemed to be in a foul mood. He simply refused to work on his language skills, and raised the pistol to my chest. "I should'a done this back in the warehouse, you miserable fuck." Well, it had been a good run. We did our best but this was not one that Chauncey or Beretta or even Mack could get us out of. Still… never hurts to try.

"Just one quick question before I check out of the picture, Mr. Hatfield. Do me the honor of explaining your earlier comment about 'making off with the money to boot.' If we ended up with a case full of newspaper, and you ended up with a case full of newspaper, then who has the fifty thousand dollars? We assumed your beautiful and talented sister pulled the double switch after we did. Perhaps we should clear up the location of the cash before I part company, just in case I can be of some assistance."

Darrell took offense at my implication, "You can go straight to hell in a shit bucket. Beula never took that money, did you, Darlin'?"

Beula had abruptly stopped picking her nose and looked over to me and Darrell with an incredulous look on her unusual face. At least I think it was incredulous. With Beula it was difficult to read, among all the other irregularities. "Darrell, you piece of shit! Fifty-thousand bucks? You told me we was making five-hundert! And I was getting' only two-fifty fer my part. You shitweed, you was gonna cheat me again, wasn't you?" She reached into a cardboard box and came at Darrell with a color printer we had seen earlier in the warehouse office. She must have practiced a bit, because she seemed to have a natural talent for slinging that unit around the boxcar by its cord and laid it upside of Darrell's head with impressive accuracy. The box exploded sending ink cartridges, plastic, and paper flying in all directions. One beautiful moment of sibling rivalry. Darrell went down for the count. He crossed the wrong chick, for once, and paid a steep price.

Beula just sat and began to cry as I picked up Darrell's gun up from the deck. I doubted if I would need it, unless Brokov got loose from Hannibal. But I held on to it for good luck. "Beula, I think you will find the officer who arrives here in a few minutes to be most understanding if you are willing to be honest with him about your business dealings. Can you do that, Beula?" It was easy to see her as partly the victim of Darrell's weird obsessions, despite her apparent complicity with whole operation. She nodded and sat crying quietly with her head down.

I pulled the police radio out of my jacket and held it up. "Officer Rodgers, Chauncey here. Send a few troops over to the tracks. I think we have what you are looking for. Over. What's your twenty? Ten-Four." I never learned proper police radio protocol.

The radio crackled back, "On the way. Be careful."

"Roger, Rodgers." I just could not let that one go by. Airplane was one of greatest ridiculous movies ever made. I had seen it too many times, apparently.

And just when I was feeling like the world order had been restored... that Perez was rubbing his head in the back of a cruiser, Darrell was unconscious at my feet, Beula was turning State's witness, Claudia was safe and still speaking to me, and Mack appeared to be free to start his life over again with his newfound sweetheart... here comes Brokov clawing his way up the open door of the boxcar, dragging a snarling Hannibal behind him by teeth that were firmly imbedded in his left butt cheek. He had given up on ridding himself of the dog, and decided to murder me in spite of the distraction.

"Brokov kill you now!" He was panting and bleeding and struggling mightily to overcome the effects of his previous injuries by Fang, his split skull from head-butting the boxcar, and the counterweight effect of a forty-pound dog hanging from his buttocks. His progress was decidedly slow getting the murder thing accomplished. Plus, I had a gun pointed at him, in the unlikely event he succeeded in gaining my boxcar elevation.

"Bustoff, how's it going there? Can I give you a hand up? Please try to keep it down… your friend Darrell is napping." I pointed at his inert boss while keeping the gun aimed carefully at his enormous head that kept bobbing up and down in the framed doorway.

"You son of pig! You vill die. And dog vill die. And den pretty little friend vill die!" He was truly pathetic. But persistent. Had to give him that. It would be shame to shoot him after all that effort. But still, it would beat the alternative if he got a hold of me. Brokov gave a mighty heave and shoved his torso up onto the deck of the boxcar bringing Hannibal up with him, still clinging tenaciously to his prize. Oh, well. Time to fish or cut bait. I raised the gun to fire as a dark flash appeared in the doorway, and a massive hand grabbed the back of Brokov's belt and held him flat to the boxcar deck. Hannibal immediately let go of his butt-steak and trotted over by my side to watch the next part of the action. Mack launched himself up onto Brokov's back and sat astride his quarry, smiling at me.

I smiled back. "Hi'ya Mack. Welcome to Mardi Gras. Thought you would never make it."

"Heard the dog. Figured you might could use a hand." He held fast to Brokov who was furiously trying to roll over and fight Mack. Brokov's engine was running on fumes, but he was one enormous human and Mack was beginning to have difficulty keeping control.

Brokov slung an arm free and struck Mack hard across the face, sending him backward toward the back of the car. Mack stood up and checked his face casually as Brokov spun around to face his antagonist. Mack did not look like a happy camper. "You shouldn't have ought to done that, Rooskie." Brokov lurched toward Mack with fist flying, but Mack drove himself forward under full steam, hands at his sides, head lowered like a battering ram. The top of Mack's bull-like head collided with Brokov's nose with a sound like a 1972 Buick hitting a telephone pole at high speed. Brokov was already halfway comatose from the earlier impact, and this collision topped that impact by several-fold. The big thug tumbled out the open door in a heap just as a herd of uniformed officers came streaming in around the boxcar, guns drawn, shouting various commands that everyone ignored.

"Down! Everybody down!" The shouts came from Officer Rodgers, running up between the railcars, gun sweeping across every open boxcar door.

"Oh, hi Frank. Over here. Jump up here and see what we found. Just use that large Russian lump there for a boost." Frank did as instructed, and hoisted himself into the car to survey the boxes of equipment, computers, and a crying, half-witted girl of questionable ancestry. "Frank Rodgers, I would like you to meet Beula Mae Hatfield, the lovely sister of Darrell Hatfield here, who is currently unavailable for social interaction, as you can see." I pointed to Darrell's lifeless form at my feet.

Beula wiped some snot from her face with her hand, then extended it graciously to Frank. "Howdy-do, officer. That there is my scumbag brother who tried to cheat me outta my share of the porno money. You can haul his ass off and keep him for good, for all I care. He ain't worth nothin' to me."

Frank's eyes widened with anticipation. "Would you be willing to offer a statement about the type of business your brother was running?"

Beula shifted her weight onto one bare leg, gave it some thought and replied, "I recon I could do that... if'n you was to keep me outta jail fer helpin'. I never thought we orta be using them young girls, but Darrell said if'n it was good enough fer me, then they could take it too. I never thought that was right. Besides, thars a whole mess of video tapes in that box thar and maybe half of 'em has Darrell hisself a'pokin away at them girls. Them tapes orta do a heap of talkin' on their own, I figure."

"That is probably true, Beula, but we would still appreciate your testimony in exchange for lenient treatment in the legal system." Frank seemed to feel a little sympathy for Beula as well.

Beula looked up at Frank and asked, "Will you make sure Boney is OK? Could you do that for me?" We all looked each other. Who the heck was Boney? Had we missed somebody? "We had to leave him behind at the warehouse, along with Secretariat, and I kinda got attached to the little guys. They really is sweet little fellers, even if they gets little randy sometimes. Just like any other dumbass male, I s'pose. Still... gonna miss the little guys."

We got the picture. Boney the Pony. How original. I wondered what kind of psychological rehab would be required for Boney and Secretariat to become productive members of society again. Horse whispering maybe. I wondered if Boney would miss Beula, too.

Frank assured Beula the ponies would be sent to a horse recovery farm in the western part of the state, and helped her down to the tracks. They sent most of the officers over to help the paramedics hoist Brokov and Darrell into two waiting ambulances, both heavily guarded with police. I hoped they would be bandaged up, and incarcerated along with Antonio Perez for a very long time.

We three amigos spent most of the night at police headquarters, giving statements about our role in the last few days of strange happenings. They divided us up, of course, but the stories must have lined up well enough, I suspect, because we were all released just past dawn and thanked for our service to the community in busting Darrell Hatfield and Antonio Perez. It had been a very, very good day for Kansas City law enforcement, but a remarkably exhausting day for all of us.

We met out in front of the station where I let Hannibal out of the truck to pee on more squad car tires. He had been a most brilliant partner through all this. He had helped me make friends with Claudia, kept me from making bad decisions in general, and prevented a large Russian psycho from dismantling my appendages. I wondered how badly things might have gone without him.

I spoke up first as we loaded into the pickup to go retrieve our other vehicles that we had left at Hauzer's Brat Haus. "I vote for sleep. Who else?"

Claudia snuggled close to me, laid her head on my shoulder and said, "Me first."

Mack clunked his head against the window, wrapped a big arm around Hannibal, and agreed with Claudia, "Me second. G'nite." Even Hannibal laid out on Mack's lap and closed his eyes.

"Now hang on a minute here, team. How come I have to stay up and drive while you lot snore off to dreamland?" All I got was a grunt from Mack and a quick, wet kiss on the cheek from Claudia. I stopped complaining after that and drove to Hauzer's. When we got there and pulled to a stop, Mack stirred out of his stupor and ruffled Hannibal back to life. Claudia showed no signs of life, so I left her snuggled up on my shoulder while Mack fumbled around for his keys. Hannibal took over the warm spot that Mack vacated and immediately crashed back into doggy dreams.

Before I headed out, Mack leaned in the window of the truck. "Look, Chauncey, I gotta tell you somethin'." I knew what was coming from the look in his eyes.

"No, you don't Mack. Let's go to sleep. You had my back just as much as we had yours. Team effort. Let's not get all sentimental this early in the morning, OK?"

Mack smiled back in appreciation. "Hey. I was just gonna tell you you're low on gas. Better fuel up later on before you get stuck somewhere."

"Thanks, Mack. I appreciate that." I glanced down at the gauge and it was on three-quarters.

"One more thing, OK? Can we meet here later, for a beer? Maybe around six?"

That sounded good. And well-deserved. "Sure, Mack. But let's make it seven. Got a date with a warm bed for most of the rest of today."

"Sure, Chauncey. Seven's great. Make sure to bring her." He smiled in at Claudia purring along peacefully. "She is somethin' else."

"Yeah, Mack, I know. See you tonight." And Mack turned off to the black sedan to head for home and a life without Perez. As I pulled away from the curb, I wondered who the next 'Perez" would be for Mack. There had to be a way out for Mack, but he was not exactly cut out for a life as a tennis pro, or a concierge, or a Walmart greeter. I was still mulling over possible career options for Mack, when I pulled up to Claudia's cabin and gently woke her up.

She pulled out of the fog gradually and asked, "My car? Did we get my car?"

"We did not, my love. You were not among the living at Hauzer's, so we left it there. It will be fine till tomorrow." I let Hannibal loose to search for Cecelia and half-carried Claudia up to her door and helped her in. The dogs ran wild outside and around the house in circles, pleased to see each other again. I gently laid Claudia across her bed and pulled off her shoes. I was still trying to be gallant, despite my own exhaustion. How remarkable she looked laying there sleepy and happy. What tremendous luck I had to find this amazing woman who weathered the entire ordeal without so much as a frown. "I shall return this evening to pick you up. We have a date with Mack to celebrate at Hauzer's. We can get your car then. Deal?"

I was not sure she was still awake, but she stirred a bit. "No deal, Chauncey," she said in a sleepy slur.

"No deal? Why no deal?" Now I was confused. I knew she would want to celebrate with us.

"Did you take off my shoes?" she mumbled out of the fog with eyes closed.

"Why, yes, I did. Anything else I can do?"

She smiled sleepily up at me, looking very much like Chessie Beretta. "As a matter of fact, yes." I moved very close to her, anticipating some amorous request. "Could you feed the dogs?" Rats. I was hoping for something a little more romantic than that. But then she added, "…and then get back in here and finish what you started." Oh… that sounded much better.

So, I sped off to complete my chores with all due haste. Cecelia and Hannibal came bounding back in at the sound of kibble hitting stainless steel, and happily shared the food from Cecelia's one large bowl. I made a quick dash to the bathroom to do whatever I could to displace the day's grunge, took a snort of mouthwash, and returned to find Claudia purring peacefully asleep, with that devilish smile still lingering on her beautiful face. I covered her up, clothes and all, dug one of her granddad's old sleeping bags out of the closet, and hit the couch, too tired to bother making a break for my apartment. Besides, maybe Claudia would wake up and need company. I could only hope.

The couch was old and funky, but fit in nicely with the Hobbit theme of the cabin. Not completely uncomfortable, and almost roomy enough for me. But not roomy enough for me and two dogs, who came thundering in after the kibble party and piled on top of me. "Off! Both of you! Be gone, beasts!" But they were not anxious to relinquish a snuggly spot with their new sleep-over buddy, so we all just scrunched in and drifted off. I thought the wildness of the day and the rustling of the two dogs would keep me awake for hours. I lasted maybe a few seconds. The last thought I had was being glad it was Sunday morning, and we all had a day to reboot.

Chapter 17

It was late in the afternoon, around five, when I finally awoke to dog slobber right in the mouth. I was hanging precariously from the couch, mouth agape, probably snoring away, when both of the dogs took advantage of my position and began to practice French kissing the sleepy human. "Akkk! Yukk! Stop! Help!" All I got was increased attack vigor and rolling laughter from across the room. Claudia was up, hair wet, wrapped in a fuzzy robe, and looking beyond gorgeous. She stood across the room, leaning against the wall with a cup of coffee in her hands.

"Morning, Chauncey. I see you are having more dog trouble. Need a hand?" I had retreated under the sleeping bag and the two mutant maulers were actively burrowing under to find me and renew the assault.

"Marphle! Snurgis! Geefersnarg!" I cried for help from beneath the covers.

I could hear Claudia laughing at the scene. "Some International Raconteur you are! Can't even fend off a couple of puppies."

I burst out of the sack, dogs jumping wildly at the opportunity to play, rolled off the couch under heavy artillery fire, and dove across the coffee table toward my target. She had only a second to stash the coffee mug on the shelf before I scooped her off her feet and hauled her squealing across the room. "Help! Cecelia! Save me!"

But Cecelia and Hannibal were having none of it. They had refocused their attack on Claudia's low-slung head as I carried her into her bedroom. "Get her, get her, get her!" I encouraged their attack but they required no such encouragement. I pitched her across the bed and both pups launched themselves on top of her to continue the fun. I joined them and we all wrestled around in a big pile of kisses, both human and canine.

I pinned her down while the dogs went for her. She giggled and tried to hide her face, but with a dog on each side, there was nowhere to hide. "Nooo…" she laughed.

"I will save you from these animals, only if you tell me what ugly name you just called me a minute ago." I had heard her mention something while I was fending off the dogs from under the sleeping bag, but it did not fully register. "Out with it, wench! Or die by slobber!"

"Noooo…" and the dogs renewed the snuffling.

"Prepare to die!"

"Noooo… what are you talking about? I called you Chauncey. Now get them off of me!"

"After that, haughty wench. International raccoon tamer? Did you call me a raccoon tamer?"

She finally got my drift. "Raconteur! International Raconteur! That's you, Bert. A great storyteller!" I let her up and the dogs jumped off the bed to chase each other for a while. They disappeared into the other room and began making noises that hinted at some unthinkable activities. I mulled over the new name as she wiped dog spit off her face and wrapped her arms around my neck. "That's you, Bertrand Chauncey. It's what got us both through that ordeal yesterday, telling great stories. Nobody can resist a great storyteller… I know I can't." And she gave me the most fantastic kiss I had ever known.

After a gradual recovery from Nirvana, I gave her Raconteur label some thought. "I like it. But I recall some pretty fine raconteuring on your part yesterday as well. That monologue with Officer Frank was Raconteur Hall of Fame material. Not to mention the knot you tied in Darrell's tail with that bit about making a video with him. Brilliant."

"Oh? How do you know that was a story? Maybe I thought Darrell was cute." She had the devilish smile back in full illumination.

"Hmmm. And all this time I thought you might want to make one of those videos with me." I was doing my best to return the teasing.

She just planted another wet kiss across my lips and replied casually, "Who needs a video?"

Needless to say, we were a little late getting over to Hauzer's to meet Mack at seven, as we had arranged earlier in the wee hours of morning. But now it was already getting dark, and we could see the old rooms lit up brightly as we pulled in. Sunday was a busy night at Hauzer's Brat Haus, and the rooms were filled with folks having fun, eating bratwurst and sipping frosty beers. We noted Claudia's red Honda parked peacefully where we left it, so we went in and found Mack in our usual room in the back. He had taken the two cameras down from the beer stein and the house plant and was packing up the other equipment. The main recording unit from Hauzer's office was already back in the box. "'Bout time you two showed up. What happen, you sleep till seven?"

Claudia turned a little red and I cleared my throat, "Well, almost till then."

Mack looked embarrassed and just replied, "Oh," and then smiled. We pulled into the booth and looked over all the surveillance equipment in the box.

Claudia turned to Mack, "Thanks for packing up, Mack. Looks like new. I will return it tomorrow morning to State Electric. It was a display model anyway, so I doubt if the boss will care I borrowed it. I think that tape will work to keep Perez on ice for a long time… especially with the gun thing."

Mack frowned a little, "I hope so. He ain't gonna be too happy with me after this. But I don't care. It feels good to be out from under that guy. Kinda weighs on you after a while."

I chimed in, "Good job yesterday, Mack. We could never have pulled it off without you. And you got immunity from prosecution. That's great."

Delores appeared in the doorway. "Prosecution fer what? He never done nothin' to begin with, but bounce around a bunch of nickel and dime lunk-headed thugs. Anybody tells different gets a load o' cast-iron up the side of the head." She whacked her head with her open hand to simulate the result of anybody stepping between her and Mack. We busted out laughing at the memory of ninety-pound Delores decking Perez with a five-pound fry pan yesterday.

I recovered and got up to give Delores a heartfelt hug. "Thank you. Your timing was impeccable yesterday. Remind me never to get on your bad side."

Delores returned the hug for a moment, then slipped back into her usual character. "Yeah, yeah. Let's not get all sentimental about it. One knot on the head ain't that bigga deal. You jokers gonna order some food or am I just standing here looking like a Christmas ornament?" Mack definitely had his hands full with this one. But he beamed at her like she *was* a Christmas ornament. Match made in heaven.

I was feeling like taking a major risk, so I decided to order first, "I believe I will have the Chateau Briand with truffle glaze, and a bottle of Dom Perignon, if you please." I sat back, trying to look aloof.

Delores never faltered. She whipped out her order pad and began writing. "Got it... German bratwurst special and a pitcher of Coors Light. Next?"

We busted out laughing again, finished our order for Delores, and watched as she sauntered off hollering brat orders at an unseen Hauzer somewhere back in the kitchen.

"I wonder how Hauzer puts up with her all these years?" I commented without giving it much thought.

Mack looked up and addressed us in a matter-of-fact tone, "He don't have to put up with her much longer."

Claudia and I stopped short and turned to Mack. "Mack, what's up? I thought she was going to work here till she dies? Is she going to quit?" I asked, with genuine concern.

Mack looked entirely too serious. "Look, that's what I wanted to talk to you guys about tonight... I could use a little advice on this one."

Now it was Claudia's turn to interrupt, "Ohmygod... Mack! You're going to marry Delores! That is so cool!"

Mack looked confused. "Whoa, whoa. Hang on. Nobody said nothin' bout marriage... well, not yet. And Delores is staying put right here... least I hope so."

I prompted him to fill us in, just as the first two pitchers came in with Delores and slid onto our table. Delores started filling glasses while wiggling her backsides in Mack's direction. "Here you go...

beer for the troops. Did Mack here fill you in yet on his next big business venture?"

Business venture? "Well, I think he may have been trying, but he hasn't gotten that far yet. Give him a couple of minutes," I explained.

Delores beamed back at Mack and slid gracefully onto one of his knees like a fighter jet landing on the USS Nimitz. "Well, I think it's just slick as owl snot! I cain't hardly wait!" She smootched him on the cheek and then launched back off the flight deck to check on the other tables, leaving all of us still hanging.

"Mack?" I prompted again.

"You know that little caper we got into yesterday?"

"Yes, Mack, I seem to recollect some activity we were all involved in. Go on…"

"Anything 'bout that you two find puzzlin'?" He waited patiently for our reply. I looked at Claudia who looked back blankly.

Then she caught a thread and asked, "Mack… where did that fifty-thousand end up, do you, think?"

Mack looked down and rubbed his fingers nervously. "Well, here's the deal. *If* that money was to turn up somewheres, I figure it's an even split… three ways. S'pose one of us was to find that cash, say under their mattress, then we oughta divide it up even… maybe even a little heavy to you two, as all this was your plan, after all."

I began to smile as the pieces to that puzzle started falling into place. "Mack… *if*, hypothetically, fifty grand were to materialize under your mattress, I would be delighted to see you make good use of all that money. You old dog." I looked over to Claudia to check her reaction to the news.

"Mack, I am with Bert on this one. I would not want any of that hypothetical money in my bank account." She was enjoying this turn of events as much as me. "But tell us something Mack, if all that cash were to magically appear, what were you and Delores scheming to do?"

Hauzer came in with a giant tray of bratwurst specials and Delores followed close behind. "Deez brats are on me tonight! I buy 'specially for das big fella over dere!" He gestured toward Mack and slid three large brats in front of him. "I am so happy to get to finally zee my family again!"

I had not been so confused since... well, yesterday. "Will one of you three tell Claudia and me what the hell is going on?"

Delores re-landed on Mack's lap and took over, "Mack wants to buy out Hauzer's interest in the Brat Haus and work here with me. Hauzer wants to retire and go back to visit his kin in the old country, but he cain't afford to. But Mack told us he has to get your OK first. So, we're gonna clear out and come back in a bit to check progress. C'mon, boss, we got customers to feed." Delores took Hauzer by the arm and pulled him out of the room, while we all sat in stunned silence, watching them go.

Mack picked up where Delores left off, "Yeah. I talked to Hauzer this afternoon. Delores told me he wanted to go back to his hometown for a while, and maybe retire from the restaurant biz. She said he loves all the people here, but misses his daughter and old friends back home. So, when I seen that case of money sitting there, I started thinkin' maybe that money could help Hauzer. I don't like much where it come from, but if it'll do some good somewhere, then I got no problem with that." Mack began to jam one of the brat specials into his cavernous jaws.

"OK. I follow you so far. But how did you end up with the cash? We thought Beula pulled a fast one on us after Claudia... er, Chessie, here switched the two cases. You were all the way over by the office door, blocking Darrell's view."

Mack nodded in agreement. "Yep. Sure was. But in my line of work, guy has to watch his back, you know? Remember what kinda windows that creep had in the office room?"

A smile crept across Claudia's face. "One-way mirror glass... you were watching Beula make the switch, even with your back to her. You sneaky devil, you."

"Yep. I saw her switch them around. That's why I backed out of there while you all was deleting them videos. Had to make one more little shuffle of the deck. I figured if I got in the right position and bent over like I was going for the floor case, no-one would see me take the desk one instead. Piece of cake." It was true… seeing anything around Mack would be a challenge without aerial reconnaissance.

I still couldn't figure one thing. "But we opened the briefcase in front of Perez and it was full of paper, not cash. Where did the cash go?"

Mack smiled, "Don't you remember? We had all those stacks of newspaper and only used what we needed to balance out the two briefcases. The rest of the paper wads we left in the car. On the way over here last night, I stuffed the cash in the seat crack and shoved the rest of the newspaper in the case. Sorry I didn't tell you guys. I was gonna, but then Perez walked in. It worked out good, 'cause you two was pretty shocked when Perez opened the case. Wished I'd hadda camera. Perez bought it, 'cause it weren't no act. You had no idea what happened to the dough."

Claudia leaned across the seat and gave Mack a hug and kiss on the cheek. "Thanks for covering for us. We were probably lucky to get left in the dark. The Beretta-Chauncey International Raconteurs can only carry the act so far, you know." She smiled at me and grabbed my hand under the table.

I feigned taking offense, "What's this? I was under the distinct impression we were to be the Chauncey-Beretta International Raconteurs." I squeezed her hand and could not remember being in a better mood than right at that moment. Well, except for that one mood about an hour earlier.

Mack looked confused. "I don't know nothin' 'bout no raccoon tours, but I sure hope you two are gonna team up like me and Delores are plannin'. You guys make a good act. I ain't never seen anybody bullshit their way through a snake pit like you two. Beats anything I ever seen."

I agreed with Mack, "I believe that will be our new motto: *'Chauncey-Beretta… Let Us Bullshit Our Way Through Your Snakepit'*." It did have a lovely ring to it.

Claudia laughed but corrected me again, "A perfect motto for *Beretta-Chauncey*, I quite agree. But I am worried now, Mack, that your new business venture will leave you too busy to participate in our adventures. Do you think you can find time to help us with our raconteuring, if we really need you?"

Mack thought about the offer for a minute, then started slowly, "No, I'm done with all that. Once I start over that side, it's a long slide down to the bottom. Never thought I could ever get outta that hole, but here I sit with you two, and Delores, getting' ready to start something that I can go to sleep at night and not wake up feelin' like a jerk." Then he went silent and gave it a little more thought. "But maybe you could still meet here, while me and Delores serve up the bratwurst and beer, and maybe we could help plan the next raccoon tour!"

"Perfect!" Claudia and I shouted in unison. We raised the beer mugs skyward, clinked glasses, and toasted, "To the next raccoon tour!"

Epilogue

Life is good back at State Electric Supply, bastion of all that is normal and stable. It actually seems a lot more tolerable than it did a few months ago, when I launched into the 'raconteuring' business with Claudia and Mack. If I had only known…

But no regrets. Mack is busy learning his new trade, while Hauzer is busy packing for an extended stay in Bavaria. I have never known either of them to be so happy. Not sure if Mack is always smiling because he finally got out of the underworld of criminal activity, or because Delores keeps him in such a good mood. They have already given up one of their apartments. Mack moved into the bigger one with Delores, although Delores complains constantly about Mack filling up two of the rooms, just by standing upright.

Claudia and I are down to one place as well. Her cabin, of course. It was between my lovely leaning abode owned by Francisco Rodriguez Hernandez Shapiro and her grandfather's hobbit cabin. Easy choice. Although Francisco Rodriguez Hernandez Shapiro did try to enforce the lease agreement and extort another $800 when I moved out. But I was able to cut that short with a little of my newfound raconteuring skills. I just mentioned that he could pick up the $800 check from my friend Brokov. He turned very pale and ran for his car. Next day I had a check slipped under the door for twice my security deposit and a note thanking me for living in his building for so long. I guess he hadn't heard that Brokov was not on the street anymore.

Claudia and I picked up an upper level night class at University of Kansas… *English 430: The Art of Storytelling*. I guess we are hoping to refine our skills. I'm even looking into Grad School if everything falls into place. Just having a hard time selecting the right department. A Masters in Raconteuring is not offered at Kansas. Pity.

As for Antonio Perez, well, the DA is still trying to tally up all the charges. Bail was set at a small Central American nation, so it looks like he is going to have to get comfortable with his new cellmate, Skull. Mack is ready to give testimony about all of Perez's shady business dealings, as promised, in exchange for his freedom.

But it would be highly unlikely that the Kansas City police force or the DA would find any reason to retract their agreement with Mack, now that they enjoy a 20% discount at the Brat Haus. Mack kept the name Hauzer's Brat Haus in homage to Hauzer... plus it sounded a lot more authentic than 'Mack's Brat Haus'.

As for our friendly neighborhood bartender Walter, he has decided to contribute to the DA's list of charges against Perez. Seems that the dumpster in the parking lot was composting some of Mr. Perez's former clients, and Walt decided that keeping Perez in the pen might keep Walt out of the dumpster. Wally re-evaluated his career options and took a job with the city. Public relations manager, in fact. The Palm Frond Saloon was boarded up and the dumpster confiscated for State's evidence against Perez. They lifted it onto a flatbed with an excavator and hauled it to the State police compound for forensics testing. The entire police force has threatened to walk off the job unless it is moved to a remote location downwind of headquarters.

Beula got probation, after agreeing to hang her dirtbag brother Darrell out to dry with the laundry. She went to work taking care of the horses at the rehab farm across the state, and I am sure Boney and Secretariat were glad to see her again. Speaking of unnatural romances, I have heard rumors that Darrell is intimately involved with Perez's roommate Skull, although not by choice. Maybe I will wait for it come out in video. Ah, hell no.

Finnegan and Tommy went in together to buy an ice cream truck from the old guy who used to cruise through the neighborhoods of Kansas City during the summer, selling Eskimo Pies to street urchins. Within a month they got busted selling pot out of the back door of the truck to the twelve-year-old son of the police chief. I'm sure it was a tearful reunion with their bosses at the state pen.

Claudia and I renegotiated our hours at State Electric to include a long lunch break so we could make the run to Hauzer's and talk over our raconteuring plans with Mack and Delores. The boss also let us construct a big kennel alongside of Hannibal's favorite spot near the tracks, so he and Cecelia could spend all day plotting their next adventures with us.

Naturally, there were a few questions that came up regarding the whereabouts of an alleged briefcase full of cash, but nobody was too upset about Antonio Perez losing a little profit from his business dealings. Officer Frank Rodgers was promoted to Captain and became a very regular customer at Mack's. In fact, he was just in there today, sitting in the back room with us, having a brat special and a coffee. And he just happened to mention a little problem, trying to track down information on a rough Asian gang who was preying on older people in a local trailer park. Seems these guys were stealing Social Security checks and making threats if anyone talked to the police. Frank was just wondering if maybe… a little raconteuring might be in order?

Made in the USA
San Bernardino, CA
22 March 2017